D0065757

THE
ACCOMPLISHED
GUEST

STORIES

ANN BEATTIE

F
B369

SCRIBNER

New York   London   Toronto   Sydney   New Delhi

For Harry and Marie Mathews

XXXIX

The soul should always stand ajar,
    That if the heaven inquire,
He will not be obliged to wait,
    Or shy of troubling her.

Depart, before the host has slid
    The bolt upon the door,
To seek for the accomplished guest,—
    Her visitor no more.

                        —Emily Dickinson

CONTENTS

THE
ACCOMPLISHED
GUEST

THE INDIAN UPRISING

"There's no copyright on titles," he said. "It wouldn't be a good idea, probably, to call something *Death of a Salesman*, but you could do it."

"I wanted to see the play, but it was sold out. Tickets were going for fifteen hundred dollars at the end of the run. I did get to New York and go to the Met, though, and paid my two dollars to get in."

"Two dollars is nicer than one dollar," he said.

"Ah! So you do care what people think!"

"Don't talk like you're using exclamation points," he said. "It doesn't suit people who are intelligent. You've been fighting your intelligence for a long time, but exclaiming is the coward's way of undercutting yourself."

"Cynicism's better?"

"I wonder why I've created so many adversaries," he said, then did a good Garth Brooks imitation. " 'I got friends in . . . low places . . . '"

"George Dickel interests you more than any person, every time. We used to come see you and we had a burning desire

1

to talk to you, to pick your brain, find out what to read, make you smile, but by the end of every evening, it's clear who's your best friend."

"But pity me: I have to pay for that best friend. We don't have an unlimited calling plan."

"How can you still have so much ego involved that you hate it that my father's company pays for my cell phone and doesn't—what? Send someone to come rake your leaves for free?"

"The super does that. He doesn't have a rake, though. He refuses to think the maple's gotten as big as it has. Every year, he's out there with the broom and one black garbage bag."

"Made for a good poem," I said.

"Thank you," he said seriously. "I was wondering if you'd seen it."

"We all subscribe to everything. Unless we're as broke as I'd be without my daddy, as you so often point out."

"If the maple starts to go, the super will be thrilled, and as a good citizen, I promise to chop and burn the wood in the WBF, not let it be made into paper. Paper is so sad. Every sheet, a thin little tombstone."

"How's Rudolph?"

"Rudolph is energetic again, since the vet's found a substitute for the pills that made him sleep all the time. I envied him, but that's what the old envy: sleep."

"Is this the point where I try to convince you seventy isn't old?"

"I've got a better idea. I'm about to turn seventy-one, so why don't you get Daddy to fly you here and we can celebrate my birthday at the same restaurant where Egil Fray shot the bottle of tequila and then offered the bartender a slice of lime as it poured down from the top shelf like a waterfall. Egil was funny."

Egil, back in college, had been the star student of our class: articulate; irreverent; devoted to books; interested in alcohol, bicycling, Italian cooking, UFOs, and Apple stock. He'd been diagnosed bipolar after he dove off the Delaware Memorial Bridge and broke every rib, his nose, and one wrist, and said he was sorry he'd had the idea. That was years ago, when he'd had insurance, when he was still married to Brenda, when everybody thought he was the brightest boy, including his doctors. He'd gotten good with a slingshot—none of that macho shooting the apple off the wife's head—but he'd caused a significant amount of damage, even when taking good aim. He was finishing medical school now.

I said, "I wonder if that's a sincere wish."

"It would be great," he said, and for a second I believed him, until he filled in the details: "You'd be in your hotel room on your cell phone, and I'd be here with my man Rudy, talking to you from the Princess phone."

He really did have a Princess phone, and he was no more wrong about that than Egil had been about Apple. Repairmen had offered him serious money for the pale-blue phone. His ex-wife (Carrie, his third, the only one I'd known) had asked for it officially, in court papers—along with half his frequent-flyer miles, from the days when he devotedly visited his mother in her Colorado nursing home.

"You know, it would be good to see you," I said. "I can afford a ticket. What about next Monday? What are you doing then?"

"Getting ready for Halloween. Looking in every drawer for my rubber fangs."

"Can't help you there, but I could bring my Groucho glasses and mustache."

"I'll take you to the finest new restaurant," he said. "My favorite item on the menu is Pro and Pros. It's a glass of prosecco and some very delicious hard cheese wrapped in prosciutto. Alcoholics don't care about entrées."

"Then we go dancing?" (We *had* gone dancing; we had, we had, we had. Everyone knew it, and every woman envied me.)

"I don't think so, unless you just wanted to dance around the floor with me held over your head, like Mel Fisher on the floor of the ocean with his buried treasure, or a goat you'd just killed."

"You live in Philadelphia, not Greece."

"There is no more Greece," he said. "They fucked themselves good."

Pretty soon thereafter, he had a coughing fit and my boyfriend came into the kitchen with raised eyebrows meant to ask: Are you sleeping with me tonight? and we hung up.

I took the train. It wasn't difficult. I got a ride with a friend to some branch of the Metro going into Washington and rode it to Union Station. Then I walked forever down the train track to a car someone finally let me on. I felt like an ant that had walked the length of a caterpillar's body and ended up at its anus. I sat across from a mother with a small son whose head she abused any time she got bored looking out the window: swatting it with plush toys; rearranging his curls; inspecting him for nits.

The North Thirty-fourth Street station was familiar, though the photo booth was gone. We'd had our pictures taken there, a strip of them, and we'd fought over who got them, and then after I won, I lost them somehow. I went outside and splurged on a cab.

Since his divorce, Franklin had lived in a big stone building with a curving driveway. At first, as the cab approached, I thought there might be a hitching post, but it turned out to be a short man in a red vest with his hair slicked back. He took an older man's hand, and the two set off, waved forward by the cabbie.

This was great, I thought; I didn't have to worry about parking, I'd gotten money from a cash machine before the trip and wouldn't have to think about that until I ran short at the end of the month, and here I was, standing in front of the imposing building where my former teacher lived. Inside, I gave the woman behind the desk his name and mine. She had dark-purple fingernails and wore many bracelets. "Answer, hon, answer," she breathed into her phone, flicking together a couple of nails. "This is Savannah, sending you her 'answer' jujus."

Finally he did pick up, and she said my name, listened so long that I thought Franklin might be telling her a joke, then said, "All right, hon," hung up, and gave me a Post-it note with 303 written on it that I hadn't asked for. I sent him Royal Riviera pears every Christmas, books from Amazon, Virginia peanuts, and hell, it wasn't the first time I'd visited, either. I knew his apartment number.

Though the hallway looked different. That was because (I was about to find out) someone very rich had been irritated at the width of the corridors and had wanted to get his antique car into his living room, so he'd paid to widen the hallway, which had created a god-awful amount of dust, noise, and inconvenience.

It was funnier in Franklin's telling. We clinked shot glasses (mine brimming only with white wine), called each other Russian names, and tossed down the liquor. If everything we said had been a poem, the index of first lines would have formed a pattern: "Do you remember," "Tell me if I remember wrong," "There was that time," "Wasn't it funny when."

When I looked out the window, I saw that it had begun to snow. Rudolph had been the first to see it, or to sense it; he'd run to the window and put his paws on the ledge, tail aquiver.

"I hated it when I was a kid and this happened. My mother made me wear my winter jacket over my Halloween costume, and that ruined everything. Who's going to know what gender anybody is supposed to be under their Barbour jacket, let alone their exact identity?"

"The receptionist," he said, "is a guy who became a woman. He had the surgery in Canada because it was a lot cheaper. He had saline bags put in for tits, but then he decided flat-chested women were sexy, so he had them taken out. I asked for one, to put in a jar, but no go: You'd have thought I was asking for a fetus."

The bottle of bourbon was almost full. We might be sitting for a long time, I realized. I said, "Let's go get something to eat before the snow piles up. How far would we have to go to get to that restaurant?"

"You're afraid if we stay here, I'll have more to drink and try to seduce you."

"No, I'm not," I said indignantly.

"You're afraid I'll invite Savannah to come up and give us all the gory details. Savannah is a former Navy SEAL."

"If you like it when I speak in a monotone, don't tell me weird stuff."

"Listen to her! When the only buttons I ever push are for the elevator. I don't live by metaphor, woman. Don't you read the critics?"

He kicked his shoes out from behind the footstool. Good—so he was game. His ankles didn't look great, but at least they were shoes I'd have to get on his feet, not cowboy boots, and they seemed to have sturdy treads. I knelt and picked up one foot, opened the Velcro fastener, and used my palm as a shoehorn. His foot slid in easily. On the other foot, though, the arch and the ankle were swollen, but we decided it would work fine if the fastener was left open. It was a little problem to keep the Velcro from flipping over and fastening itself, but I folded the top strap and held it together with a big paper clip, and eventually we got going.

"An old man like me, and I've got no scarf, no hat, only gloves I bought from a street vendor, the same day I had a roasted chestnut and bought another one for a squirrel. I can tell you which one of us was happier." He was holding the crook of my arm. "Only you would take me out in the snow for a meal. Promise me one thing: You won't make me watch you make a snowball and throw it in a wintry way. You can make an anecdote of that request and use it later at my memorial service."

He'd had a triple bypass two years before. He had diabetes. He'd told me on the phone that he might have to go on dialysis.

"Is this the part of the walk where you tell me how your relationship is with that fellow I don't consider my equal?"

"Did I bring him up?" I said.

"No, I did. So is he still not my equal?"

"I feel disloyal talking about him. He lost his job. He hasn't been in a very good mood."

"Take him dancing," he said. "Or read him my most optimistic poem: 'Le petit rondeau, le petit rondeau.' That one was a real triumph. He'll want to know what *rondeau* means, so tell him it's the dance that's supplanted the Macarena."

"I wish you liked each other," I said, "but realistically speaking, he has three siblings, and the only one he talks to is his sister."

"I could wear a wig. Everybody's getting chemo now, so they're making very convincing hair."

We turned the corner. Snow was falling fast, and people hurried along. He wasn't wearing a hat or a scarf. What had I been thinking? In solidarity, I left my little knitted beret folded in my coat pocket.

"Let's go there," he said, pointing to a Mexican restaurant. "Who wants all those truffles and frills? A cold Dos Equis on a cold day, a beef burrito. That'll be fine."

I could tell that walking was an effort. Also, I'd realized his shoes were surprisingly heavy as I'd put them on.

We went into the Mexican restaurant. Two doctors in scrubs were eating at one of the two front tables. An old lady and a young woman sat at another. We were shown to the back room, where a table of businessmen were laughing. I took off my coat and asked Franklin if he needed help with his. "My leg won't bend," he said. "That's happened before. It locks. I can sit down, but I'm going to need an arm."

"Seriously?"

"Yes."

The waiter reached around us and put menus on the table and rushed away. I pulled out a chair. How was I going to get it near the table again, though? I was just about to push it a little closer to the table when Franklin made a hopping motion with one foot and stabilized himself by grabbing the edge of the table and bending at the waist. Before I knew it, he was sitting in the chair, wincing, one leg bent, the other extended. "Go get those doctor fellows and tell 'em I swallowed Viagra and my leg's completely rigid," he said. "Tell 'em it's been this way for at least ten hours."

I dropped a glove, and when I bent to pick it up, I also tried to move the chair in closer to the table. I couldn't budge it. And the waiter looked smaller than I was.

"Let's see," Franklin said, picking up one of the menus. "Let's see if there's a simple bean burrito for a simple old guy, and our waiter can bring a brace of beer bottles by their necks and we can have a drink and make a toast to the knee that will bend, to Egil our friend, to a life without end . . . at least let's hope it's not rigor mortis setting in at a Mexican restaurant.

"Three Dos Equis, and you can serve one to my friend," Franklin said to the waiter. "Excuse me for sitting out in the middle of the room, but I like to be at the center of the action."

"You want me to maybe help you in a little closer to the table?" the waiter said, coming close to Franklin's side.

"Well, I don't know," Franklin said doubtfully, but he slid forward a bit on the chair, and with one quick movement, he rose slightly, the waiter pushed the chair under him, and he was suddenly seated a normal distance from the table.

"*Gracias, mi amigo,*" Franklin said.

"No problem," the waiter said. He turned to me. "You're going to have a Dos Equis?"

I spread my hands helplessly and smiled.

At that exact moment, my ex-husband and a very attractive woman walked into the back room, followed by a different waiter. He stopped and we stared at each other in disbelief. He and I had met at Penn, but for a long time now I'd lived in Charlottesville. Last I'd heard, he was living in Santa Fe. He said something hurriedly to the pretty woman and, instead of sitting, pointed to a different table, in the corner. The waiter complied with the request, but only the woman walked away. My ex-husband came to our table.

"What a surprise," Gordy said. "Nice to see you."

"Nice to see you," I echoed.

"I'd rise, but I took Viagra, and now I can't get my leg to move," Franklin said. He had settled on this as the joke of the day.

"Professor Chadwick?" Gordy said. "Franklin Chadwick, right? Gordon Miller. I was president of Latin Club."

"That's right!" Franklin said. "And back then we were both in love with the same girl!"

Gordy blushed and took a step back. "That's right. Good to see you. Sorry to interrupt." He was not wearing a wedding ring. He turned and strode back toward the faraway table.

"Why did you say that?" I asked. "You were never in love with me. You were always flirting with Louisa Kepper. You paid her to cut your grass so you could stare at her in shorts and work boots. She knew it, too."

"I wasn't in love with you, but now it seems like I should have been, because where are they now? Who keeps in touch? I never hear, even when a poem is published. It was just a job, apparently. Like a bean burrito's a bean burrito."

"Here you go, three beers. Should I pour for you?" the waiter asked.

"I'll take mine in the bottle," Franklin said, reaching up. The waiter handed him the bottle.

"Yes, thank you," I said. The waiter poured two thirds of a glass of beer and set the bottle beside my glass. "Lunch is coming," he said, putting the last beer bottle in front of Franklin.

"I'll tell you what I'd like: a shot of tequila on the side."

"We only have a beer-and-wine license. I'm sorry," the waiter said.

"Then let me have a glass of red wine on the side," Franklin said.

"Okay," the waiter said.

"Take it easy with the drinking. I've got to get you back in one piece," I said. "Also, I don't want to feel like an enabler. I want us to have a good time, but we can do that sober."

"'Enabler'? Don't use phony words like that. They're ugly, Maude."

I was startled when he used my name. I'd been "Champ" in his poetry seminar. We were all "Champ." The biggest champ had now published six books. I had published one, though it had won the Yale Series. We didn't talk about the fact that I'd stopped writing poetry.

"I hope you understand that he and I"—he tilted his head in the direction of my ex-husband—"had a man-to-man on the telephone, and I told him where we'd be eating today."

"I wonder what he *is* doing here. I thought he lived in Santa Fe."

"Probably got tired of all the sun and the turquoise and coyotes. Decided to trade it in for snow and a gray business suit and squirrels."

"Did you see if she had a wedding ring on?" I asked.

"Didn't notice. When I'm with one pretty girl, what do I care about another? Though there's that great story by Irwin Shaw, 'The Girls in Their Summer Dresses.' I don't suppose anyone even mentions Irwin Shaw anymore. They might, if only he'd thought to call his story 'The Amazingly Gorgeous Femme Fatales Provoke Envy and Lust as Men Go Mad.'" He turned to the waiter, who'd appeared with the bean burrito and the chicken enchilada I'd ordered. "Sir, will you find occasion to drop by that table in the corner and see if the lady is wearing a wedding ring?" Franklin said quietly into the waiter's ear.

"No problem," the waiter said. He put down the plates. He lifted two little dishes of sauce from the tray and put them on the table. "No joke, my brother José is the cook. I hope you like it. I'm getting your wine now."

The first bite of enchilada was delicious. I asked Franklin if he'd like to taste it. He shook his head. He waited until the waiter returned with the glass of wine, then took a big sip before lifting his burrito, or trying to. It was too big. He had to pick up a fork. He didn't use the knife to cut it, just the fork. I'd studied him for so long, almost nothing surprised me anymore, however small the gesture. I had a fleeting thought that perhaps part of the reason I'd stopped writing was that I studied him instead. But now I was also noticing little lapses, which made everything different for both of us. I liked the conversational quirks, not the variations or the repetitions. Two months ago, when I'd visited, bringing fried chicken and a bottle of his favorite white wine, Sancerre (expensive stuff), he'd told me about the receptionist, though that time he'd told me she'd had the surgery in Denmark.

The waiter came back and made his report: "Not what I'd call a wedding ring. It's a dark stone, I think maybe amethyst, but I don't think it's a wedding ring, and she has gold rings on two other fingers also."

"We assume, then, she's just wearing rings."

The waiter nodded. "You want another glass of wine, just let me know."

"He and I had a man-to-man last night and he promised to keep me supplied," he said. "I told you the guy with the Messerschmitt gets drug deliveries? Thugs that arrive together, like butch nuns on testosterone. Two, three in the morning. Black guys, dealers. They're all How-ya-doin'-man best friends with the receptionist. That's the night guy. Hispanic. Had a breakdown, lives with his brother. Used to work at Luxor in Vegas."

"Take a bite of your burrito," I said, and instantly felt like a mother talking to her child. His expression told me he thought I was worse than that. He said nothing and finished his wine. There was a conspicuous silence.

"Everything good?" the waiter said. He'd just seated a table of three men, one of them choosing to keep on his wet coat; he sat at the table, red-nosed, looking miserable.

Leaning forward to look, I'd dropped my napkin. As I bent to pick it up, the waiter appeared, unfurling a fresh one like a magician who'd come out of nowhere. I half expected a white bird to fly up. But my mind was racing: There'd been a stain on Franklin's sock. Had he stepped in something on the way to the restaurant, or was it, as I feared, blood? I waited until the nice waiter wasn't looking and pushed back the tablecloth enough to peek. The stain was bright red, on the foot with the unfastened Velcro.

"Franklin, your foot," I said. "Does it hurt? I think it's bleeding."

"My feet don't feel. That's the problem," he said.

I pushed back my chair and inspected the foot more carefully. Yes, a large area of the white sock was bloody. I was really frightened.

"Eat your lunch," he said. "And I'll eat mine. Don't worry."

"It might . . . it could be a problem. Has this ever happened before?"

He didn't answer. He was now using both his fork and knife to cut his burrito.

"Maybe I could run to CVS and find some bandages. That's what I'll do."

But I didn't move. I'd seen a drugstore on the way to the restaurant, but where? I could ask the waiter. I'd ask the waiter and hope he didn't know why I was asking. He might want to be too helpful, he might insist on walking us to a cab, I might not get to eat my lunch, though the thought of taking another bite revolted me now. I'd wanted to say something meaningful, have what people think of as a *lovely lunch*. Were we going to end up at the hospital? Wasn't that what we would have to do? There was a fair amount of blood. I got up, sure that I had to do something, but what? Wouldn't it be sensible to call his doctor?

"Everything okay?" the waiter said. I found that I was standing in the center of the room, looking over my shoulder toward the table where Franklin was eating his lunch.

"Fine, thank you. Is there a drugstore nearby?"

"Right across the street," he said. "Half a block down."

"Good. Okay, I'm going to run to the drugstore," I said, "but maybe you shouldn't bring him anything else to drink until—" and then I fainted. When my eyes opened, my ex-husband was holding my hand, and the pretty woman was gazing over his shoulder, as the waiter fanned me with a menu. The man in the wet wool coat was saying my name—everyone must have heard it when Franklin yelped in surprise, though he couldn't rise, he saw it with his eyes, my toppling was unwise . . .

"Hey, Maude, hey, hey, Maude," Wet Coat was saying. "Okay, Maude, you with us? Maude, Maude? You're okay, open your eyes if you can. Can you hear me, Maude?"

Franklin, somehow, was standing. He shimmered in my peripheral vision. There was blood on the rug. I saw it but couldn't speak. I had a headache and the thrumming made a pain rhyme: He couldn't rise / He saw it with his eyes. And it was so odd, so truly odd, that my ex-husband was holding my hand again, after one hundred years away, in the castle of Luxor. It all ran together. I was conscious, but I couldn't move.

"We had sex under the table, which you were kind enough to pretend not to observe, and she's got her period," Franklin said. I heard him say it distinctly, as if he were spitting out the words. And I saw that the waiter was for the first time flummoxed. He looked at me as if I could give him a clue, but damn it, all I was managing to whisper was "Okay," and I wasn't getting off the floor.

"The color's coming back to your face," my ex-husband said. "What happened? Do you know?"

"Too much sun and turquoise," I said, and though at first he looked very puzzled, he got my drift, until he lightened his grip on my wrist, then began lightly knocking his thumb against it, as if sending Morse code: tap, tap-tap, tap. He and the pretty woman stayed with me even after I could stand, after the waiter took me into his brother's office and helped them get me into an armchair. For some reason, the cook gave me his business card and asked for mine. My ex-husband got one out of a little envelope in my wallet and handed it to him, obviously thinking it was as strange a request as I did. "She didn't have nothing to drink, one sip of beer," the waiter said, defending me. "She saw blood, I don't know, sometimes ladies faint at the sight of blood."

"He's such a crude old coot," my ex-husband said. "I should be impressed with your loyalty, but I never knew what you saw in him."

Savannah the receptionist came for Franklin, and he went to the hospital—but not before paying the bill from a wad of money I didn't know he was carrying, and not before taking a Mexican hat off the wall, insisting that he was "just borrowing it, like an umbrella."

"There might be an Indian uprising if we stop him," the waiter's brother said to him. "Let him go." He called out to Franklin, "Hey, pard, you keep that hat and wear it if they storm the Alamo."

I thought about that, and thought about it, and finally thought José hadn't really meant anything by it, that a little shoplifting was easy to deal with, especially when the culprit announced what he was doing.

With the worried transgendered woman beside him, and Franklin holding her arm, it was amazing that he could shuffle in a way that allowed him to bend enough to kiss my cheek. "Awake, Princess," he said, "and thank God our minions were all too smart to call an ambulance."

He refused dialysis and died at the end of April, which, for him, certainly was the cruelest month. I spoke to him the day after I fainted in the restaurant, and he told me they'd put leeches on his foot; the second time, several weeks later, he was worried that it might have to be amputated. "You're the ugly stepsister who crammed my foot into the slipper," he said. "And time's the ugly villain that made me old. I was a proper shit-kicker in my Frye boots. I would have had you under the table back in the day. But you're right, I never loved you. Maybe you'll find something to write about when I'm dead, because you sure aren't kicking your own shit while I'm still alive."

If you can believe it, that Christmas I got a card from the Mexican restaurant signed by staff I'd never even met. It could have been a crib sheet for remembering that painful day: a silver Christmas tree with glitter that came off on my fingertips and some cute little animals clustered at the base, wearing caps with pom-poms and tiny scarves. A squirrel joined them, standing on its haunches, holding sheet music, as Santa streaked overhead, Rudolph leading the way. Rudolph. What had become of Rudolph?

There was no memorial service that I heard of, though a few people called or wrote me when they saw the obituary. "Was he still full of what he called 'piss and vinegar' up to the end? You kept in touch with him, didn't you?" Carole Kramer (who'd become a lawyer in New York) wrote me. I wrote her back that he'd had to give up his boots, but I could assure her that he was still full of piss and vinegar, and I didn't say that it was an inability to piss that finally killed him, and that he'd drunk himself to death, wine, vinegar, it didn't really matter.

He'd mentioned squirrels the last day I'd seen him, though, so now when I saw them I paid more attention, even if everyone in Washington thought of them as rats with bushy tails. I even bought one a roasted chestnut on a day when I was feeling sentimental, but the squirrel dropped it like it was poison, and I could see from the gleam in the eye of the guy cooking the nuts that he was glad I'd gotten my comeuppance.

Then winter ended and spring came, and I thought, Even if I don't believe there's a poem in anything anymore, maybe I'll write a story. A lot of people do that when they can't seem to figure out who or what they love. It might be an oversimplification, but they seem to write poetry when they do know.

FOR THE BEST

The Clavells weren't the sort to play pranks, so the printed invitation to their annual Christmas party arrived after what Gerald and Charlotte's son, Timothy, would call a "heads-up," sent by e-mail, letting them know that both were invited to the event, at the Clavells' apartment, on West Fifty-sixth Street. Gerald hadn't seen Charlotte since their divorce, thirty-one years before, and this was the first time he'd seen her e-mail address. Whether she was on any social media, he wouldn't know, as he was not.

It was a rather jaunty message from the Clavells, who were not jaunty people. Intellectually, they were clear thinkers, and as for jauntiness, Rorra Clavell had never totally recovered from a hip replacement years earlier, and her husband constantly fretted about why anyone would read a book on a Kindle. The brief e-mail message featured not one but two exclamation points and offered no explanation as to why the Clavells had decided to invite them both. It seemed odd, but although Gerald did have some curiosity about how

Charlotte looked and what she was doing, it did not keep him awake at night.

Gerald lived in a two-bedroom apartment on the East Side, next door to his oldest friend and former college roommate, Willers Caton, and his dog, Alexander the Great. A few days before the party, he happened to mention to Willers that he'd accepted an invitation to an event that Charlotte might also be attending. Without a second's hesitation. Willers said, "She won't show up. Watch." Since Willers wasn't usually a skeptic, Gerald asked how he could be so sure. To his great surprise, he found out that Charlotte and Willers had a psychiatrist in common, a Dr. Frederick Owls, known as the Owl, on Central Park West.

The day before the party, Gerald got a good jump on the season. He took a cab down to Kiehl's, then worked his way back uptown, stopping at various stores, including the newly relocated Rizzoli. At each place, he picked out presents to be wrapped and mailed directly to his list of nineteen friends. (He counted his four cousins as friends, since he was not close enough to any of them to consider them family.) Outside the bookstore, he saw a man walking with a cane, his head bent in the wind. Was it Ned Farnsworth, his former accountant? He doubled back and managed to get a look at the man's long, sharp nose as he was waiting for the light. He said Ned's name, and the two warmly embraced. If such an embrace had happened with his son, Gerald would have had to suffer a series of violent thumps on the back, since young men who were affectionate in this way tended to act as if the other person were a baby in need of burping.

Gerald and Ned had coffee and caught up. (Ned had

retired years before.) Ned said that he'd sold his beautiful Victorian upstate but was enjoying life on the twentieth floor of a new building in midtown that came complete with a dry cleaner, a lap pool, a gym he never used, and a concierge so eager for tips that he wrote thank-you notes for the simplest kindnesses—such as a resident remembering what team he wanted to win the World Series—then leaned them, in parchment envelopes, against the door to your apartment at night. Ned laughed heartily while telling him this. Years before, it had been Ned who'd recruited Gerald to pose in another client's ad—almost to be mischievous, initially, but the ad had been so successful that Gerald had made a late career of modeling for others. As Ned gossiped, Gerald's attention floated away. Might Ned also have been invited to the Clavells'? If memory served, he had been the Clavells' accountant, too. But how to find out without risking making Ned feel excluded?

"Tell me the holiday party you're most looking forward to!" Gerald exclaimed, thinking himself rather clever to have asked in such an open-ended way. "I don't think I'm invited to any," Ned replied, crestfallen. How rude of me, really unforgivable, Gerald thought, so he said, "Well, I'd like to invite you to dinner at my favorite Italian restaurant, on Fifty-fifth Street. Perhaps early January, when all the craziness has ended?" Oh, Ned said, he couldn't eat much anymore; such an evening would be wasted on him, though he'd be happy to meet for coffee again. It would be something to look forward to. He produced his card, which Gerald pocketed with thanks. He found, to his surprise, that he had no card of his own in his wallet, so he jotted down his phone number on the back of a receipt. They parted with a firm handshake and a promise to meet again.

Late that same afternoon, Gerald had another thought. Or not so much a thought as a dream. He and Ned were swimming in the ocean, and he knew, though Ned did not, that a shark was lurking nearby. He tried to warn Ned, but some woman in the dream, an idiotic tourist, kept blocking his view, telling him that *Jaws* had scared an entire generation, and he really should shut up. However much he tried to look around her, or move to the side, no one seemed to notice him; nor was his shouting audible anymore. The dream ended abruptly when the heat turned on, with a series of little clicks, as it had been programmed to do, at five P.M. Gerald sat on the edge of the bed, sweating, distressed to have had such a vivid, disturbing dream, which he hoped was not a premonition.

The night of the party, Gerald nicked his cheek—with an electric razor, no less—and had to find the styptic pencil to stop the bleeding. He was perhaps more nervous than he'd thought. He showered, dried off, and dressed, making it a point not to care which of his white shirts he selected, except that regular cuffs seemed fine; hardly anyone still wore cuff links.

Alonzo got him a cab with the first blow of the whistle. He might have walked to the party had he set out earlier, but it had rained all day, and more was predicted. Also, he didn't want to arrive sweaty. It was early in the month for a Christmas party, though many people were sure to be out of town, or harder to get, closer to the holidays. His son had asked him to visit, but Seattle was too much in the winter— both the travel and all the rain.

The Clavells' lobby already had its Christmas tree up, resplendent in green and white lights, though it dangled no Christmas balls. At the top was an angel with sparkling white wings. She'd fallen forward a bit, so she looked as if she were about to jump. "Darling!" Brenda Hampton called to Gerald, rushing in with a young woman she introduced as her goddaughter. They'd had their hair styled the same way, with a curly tendril hanging below one ear and the rest neatly wound in a French twist. Each wore bright-red lipstick. "Brenda!" he exclaimed. The goddaughter extended her hand as if it were a gift. Indeed it was, with its slim fingers, absent of jewelry, its smooth skin and glossy fingernails. He raised her hand and kissed it, which made her blush. "I'll have to stick out my hand next time we meet, instead of hurling myself into your arms," Brenda said, laughing.

The Mitchums were in the living room, standing beside Joe Jaye and Hubert Gunderphaal, deep in conversation. Ed Mitchum had a four-pronged cane (such canes had a name that Gerald couldn't remember). Sarah Mitchum's foot was in a cast—she had broken her ankle *simply stepping off the curb*, she told Gerald immediately, grabbing his hand in greeting while rolling her eyes. "You're looking splendid!" Ed exclaimed, clapping Gerald on the back. He took the compliment, though talk of his appearance always made him desperate to move on to another topic.

That topic was quickly found: the horrible news of the shooting in California, which he knew nothing about, having watched no television, having not even wandered out until evening. What had he done all day? A crossword puzzle. He'd also spoken to Timothy on the phone, and exchanged e-mail messages with several people. He'd napped. To be honest, he'd watched unabashedly as two women in an office across the street seemed to have simultaneous temper tantrums, throwing crumpled sheets of paper in the air; strangely, neither of them had confronted the other or seemed to register her presence. When a man entered the brightly lit room, the tossing of paper instantly stopped and the women returned to their desks, sitting up straight in their chairs, staring at their computers.

Janice Evans and her second husband, Tim something-or-other (Gerald remembered the first name because it was the same as his son's), arrived. Tim had acted in his youth and still occasionally had a minor role off Broadway, but what he obviously devoted his time to now was having work done (as was the euphemism): He looked like someone with a mask stretched tightly over his face, cheekbones protruding. He wore a gold ring on his pinkie—a clunky, unattractive school ring. His knuckles were so swollen that he must have had to shift it over from his ring finger. Janice, always standoffish, shook Gerald's hand, then joked that in flu season one should really only rub elbows. From the many speakers of the Bose system, Frank Sinatra brayed Christmas carols, his band never as good as one might wish.

Inevitably, the looming election got many people involved in the same conversation, except for Brenda's goddaughter, who'd discovered that Ed Mitchum had attended Princeton's Woodrow Wilson School of Public and International Affairs, where she was studying, and pulled him aside to talk. Their discussion seemed lively, as they debated the pros and cons of changing the school's name. Gerald accepted a flute of champagne and thought, Goodness, I forgot that Charlotte was even coming! He looked around in case he'd missed her entrance. Seeing him searching the room, Tim walked over and told him that he looked like he'd gotten lost in a department store. The implication was that Gerald looked like a desperate child. One way or another, Tim's conversation, Gerald now remembered, was always centered on youth. At a Fourth of July party in Maine, Tim had shown Gerald a photograph of a young actor he was mentoring and asked whether Gerald didn't think he looked much younger than thirty. Indeed, Gerald had assumed that he was a teenager. He had also assumed more than that.

"What's at the top of your list for Santa?" Tim whatever-his-name-was asked. They had little in common, but Gerald gave him credit for coming over to talk. "Anything but a lump of coal," he replied, "since fossil fuels have to be done away with." Tim smiled and began talking about the conference on global warming. He seemed very well informed. Brenda drifted over and joined in. Gerald excused himself and greeted Todd Browne, who was without his longtime live-in boyfriend. "How's the stock market going to treat us in 2016?" Todd asked. "Or is the subject of money out of bounds?" Gerald did his best to provide an answer that was at once concise and ambiguous. For many years, he'd worked at Dean Witter Reynolds—a financial institution that no longer existed. Todd was a tall black-haired fellow who wore brightly colored bow ties and the very newest shoes.

Tonight's were ridiculous, with squared toes, made of some sort of animal skin that had to be deeply politically incorrect.

The Orrs came. Henrietta House walked in alone. An hour after the party started, another flood of people arrived—"flood" being the operative word, as the woman at the door struggled to keep up with all the wet umbrellas. For some reason, she was intent on putting them in tall ceramic containers instead of allowing them to be left in the hallway with the coats. She was bent over nearly double, rolling out another container from the kitchen. Gerald had been distracted, but tuned in to a conversation about Hillary Clinton that seemed to have just concluded. Now Brenda was inviting Tim to the Museum of Natural History for the private unveiling of a recently donated skeleton of a feathered dinosaur. She should have spoken more softly, since her invitation extended to no one else. "After all the years, I can't bear the tears to fall," Sinatra sang. He'd obviously moved on from Christmas music.

Sometime during the next hour, when everyone who was going to get a bit tipsy already had, the music changed to the Hallelujah Chorus. "Did you know," Todd said to Rorra, "that the Hallelujah Chorus was first performed in Dublin?"

"I certainly did not. You are a fount of information," she said, though from the tone of her voice, it was clear that she found him tedious. Gerald accepted a small Swedish meatball, already speared with a toothpick. With his other hand, he took a golden olive on a tiny silver fork, which the server waited for him to replace on the tray. When he looked up again, he caught sight of Ned, who had been invited after all and was beckoning Gerald over with his cane. No, no, it wasn't Ned . . . It was someone he didn't know. The man was summoning someone else. The woman at the man's side was in her thirties or forties, wearing a short blue shot-satin dress and boots with high silver heels. She was laughing at her own joke, unless the bird sconces had become animated and were chirping. Gerald remembered how furious it had made Charlotte when he engaged in this kind of fantasy. "You're no poet!" was the way she'd expressed her objection those times when he pretended that oncoming cars bearing down on them were just toys, or that Monopoly was actually a way to contact the spirit world. "Don't say such asinine things in public! It's far from charming."

Late in the evening, two thirds of the way through, if one paid attention to the time listed on the invitation, there was still no sign of Charlotte. Was the champagne interacting with his blood-pressure medication? He felt a little queasy and confused, though he couldn't focus on what, exactly, was confusing. His line of thought was cut off by Brenda's goddaughter coming to his side, asking if he thought Janice Evans might have had too much to drink, because she'd more or less, sort of—well, actually, she *had*—accused the goddaughter of being in league with the enemy, for attending a school named for Woodrow Wilson, one of our most contemptible presidents. "I wouldn't want to hear what she thinks about Jefferson!" the goddaughter said. Food and drink had removed her lipstick. She was equally pretty without it. A natural beauty. "She must be drunk if she spoke to you that way, yes," Gerald said. "Pay it no mind. We get to a certain age and we think everyone wants to hear our opinion."

"You aren't that way at all," she said.

What did she mean? They'd hardly spoken. Now she was clinging to his side. "Didn't you . . . Brenda said you used to teach at Princeton," she said.

"Ah. As a graduate student. Then I became a stockbroker for a time. Later, I was at Yale, in New Haven." Good God. As if she wouldn't know where Yale was. "I don't know why I said that," he said. "I don't take you for a fool."

"My fiancé, who just broke up with me, was at Yale. He won some fellowship to Italy, and got on a flight, then never showed up where he was supposed to go," she said. "I was engaged to be married to someone that mean."

"I'm so sorry. It sounds as if he might have had some sort of breakdown."

"I know," she said glumly. "But it's easier to think that it was just malice. If I thought he'd flipped out, I'd have to be even more worried about him. To be perfectly honest, a friend of mine sent me a picture of him at a party in Rome last week, so I know he's alive."

"What mysteries people can be. Who in his right mind would leave you?" he asked.

"You're sweet," she said. "Thanks for talking to me."

She walked away without saying goodbye, though her smile lingered. It was an enigmatic smile, one sometimes seen in Botticelli paintings. Gerald went to all the museums regularly, though he'd not yet made it to the new Whitney.

The Mitchums stood at the door, saying goodbye to their hosts. Brenda was approaching the door, the goddaughter trailing behind her. The girl had loosened her hair, which fell to her shoulders. Really a lovely young woman. And so accomplished! What a world she was inheriting. No doubt there was an update on the people who'd done the California shooting—news he'd get from Alonzo. He felt drawn home, as if Alonzo were the North Star, he thought, bemused. He pictured the sturdy doorman in his hat and gloves, so padded they made him look as if he were about to enter a boxing ring.

Gerald took his leave, kissing Rorra lightly on both cheeks and asking her to thank her dear husband for him. The door closed behind him, and he found himself at the coatrack, where Brenda and her goddaughter were still putting on their coats. The Mitchums had preceded them to the elevator but were waiting until they arrived to push the button. "Is something the matter?" he heard Brenda ask the goddaughter. "No, I just, I just don't know . . . it's just the damn zipper, that's all," she replied, though she'd gotten her coat zipped on the first try.

"Mark my words, things will turn out for the best," he said in as consoling a whisper as he could manage, steering the young woman toward the elevator with one hand placed lightly on her back. He felt a real bond with her. He hoped he'd see her again. She was one of those pretty women who didn't give any indication that she knew it or cared. But how had she intuited that she liked him, since he'd said almost nothing to her and there must have been little to differentiate him from the other party guests? Lost in his thoughts, he was frowning as the elevator doors parted on the ground floor.

"Boo!" Charlotte said, jumping out from behind the lobby Christmas tree.

"Oh my God! Oh my God, *Charlotte!*" Sarah Mitchum

said. "What are you doing? Were you *really* lying in wait behind the tree?"

No words came. It was as if Gerald's eyes were hiccupping—they batted so many times. "Charlotte," he finally echoed.

Whereupon she threw herself into his arms, her gray coat trailing its belt, her hair damp and frizzy, her breath reeking of alcohol.

"The lady insisted," the man behind the desk said, wide-eyed and clearly nervous. Whatever was going on, the doorman suddenly knew that the lady had not leveled with him. Sarah continued to gawk at Charlotte while her husband strode on as if he knew neither of them. She said, "Charlotte, that wasn't funny. I can hardly walk as it is," her voice quavering as she spoke. Go on, go on, Gerald tried to signal to Sarah with his eyes, because Charlotte had released him and he didn't know what to do. Brenda, exasperated, was tugging her goddaughter forward, though the girl was looking over her shoulder at Gerald with an expression of real concern. As she was led away, their eyes briefly locked. Then she turned, and she and Brenda more or less staggered across the lobby.

Behind Charlotte, who was now standing very still, the green and white lights on the tree with its falling angel suddenly looked garish and out of place. He could *think*—he was empathizing with the tree, for heaven's sake, for having been taken out of the woods and into New York City, where it was foolishly clad—but he really could not speak.

Todd Browne exited the elevator, whistling, as Charlotte moved in for a second, firmer embrace of Gerald. "Merry, merry," Todd said, nodding as he passed.

Charlotte held Gerald tightly around the waist and was crying against his lapel. "You and your wonderful clothes, your perfect clothes, your perfect friends, your uptight, ruinous friends," she said, her head thrown back, her mascara-streaked eyes looking directly into his.

Ruinous friends? She was wearing stockings with a run down one calf, and short red boots. Her eyes were as red as her footwear. That was hyperbole; still, her eyes were alarmingly red from such a brief burst of crying.

"Let's get a drink," he said, finally finding his voice and leading Charlotte to the door. "Merry Christmas," he said, nodding to the soldier-straight doorman as they walked past him. "And to all a good night," he heard himself adding. He turned toward Charlotte, giving her a false smile. "And laying his finger aside of his nose . . ."

"Oh, why don't you just admit you're discombobulated, instead of talking nonsense, like some proud little schoolboy who's memorized his lesson," she said when they got outside. "If you can't tell, the last thing I need is another drink. I wasn't even able to come upstairs. Let's go to Rockefeller Center. The tree's being lit tonight. It's what people do in New York at Christmas. They have cocktail parties and they go off to see the tree. I had my cocktail party alone, while you had yours with your wonderful friends."

He put his arm around her shoulders. There were many puddles, though it was not, at the moment, raining. It was difficult to walk with his arm around her shoulders, her gait was so irregular, so he let go and clasped her hand. What had she called him? A proud schoolboy, was that it?

"We do have a son in common, you know," she said.

"I'm quite aware of that. A wonderful son," he said.

"We could have had more children, if you hadn't been so selfish."

"One seemed like all we could cope with," he said.

"Oh, I don't know about that. Speak for yourself."

He had no intention of reminding her how exhausted she'd been. She hadn't been young when Timothy was born, but she was the one who'd wanted to go back to work. She'd insisted: No staying at home with the howling baby. She was the one who'd voted no to everything: a cat, a dog, a summer house, another child. He'd given her more than he'd been required to in the divorce. At first he'd intended to keep their place in Redding—she'd gotten their apartment and the Florida bungalow they'd hardly ever gone to—but that, too, he'd relinquished, along with Pet, his dog, Pet, never to see him again, not even when he went to get Timothy, because she always had the dog shut in another room.

Police were everywhere on Sixth Avenue: on motorcycles; flanking the barricades by Rockefeller Center; many on foot; one on horseback. Was this—it had to be—because of the terrorist attack in Paris? Only one sidewalk was open. Finally they walked east, cutting through the dense crowd to get a side view of the tree, its blue and green and white lights blinking. "It's always so beautiful and so unexpected, even though you know exactly what you're coming to look at, isn't it?" Charlotte said. He nodded. His thoughts were more about his son, his capable, seemingly contented son, who had no tattoos, no body piercings, who'd been born after the draft was abolished, and was a graduate of Gerald's own alma mater, not a neo-Nazi or even a surf bum.

"Did you bring Timothy to see the tree?" he said.

"He's in Seattle," she said.

"I know where he lives," he said, trying to keep his voice level. "I meant when he was a child."

"I suppose," she said after a moment. "Didn't you?"

They stood with their backs to a building on Fifth Avenue. Music had begun to play, and a light show projected images onto the blanched facade of Saks. Ingeniously, someone had used the architecture to create a landscape, with stars appearing and constantly changing colors transforming the building. iPhones were everywhere, glowing, like the Cheshire cat's smile—disembodied, floating.

"That old windbag Henrietta House came into the lobby and had a spat with some man who was with her, and he stormed out, and she made fists and all but jumped up and down. That was right after I hid behind the tree," she said.

"You made the man at the desk quite nervous," he said.

"Yes." She smiled. "Did I embarrass you?"

"No," he said. Of the many things he'd felt, embarrassment hadn't been one of them.

"Oh, if only I hadn't had so many drinks, we could go to the Warwick, the remodeled Warwick, and sit in their nice bar," she said. "Or walk over to the Parker Meridien and go to that strange Moorish bar where the sofas are so comfortable and all the Eurotrash hangs out."

"Eurotrash?" he said with surprise.

"Did the Orrs come to the party? I'd have liked to see them."

"They were there. We didn't really get to talk."

"Horrible, long-suffering Sarah Mitchum. If it's not her foot, it's something else—so long as she's the center of attention. You tell me: Who seemed more likely to divorce, the Mitchums or us? But they're still together, and he's still pussy-whipped."

"Really?" he said. "I thought they had a good marriage."

"So good he tried to get into my pants once," she said.

"Really?" he said a second time.

"No, I'm making it up because I want us to remarry, and I know you'll feel all sorts of jealousy and protective impulses toward your seventy-year-old ex-wife."

"It isn't always easy to decipher your meaning," he said.

"You love to appear dense. It's part of your defense system. You've also always been something of an ass."

"Please. It's Christmas."

"It is not. It's the second of December."

Beside them, a man in a cloak sat down, as quickly and gracefully as a dancer concluding a twirl. From under his cloak he pulled a piece of cardboard, which he propped up on the wet sidewalk. Again, the lights at Saks began to blink. The man's sign said, NEED $22 TO GET HOME TO WEST VIRGINIA. The second 2 had been drawn over a 1. Beside the sign, the man placed a cup wrapped entirely in masking tape. He was wearing a hoodie underneath the formless, dirty cloak, which he retreated into like a wet bird, ducking his head until his face could no longer be seen. His final gesture was to remove one hand from inside the cloak to check his cell phone.

Charlotte had noticed none of this. Her eyes were riveted on the scene projected in front of her. The light display was at its apogee, so now all it could do was gradually disappear. She didn't look her age, Gerald thought. Still, she was hardly young. What must he look like, nearly ten years older? ("Why do you always say ten years? You are nine years and one day older," she used to say irately.) Had Ed Mitchum propositioned his wife?

"That was amazing," she said when the light show was over. "The perfect evening after all. Find me a cab and send me home now, will you?"

"We could go to the Warwick and have a Perrier, then I could put you in a cab," he said.

"No. Just the cab, please."

It was now incumbent upon him to find her a cab, on a crowded, blocked-off Fifth Avenue that looked like a double-page spread in *Where's Waldo?* It would be next to impossible, though he supposed that if they returned to Sixth—the Avenue of the Americas, as no one called it—they might join the line and get a cab at the Hilton, should they fail to find one sooner. He discovered, though, that they could not retrace their steps. Because of new blockades, they'd need to walk uptown until they found an open cross street.

She moved where he steered her, less conscious of puddles than he. Stupid to have worn his Belgian loafers when he'd known what a ghastly night it was going to be. Again, he clasped her hand with no resistance. Oh, the feel of that young woman's skin at the party! He didn't even know her name. Rudely, Brenda had said only what relationship the woman was to *her*: her goddaughter.

They got a cab almost immediately. That was what you had to love about New York: It always defeated your expectations. The driver was letting out someone at the corner of Fifty-third and Sixth who smiled and said, "All yours," leaving the door open. "Goodbye!" Gerald said as Charlotte dove into the back. She was certainly agile. As slippery as a fish. She was lucky that a boot dangling from her foot didn't come off entirely. When last he saw her, she was simultaneously pulling the boot back on and closing the cab door.

He stood on the corner. All the talk around him that wasn't flirtatious or drunken, or flirtatious *and* drunken, was not about the tree but about the fourteen people dead and more wounded in California: Yet again, helpless people had been shot by crazies who were either terrorists or disgruntled, well-armed workers. One man passing by *knew* they were terrorists. "How stupid do you have to be not to know that?" he asked his buddy. Gerald thought he heard someone else say that a baby had been left behind by the shooters. He could imagine Obama's next press conference. Gerald once passed up an exciting job in California because Charlotte wanted to stay on the East Coast. Where had she come from tonight, and where was she returning to? He had no idea. He hoped—he assumed—she'd be fine and not too embarrassed the next day. In any case, the Owl—what a nickname!—could fix her up.

Of all people, Todd Browne appeared. "Happy to see you again. Sorry we didn't get to talk earlier," he said, extending his hand. "I have an aversion to Sarah Mitchum. Every time I was going to come over, she seemed to be there."

"Many people feel that way. I understand," Gerald said, adding, "Lovely party. I was just looking at the tree. You really must see it."

"I think they turn it off at eleven-thirty," Todd said, looking at his watch. "My driver's around the corner. Can I give you a ride? I was having a quick drink with a client. Imagine running into two people I know on the same corner, on the same night." He turned his palm outward to indicate that Gerald should precede him to the waiting car. What was this—some moment in a Woody Allen film? Would the car be a chariot? "Awful about what happened today," Todd said. "My husband had to go back to the office." Were the two things connected? Todd's meaningful look suggested that they were. "Apparently both of the killers were shot dead."

"Someone was saying there might have been a third person," Gerald replied.

"I don't know. I didn't hear that," Todd said. "In any case," he added, then didn't finish his sentence.

The driver was leaning against the car, a shiny black Volvo SUV, smoking. Seeing Todd, he reacted like a marionette being lifted, rushing to open the back door. Todd climbed in after Gerald. Neither spoke as the car pulled into traffic. What if it's not just my ex-wife? Gerald wondered. What if I can never think of anything to say to anyone ever again? It was really unfair of Charlotte to say that he'd always been an ass. "Your address?" Todd asked. Gerald told him, speaking loudly enough that it didn't have to be repeated to the driver. Except for Todd remarking that the weather was supposed to get colder the next day, they said nothing else until they got to his building. The ride was a quick one because they made every green light.

The driver hopped out so fast at the curb that Gerald

didn't even have to figure out how the door opened. "I appreciate the lift, Todd," he said.

"Of course. My pleasure," Todd said, sliding over to take up more of the seat. From out of nowhere, Alonzo had appeared. He was holding his big umbrella over his head and Gerald's. "I know I probably shouldn't say this, but my parents pointed you out to me years ago, in one clothing ad or another," Todd said. "I remember your Breitling ad. That's what I wear now, so I wonder if you influenced my life more than I realized. I'm always flustered when I meet a celebrity."

"Hardly that," Gerald said, reaching in to shake Todd's hand. Then the door closed. The SUV pulled away.

"Welcome back," Alonzo said.

"Quite a night," Gerald replied, walking toward the front door. He was tired. Tired and still more than a little perplexed.

"It's another incident that gives foreigners a bad name," Alonzo said. "That's what Americans think—that foreigners are the problem. More and more people don't want to let them in."

"Troubling," Gerald said. In the short walk to the door, he'd stepped in a puddle. Now his shoes were sopping wet.

In the lobby, Alonzo closed the dripping umbrella and shook it mightily. He stood staring into the street rather than at Gerald. "And I was born in the United States. I was my mother's first son, born in Buffalo, New York, on her birthday, April eleventh, 1950. Right there, in Buffalo."

Gerald nodded. "No one has said anything unkind or prejudicial to you, Alonzo, I hope," he said. It had been a night of slow thinking and near-paralysis with words, yet he'd managed this, which was essentially what he'd intended to say.

"Me, somebody else, an African, a Muslim, an Englishman who talks with a funny accent—people have their thoughts, whether they say what they're thinking or not."

"I suppose that's so. We just have to hope that at least some of them are intelligent and not quick to judge. That they don't act on their baser instincts, I mean."

"You're not that kind of person at all," Alonzo said. "But this country? Even our allies are coming to think we're crazy, with all this shooting! They're losing heart that we'll ever change, I think. I wouldn't say this to anyone but you," he added, gesturing to the empty space around them: the marble walls, the chandelier.

Gerald leaned forward to hear what Alonzo was about to say, a sick feeling in his stomach. But Alonzo said nothing; he'd already spoken. Relieved, he nodded, vehemently agreeing with Alonzo. Oddly, he found himself lingering. He said, "You know, tonight was one hell of a night. My ex-wife was at the party. Not even at the party but at the building where the party was given, and do you know what she did? She jumped out from behind a Christmas tree."

"What?" Alonzo said.

"Yes, she did. As a sort of joke. I mean, what else could it have been? To be fair, I went to the party knowing that she might be there, but what sort of a fellow would I be if, after thirty-some years, I was too afraid to be in a room with my ex-wife? That would be ridiculous."

"I don't think I would have gone," Alonzo said.

"No? Do you have an ex-wife?"

"You don't know, because I never talk about her, and I still wear my wedding ring." He took off a glove and held out his hand. Gerald had seen the silver band before. He wore it on his right hand, not his left, but since some European men did that, Gerald had assumed it indicated that he was married.

"She died eighteen years ago. The same year you moved into the building. She told me, 'That man's a model,' and I didn't know what she meant. But then she showed me your picture in *Esquire*. She did! She recognized you from your picture. It was you!"

"Oh, a lot of people seem to have seen that ad. I think the Jaguar attracted their attention."

"Another one was in *The New York Times Magazine*. The one where you're standing by a pool table."

"Yes. I remember that."

The lobby was not yet decorated, though sometime that evening a Christmas tree wrapped in netting had been brought in. Tall and slim in its binding, it lay beside the reception desk. No one staffed the desk at night. When Alonzo went off duty, the building was protected by an alarm system that sometimes went off for no reason. The residents had had many meetings about what should be done, but of course no one wanted to pay for a night person. Alonzo had been given more money to stay an hour later, and the sensors on the alarm system had been tinkered with so that it wouldn't malfunction. Or, in theory, it wouldn't. Gerald noticed that the elevator was descending. Someone was coming down, so it was a good time to take his leave. He felt chilled and exhausted—just what he'd tried to avoid all day by being sensible and staying inside.

He said, "I'm sorry about your wife. She came here, and we apparently saw each other a time or two?"

"That's right. She was going to work at the dry cleaner owned by the French people. We moved out of Washington Heights to be closer to my job. Then she got sick. She got too sick to even read a magazine. They tried everything. They sent her to Mount Sinai, but she died."

"I'm awfully sorry," he said. "Imagine my not even knowing that."

"I'm a professional. I know not to talk about my family or things like that."

"Of course," Gerald said, though he said it only to agree. He didn't know what to say. Inequality was a problem. Keeping one's distance wasn't always a good thing. Any sensible person knew that. "We're friends, and if there's anything you'd like to discuss, I'm always ready to listen," he said.

"I appreciate that," Alonzo said.

The elevator doors began to open.

"Yes, of course. Let's talk more tomorrow," he said. By then he hoped to have sorted out his feelings about seeing his ex-wife. He didn't think he'd say anything to Timothy. He'd let her do that, if she was so inclined, and let whatever story she told remain uncontested.

"Al, I am really, *really* stressed," a teenage girl said, rushing up to Alonzo, holding an iPhone in one hand and a leash attached to a little white dog in the other. "If you could pretty pretty please take Duckie for a walk, I would totally love you forever."

She was wearing an enormous T-shirt over pink leggings. A Celtic cross on an obviously fake gold necklace hung between her breasts, her nipples protruding underneath the shirt. Her toenails were bright red—as smooth and shiny as the surface of that Jaguar. She was standing there in December, barefoot, her hair messily gathered in a sparkly hair clip, the little dog staring up at her, panting. As Alonzo reached for the leash, she heaved a dramatic sigh of relief and pulled some crumpled money out of her waistband. She pressed it into his hand, pirouetted, and raced back to the elevator, her ponytail bouncing.

"His name is Alonzo, not Al," Gerald called after her.

"Pardon?" she said, turning as the elevator doors opened.

"Alonzo," he repeated.

"What*ever*," she said. "You need me to hold the elevator?"

"No," he said decisively. "No, thank you."

She kept her back turned even after she'd stepped inside. She was heading to the thirty-fifth floor, the penthouse—she was the Baileys' niece, who'd come to live with them when she was thrown out of private school in D.C. He hadn't seen her in months. He'd assumed she'd left.

Outside, Alonzo stood under the umbrella. He turned right and headed toward the nearest tree box, which wasn't so near. Seen through the lobby's windows, he seemed to grow smaller quickly, the way people did if you watched them walk away.

For a while, Gerald waited for the doorman to return. He felt as though their conversation had not really concluded when the girl had so rudely interrupted. But, as time passed, he realized that Alonzo must be taking the little dog for a longer walk. It was a kind thing to do, not to punish the dog because its owner was a mindless young fool.

How had he and Alonzo's wife met? he wondered as he summoned the elevator. Had they exchanged pleasantries?

Why had none of this ever come up in all these years? He was incurious—an accusation that Charlotte had leveled at him repeatedly, though what hadn't she accused him of? Well, he supposed she'd never accused him of not loving her. She hadn't been that irrational. Nor had she said that she'd stopped loving him, even when she'd become so shrill and angry under the tutelage of whatever Owl she'd seen back in the day—just that he was impossible, uptight, set in his ways, a rich, self-satisfied snob. But she'd been delighted that he was rich. It was one of the reasons she'd married him. He shook his head over the illogic of that, unaware that he was doing it until he caught sight of his reflection in the mirrored wall of the elevator, and it was as he'd thought: He'd grown old.

THE ASTONISHED
WOODCHOPPER

John decided to leave for the wedding on Thursday night in order to avoid the Friday traffic. They'd encounter it on their return, no way around that, with thousands of cars on I-95 regardless of the high price of gas.

John's brother, Randolph, was remarrying after seven years living on his own at the family summer house, which absolutely no one was pressuring him to vacate, as none of the children who'd inherited it wanted to sell it or inhabit it, and they weren't contentious people, anyway. But in his telephone call to John on John's April Fool's birthday, Dolph had told him that he'd been seeing a woman for a year—not a local woman; a journalist, who traveled—who lived twenty minutes from the lake house. Ruth had a son in boarding school in Massachusetts, her husband had died prematurely from wounds he'd gotten in Vietnam, and she was fifty-four, which made her several years older than Dolph. John was surprised by the information: His wife had convinced him that his brother was a real loner, not interested in women because they were too dangerous. He himself knew his brother to be shy, inordinately bitter about the breakup of his marriage, and he'd come to agree with Jen. No one in the family except—it turned out—their daughter, Bee, had ever met Ruth, who had gone with Dolph to visit Bee when she started at Harvard. Apparently, Ruth had not only recommended several books Bee might like, but had taken them, after dinner at an Indian restaurant (Dolph?!), to the Harvard Book Store, where she was able to purchase two books as gifts for Bee. At the end of her freshman year, Bee had moved in with her boyfriend in Somerville, behind Porter Square. In the fall she would start her second year of college. Bee gave Ruth a thumbs-up: intelligent, restless in a good way, cryptic in a funny way, and totally devoted to Dolph. (This devotion, too, she might have said, was "in a good way"—one would not want "in a funny way"; since childhood, Bee had offered such elaborations. A third-grade teacher who had urged her to always be specific had really made an impression on his daughter.)

Bee and her boyfriend, George, would be flying to Port-land—these kids: too lazy to drive!—where John and Jen would pick them up for the drive north to the wedding. But tonight John and Jen would be in a Portland hotel; they'd check out the good used bookstores and some antique stores, then have dinner at one of Jen's favorite restaurants, Back Bay Grill. Maybe there would be something good at the movies. Or some music. In any case, he didn't want to fight Friday-morning traffic heading north, then Saturday-night traffic returning to Boston. The wedding would be at two o'clock on Friday. The couple planned to honeymoon in

Virgin Gorda. Dolph would board up the lake house during the winter and move in to his new wife's house. They would go out on weekends to make sure it was okay. In retrospect, Dolph had told him more about the family house than about his fiancée.

"I find it hard to believe Dolph would have sex outside of marriage," Jen said. "He's such a prude."

"Well, we don't know that they have had sex," John said. "Let's try to share one suitcase, and I'll put our wedding things in a garment bag and lay them flat in the trunk. Don't pack your big jar of wrinkle cream."

A joke: Jen did not use wrinkle cream. She cleaned her face with Neutrogena and used Kiehl's moisturizer.

"Don't pack extra jockstraps," she said, disappearing into their bedroom.

A joke: He'd had testicular cancer and—after the double orchiectomy—most certainly did not need a jockstrap. Nor did he play tennis anymore. When he'd stopped smoking, he'd gained fifteen pounds, which showed in his face and in his ass, of all embarrassing things.

"Who would go all the way to Virgin Gorda and not have had sex?" she called. He could hear the closet door sliding back.

"What do you mean? No virgins in Virgin Gorda, because it would be too ironic?"

He stood watching his wife push hangers aside, looking perplexed and preoccupied. This August, they would be married twenty-four years. His wife's first marriage, to a harmonica player, had "ended in divorce," as the *New York Times* wedding column would say. Jen was John's only wife, though he'd lived with two women, each for about six or seven years, and the last one he'd had to pay to go away. Actually, his father had paid her to go: a not insignificant amount of money. His father had had a lawyer draw up an agreement. The woman had brought a fountain pen to the lawyer's office and had—as the lawyer told him—deliberately made a big splotch where she was to sign, so that the contract had to be redone. Violet was an English girl he'd met at a photography workshop in Santa Fe when he'd been under the delusion that he might change careers and become a photographer. In addition to money, she'd also gotten the Edward Curtis. The earlier girlfriend's name had been Bonnie. She had become adamant about a wedding ring and a baby, though not necessarily in that order. He had opted instead for a sports car and a cat. A kitten, actually, an abandoned kitten that showed up one night at his back door, though he'd soon realized he was allergic to it and had taken it to the SPCA when he'd moved from Michigan. Things had worked out so that not only was there no baby, but any lunatic could have adopted the cat. His sports car had broken down as cosmic punishment, no doubt. He'd had to spend three days in Ohio, on the way back to his parents' house in Boston, getting it fixed. He remembered those frustrating days in a motel much more distinctly than he remembered Bonnie.

"Green isn't my color. Why do I buy so many green things?" Jen said.

"Wear that blue dress. You look great in that," he said.

"I do?" she said. "Are you just saying it because you hate to watch me flip through clothes?"

"I don't mind watching you flip through clothes unless I'm in a store," he said.

She took out the dress he'd pointed to, hung by two narrow blue ribbons from the neck of the hanger. She put the hanger on a hook, tugged lightly at both sides of the waist. "I'd be lucky if it fit," she said. She pulled down her shorts and pulled her T-shirt over her head. She stepped out of the shorts and tried on the dress, braless. Those weird Frisbee pads would be sticking over her breasts if she wore the strapless dress, he remembered: little white circles that looked like they'd as easily hold falafel as breasts. How did the things adhere to flesh? He realized that she realized that he was staring at her nipples. "There's a special bra," she said matter of factly.

"It's great. You look great," he said. She handed him the dress and began rummaging through her dresser drawer. He went to his own closet and took out the garment bag, hung the dress inside it. He had only one summer suit, a nice Bilzerian linen one, so he found that hanger and put it in the same bag.

"Don't forget grown-up shoes," she said. "That was ridiculous, that time we went to Jennica's wedding and we had to stop and buy you oxfords."

He liked his clogs, had worn them everywhere for years, even to work. His surgeon had been wearing red clogs encased in bags the day he was operated on. Surgeon's choice, Mozart, had already been playing as he was wheeled into the OR.

"I'll wear those new high-heeled sandals," she said, mostly to herself.

"Don't paint your toenails some color that makes you look like a whore."

She turned and threw something that fell far short of striking him. It was a sachet in blue netting, he discovered. Filled with lavender. He closed his eyes as he sniffed. Just a few seconds of nothingness were needed: giving no advice, making no jokes, remembering nothing, anticipating nothing. He told himself to inhale deeply.

"It was a good idea to avoid the traffic," she said. "I'll call the restaurant before we leave. Seven-thirty, eight?"

He handed back her sachet without answering. It wasn't really a question, and it didn't really matter what time they ate dinner. And though his wife wasn't frantic at the moment, he turned and left the room because he knew she would be soon: Where were her new reading glasses? Should she take her book or leave it as something she'd be dying to get back to? No lipstick would be right: She'd look at the tubes as if she'd never seen such colors before, as if none of them could even exist on the color spectrum, each one very wrong. The sandals . . . who, but a woman as stupid as she, would not place new sandals on the closet floor with every other pair of shoes. At their own wedding, mercifully, they had worn blue jeans and been married on the beach. Now his wife had become rather materialistic, but back then the few guests had stood around in shorts, each with his or her own kite, the coolers holding champagne bottles and plastic glasses resting on the sand, seagulls spreading their big wings, circling for a handout, the JP's gold bracelet sparkling in the sun. ("Is he under house arrest?" Jen had said wittily after they visited the justice of the peace several days before the event.) Worry was the price Jen paid for materialism.

His shoes were where he'd stepped out of them in the entryway days before, coming in from the rain. He took them, with the garment bag, out to the car. The neighbor's strange son was headed down the dirt road with a butterfly net. The young Nabokov, off to capture—and in this case, probably squish—the butterflies that rose like champagne bubbles from the dust at the shoulder of the road.

John had asked Jen not to tell Bee the details of his surgery, but of course she had—no doubt also cautioning Bee to lie if he asked her directly what she knew. White lies: as prevalent in this family as white noise on the highway that drifted across the meadow toward their house. He had wanted a more secluded house; Jen had said she liked to be nearer to what she called "civilization"—the same environment she now damned as being filled with "idiot tourists and Maine-iacs in their tortoiseshell SUVs, driving like lunatics because they can't imagine they'd ever go belly-up." Just the week before, a man had died, not at all protected by his SUV as it rolled.

"Have you seen that red box that came last week with my sandals in it? Bright red, no one could miss it, but it is not . . ." She realized midsentence that he knew nothing. She went back into the house. He tilted his head, studied the cloudless sky, which almost immediately began to shake—the sky!—as his neck twitched, reacting to the cell phone's vibration in his pants pocket. But it would be a missed call. He liked that concept. As if by missing a call, you could shape your destiny.

Lately, he wasn't interested in talking to anyone. He'd

listen if Bee called him, specifically, but if he were around when she called her mother, he'd catch Jen's eye and move his hand sideways. Had they been at an auction—that was the way they'd bought so much furniture for their house, way back when—he would have been bidding by half-step increments. The phone had stopped vibrating, the sky was safe. Into the house went Chicken Little, silent, as Jen had pointed out that he now so often was.

"Shall I call the restaurant?" he called.

"I already did, thanks. Eight o'clock."

"Should I double-check with Bee and make sure she knows not to call until the plane actually lands?"

"You know I hate screaming between rooms," Jen said, coming out of the bedroom with a patent-leather purse he'd never seen dangling from one hand. "What?"

"I said, 'Fantastic weather for what I hope will be a perfect wedding.' Whatever 'a perfect wedding' means."

"Remember when an interviewer asked Prince Charles if he loved Diana and he said he did, 'whatever love means'?"

"Prince Charles?" He frowned. "What would make you think of him?"

"I suppose because William just got married."

"We'll bang around for hours if you don't pack," he said. "And while you're at it, would you put in my pajamas and two pairs of socks?"

"I'm wearing patent-leather pumps," she said. "I'm not looking for those stupid sandals any longer."

As she turned, he thought, She assumes I can always concentrate enough to drive; she's always up for an adventure, even if that only means leaving a day early; she'd act like she was playing Russian roulette and sweat bullets if her phone vibrated and she didn't even look to see who was calling. She thinks that if she, personally, is orderly, things will be fine; she'd get implants if, God forbid, she had to have a mastectomy, then she'd tell everyone about every minute of it, holding nothing back. Though if that really happened to her, it might make her look at the sky more often. It certainly might.

The Portland Superior Hotel looked out over downtown. Their room had a king-size bed, both blinds and curtains, and a walk-in shower on one side of the hall and another room with a door and a toilet and a sink on the other side. He picked up the soap and smelled it. It smelled like a field in France. He thought that he would prefer to be buried in France, then corrected his thinking: he wasn't Jim Morrison. They wouldn't want him. But she could scatter his ashes. She could be the sad, lovely widow, the ashes disguised as something clever, something that would make it through security. The surgeon in the red clogs emphatically did not think he would die. The chemo had been bearable, as the doctor had said. It was an advantage to have been almost bald for ten years. His hair, what he had of it, had grown back rather coarse and curly. It had pleased him to let it grow until he could make a ponytail that protruded an inch from the rubber band. It could have turned into a horse's tail for all he cared, but his hair simply grew no longer.

He regularly picked up the antidepressant the doctor had ordered, but threw it away and put multivitamins in the bottle in case Jen picked it up and wondered. He thought he deserved to feel sorry for himself and also deserved to realize that he had pretty much made a mess of his life, even if he had earned good money. He was amused to wear the yellow rubber bracelet Bee had given him that said WHATEVER. This was his little joke, though it had no particular point. His wife had said, "Why don't you get another one that says YOU SAY, and make me happy?" Now, his wife was having a Scotch from the minibar, sipping from the bottle, looking out over Portland. Was she thinking about the wedding? If he hadn't married her so many years ago, would she want to marry him now? The vitamin pills did not lead him to think she necessarily would. But it was his plan to pretend to be taking the pills, to pretend to be less depressed, so he said, "Shouldn't we go to the bar upstairs and look out over the city? Or do you really want to drink that here?"

"Both," she said, shooting him a sly smile.

So he flipped through the free *USA Today* as she stood and sipped—by mutual agreement, neither of them went into a hotel room and automatically turned on the TV—then she smiled and extended her hand. He smiled, genuinely, seeing how bright her eyes were, how lovely her hair. He grabbed the keys and they went out, walked to the elevator, and got on, pushing the button for the top floor. And as the elevator door opened, who should be standing smack in front of them but Dolph and his bride-to-be, who had decided to spend the night at the same hotel. The bride-to-be, Ruth, had been expecting her sister to emerge from the elevator. She'd called—as they learned—from the parking lot to say they'd arrived. Ruth was tedious about details, John could tell from her first minutes of gushing, as if every action needed to be explained or she might be found guilty of something. She wore a miniskirt and had not-bad legs. She was tall, with those overplucked eyebrow arches everybody had now, wearing frameless glasses and what turned out to be a rather impressive diamond engagement ring (Jen's was modest; it had been a "dinner ring" that belonged to his grandmother). Jen, at least, had the sense to throw herself into Ruth's arms, while he stood back as if they were being ambushed. He finally gave his brother a man hug, slapping his back, along with a knowing glance about the two squealing women, already exchanging information.

The sister did not emerge from the next elevator, or the one after that. "Honey, she knows where we are. They're probably freshening up. Come, let's sit at a table," Dolph said. The only "honey" to follow him was John, who was glad that the two women had met and gotten along so well, but really . . . or did only drag queens say "really"? Drag queens imitating actresses in old movies who had cigarette holders and fox stoles. He thought of drag queens because he was used to passing them by, when he and Jen went to their little Key West house, just down the street from the 801 where the "girls" gathered every night. Yes, they'd shriek things like "Re-ah-llllly!," pointing their big hands with their long red fingernails at any mom-and-pop tourist who walked by in a tropical shirt. John they left alone, except for sometimes asking for a light or giving some perfectly pleasant greeting; they knew he was local.

He made the magnanimous offer of ordering a bottle of Cristal—in their instant bonding, Jen and Ruth had run off to the ladies' room—but Dolph said it was an unnecessary extravagance, there would be plenty of bubbly (as he called it) the next day, and he was a bourbon man himself. Yes, of course John knew what his brother drank, but on the eve of his wedding . . . John thought Dolph should simply have said yes, because the women would have liked it so much. But he was not about to order a whole bottle just for the two of them, especially not in their absence. He, too, might have a Maker's Mark, he supposed. To him, it was indistinguishable from Irish whiskey, but if you ordered that, the bartender would pressure you to try some boutique malt, a hundred years old and packed in cow flops or something, and it was exhausting, protesting that you didn't want it and knowing the bartender just wanted the big tip, he didn't care if you drank liquid peat moss from Dingle Peninsula. To hell with the now-suffering Celtic Tiger and its single malts. He'd have a Maker's, straight up. Dolph ordered a Jim Beam with water on the side.

John almost said the obvious—that who could imagine such a coincidence?—but it seemed lame, a girly thing to say, and anyway, it wasn't that much of a coincidence, since the Portland Most Exemplary (as Jen called it) was a big hotel not far from where the wedding would take place the next day. Why shouldn't Dolph have thought of the same hotel? Yet he wouldn't have thought Dolph would stay at a new, glitzy place. They were different: Dolph drank Jim Beam; John ordered Maker's Mark. Their parents had always pointed out how dissimilar their two sons were. If they had more similarities, they probably kept the lid on them because their parents seemed to be so taken with what different people they'd given birth to. Their older sister, from whom both were estranged, had not figured in this equation at all. She was simply, to the parents as well as to the brothers, "troubled."

Where were Jen and Ruth? Peeing a waterfall?

"Last night of freedom!" John smiled, raising his glass. "To your joining the ranks of the sorely oppressed."

"That is an idiotic toast," Dolph said. "I know you've been depressed, but don't take it out on me, and none of that sexist stuff when Ruth gets back." He added a trickle of water to his glass, stirring with the plastic stirrer before sipping tentatively.

This remark surprised John, it certainly did. But he thought it would be best to sidestep the whole issue, to change the subject.

"Will you go to the lake house after your trip, or—"

"Ruth's son, who is a senior in high school, will have been there for a week by the time we get back. They're in Switzerland now, on a class trip—couldn't make the wedding is the official story, but I happen to know he's showing up tomorrow as a big surprise. Nice kid. He's something of an athlete. Very good values, nobody to worry about in the lake house. The father was an alcoholic, and it made both of them super-cautious."

"I wasn't worried about the house."

"We have so little to say to each other. I know. I know how it is."

"What? Dolph—I have never felt we had little to talk about."

"I called you three times through your whole ordeal. I didn't know what to say. Can you still fuck? That was what I wanted to ask you, and I might as well ask now, so you can't blame it on my drinking."

"Yes, Dolph, I can. I'm not much inclined to, though. But since you're reaching out for some male bonding, I think it's sissy to take antidepressants, so I put vitamin pills in the bottle so Jen won't find me out, and I approximate a contented human being as best I can. Not that you care about that, apparently—only whether I can fuck."

"I'm very relieved to hear it," Dolph said, taking a big sip of his drink and pushing the glass away. "Okay, important business settled before the ladies get back."

"You know, Jen didn't think you'd have sex without being married. So can I tell her she's wrong?"

"You most certainly can. My relationship with Ruth is based on sex."

"Dolph—is this your first drink?"

"It is, and it's my last. She's always worried every man is going to boomerang her back to the kind of life she had with her husband. I'm going to prove her wrong, but she doesn't know that yet." Dolph looked up, but it was Ruth's eyes he met across the room: Ruth, Jen, and some woman who was a shorter, fatter version of Ruth but otherwise looked very much like her. As they arrived at the table, John saw that Ruth's sister was wearing cornucopia earrings. The 801 drag queens would have loved them. She was introduced as Belle. Her husband had a headache from so much driving and was lying down. "But that won't stop me!" she said. John scanned Jen's face, which was set rigidly in a smile. Where had they been for so long?

An attentive waiter brought first one and then a second

chair to the table, removing the salt and pepper shakers and giving them every inch of table space he could. Jen sat in a chair next to John, which he was glad of, and Ruth sat next to Belle, who sat—stupidly—next to Dolph. It would have been a grand gesture to insist on Cristal, but he doubted Belle would know what Cristal was, and he'd have to explain himself—how would he?—to Jen, later. She was materialistic, maybe, but Korbel was good enough for her.

He listened as they placed their drink orders: a white wine, a glass of prosecco (so, really, Jen might have appreciated champagne), and a rum Collins "with extra cherries" for guess who. Dolph still had most of his drink. John ordered another. "Please, no toasts," Dolph said flatly. Now Jen was searching Dolph's face—what a remark to make, sotto voce but quite audible. What could it mean?

John paid the bill on the sly as he and Jen were leaving, but that grand gesture would probably be lost, because Dolph, Ruth, and Belle remained. Belle, it seemed, meant to make it a night of drinking. "Oh, we have reservations at eight," Jen had said suddenly—and how good she'd remembered. She'd stood immediately, and John had sprung up beside her.

"They're going to their room! That's their 'dinner reservation,'" Belle joked.

He couldn't wait to be out of there, away from the conversation about Dolph replacing pipes in the lake house. And something about a guy who reached in the woodpile and was bitten by a snake, Dolph having to get him in the truck and race him to the hospital, and people in the emergency room seeming to think he should just wait his turn . . . Crazy. But why would there have been a woodpile when the chimney had needed to be fixed for years—rebuilt, really—and they couldn't light a fire? Dolph seemed to be on very good terms with the man who'd gotten the snakebite, but all the information about how inefficient the emergency room was . . . and all the while John could have been checking his watch secretly, if he'd even remembered their reservation. Which was a reservation to eat dinner. During which he planned to drink a very good bottle of wine with his wife.

Except that no sooner had they been seated—a lovely table in the front of the restaurant, and to his surprise, the waitress remembered them from the one dinner they'd had there the year before—than Jen took a call during which she looked more and more concerned. At one point, while he was considering the wine list and thinking about a California zinfandel versus the more usual pinot noir, she rolled her eyes at him. Those times she even answered her phone in a restaurant, she always told whoever was calling that she was eating and would call back later, but she was not doing that, nor did she respond when he held up the wine list and pointed to the zinfandel. In fact, it looked like she was about to cry. "I don't understand," she said quietly. It wasn't Bee; this was not the way conversations went with Bee. Something pertaining to Jen's mother? One of her clients? He meant to order the zinfandel, but the waitress had good manners and was staying away from the table while Jen hunched over her phone. Then, after many murmurings from which he could make out only a few words or phrases, Jen said something he could not hear at all and flipped the phone shut. "George turns out to be a total beast. He's left her a note; he's taken off even though he got that summer job in the chemistry lab. He left her a joint and—this is ironic—a bottle of wine, saying she should lighten up and then wise up, I think that was what she said: that she needed to wise up and realize she needed to get her act together, but that whether she did or not, he'd be in California with his former girlfriend. She thought he'd be getting on the plane with her tomorrow—how idiotic, anyway, that they were flying—and she's devastated. A joint and a bottle of wine, and he goes back to his girlfriend and sticks her with the rent and his cat and breaks her heart without even a conversation?"

John raised a finger and, when the waitress came quickly to the table, ordered the pinot noir. "Good decision," she said, nodding, and went away. She couldn't have been much older than their daughter—their brilliant daughter who had chosen not so brilliantly her first great love. From this vantage point, though, he thought he would advise smoking the joint and drinking the wine.

He took Jen's hand and shook his head ruefully. Maybe, just maybe, Jen would recover after a glass of wine. He withdrew his hand. "Is she still coming?" he asked.

"Yes, but John, she's in a very bad way. She said horrible things about herself that are completely untrue. Go outside and call her." She reached in her purse and brought out the phone. "She doesn't want to upset you, because of everything, you know, but you're not going to be that upset, are you? Call her. Say something to console her."

He crossed paths with the waitress, carrying two enormous stemmed, bowl-shaped glasses to their table. The pinot noir was from a vineyard they'd toured. It was sure to be excellent. But he continued out the door into the humid evening. Except for the restaurant, it wasn't an interesting neighborhood. Still, he liked the old architecture, the easy parking. He opened the phone and looked at it, looked at someone just around the corner having trouble parallel-parking, felt the urge to go to their car and do it for them— such a good guy; such a humanitarian. He held the phone to his ear but did not make the call. It was even possible he might not get found out. That Bee would show up the next day, or call again, and his not talking to her wouldn't even be a subject of conversation. He had some curiosity about how cheap the wine was that George had left her. Some dreadful bottle from Trader Joe's, or had it been a meaningful bottle of wine? A lovely, fresh Fleurie? The mere name danced on your tongue. A crisp Sancerre? Two very pretty young women got out of their now-parked car, the wheels too far from the curb, closed their doors, and teetered in the opposite direction in their high heels.

Into the phone, he said, "Now, follow Daddy's advice and sip your wine until you feel better, then light the joint and feel even better, but leave some of the wine until later, in case you wake up in the middle of the night. Tomorrow you'll alight from the plane and still be our princess, and your mother will say vile things about men she thought she'd forgotten until now, and your daddy will write you a big check for the summer's rent but make it very clear that you can always come home, you're always welcome, you're the point of everything, the reason for living . . . because by then Daddy will have had a good meal and a bottle of wine and escaped his strange brother and all the goings-on that don't really matter because everything is just a little bit too contrived, isn't it? A little too superficial, symbolic in a way that assures others, maybe, but not Daddy." He shut the phone, dropped it in his pocket, and went back into the restaurant, where two glasses of wine had been poured. His wife looked up expectantly.

"She's decided that not only can she live through it, she's glad she found out now how unstable he is. She was already having a glass of wine."

"Really?" Jen said. "But even that's awfully odd, don't you think?"

"We've forgotten what it's like to be nineteen. Let's have a sip of wine and no toast, in honor of my brother."

Jen giggled. She said, "You have to wonder what would make someone say a thing like that."

Ah, his dear wife had ventured out onto the first crossing stone, stepped onto the erratic path that passed through the river of life's confusion. There would be another stone, an easy distance away, the one referred to earlier in the evening, then the even more reassuring, flat, "Isn't the wine good?" stepping-stone, and soon enough she'd have arrived at the final, non sequitur stone, then she'd scurry up the bank into his arms.

She ordered salmon. He ordered steak. Reassured by the pretty, thin young waitress (who probably lived on crackers and water with lemon) that they had chosen well, they sank a bit deeper into the comfortable seats. The smell of fresh flowers reminded him of inhaling the soap earlier, his seconds of respite. He broke off a bit of bread and breathed in its yeasty aroma; he pushed the point of his knife into some sunflower-yellow butter, well tempered, and smeared it over the bread's pocked surface. Even the touch of the wine stem in his fingers was lovely, let alone what the glass contained. Which, as he swirled and sipped, would be reassuring. Because really: What could he say to his daughter, who believed her life to be over? That she should see a doctor and get medicine that would alter her mood and, if that worked, dump it out and imitate her improved behavior? She was at Harvard. She would be fine. Her best friend was at BU. Of course Bee would call her, and she would come, like the Red Cross nurse. It would all be fine, a lot of talk trashing men, but what else was new? Daddy was exempt.

Bee arrived in Portland almost on schedule and called with a shaky yet brave voice: Yes, the wheels were really on the ground.

They drove to get her. Bee was standing outside the terminal in a dropped-waist Laura Ashley dress and bronze T-strap heels, carrying a little cardigan. She didn't even cry when Jen threw herself into her daughter's arms. In fact, she looked beseechingly over her mother's shoulder at her father, who stepped forward and clasped her hands once Jen had relinquished her. "We won't talk about it unless you do," he said emphatically, offering Bee what he hoped was a real possibility, a clue about how he'd like her to behave.

It worked. On the way to the wedding they talked about Cambridge, about the many bookstores and newsstands that used to be there when they were young, along with record stores—records!—and the wonderful Reading International that had such amazing foreign publications, and literary magazines, and of course there had been the ice-cream store, where the sundaes dripped fudge sauce onto a little plastic tray and the sauce slipped all around when you tried to scoop it up. They talked about the family trip they'd taken to Tortola the year Bee started high school, the snorkeling off of Frenchmans Cay, the Painkillers they'd drunk at Pusser's, letting Bee sip from their straws every now and then because nobody at the bar really wanted to notice she was only a girl. And those Brits who fell into the water trying to get into their dinghy. It still brought a laugh. But no, they hadn't taken the boat to Virgin Gorda, though they'd known there was a cave you could snorkel through; they'd just been too lazy, lying in hammocks, snorkeling in the late afternoon, riding around in their Mini Moke.

"Turn left onto route 302," the voice on the GPS said, and Jen—who'd felt like driving, she'd simply felt like driving—turned the Lexus onto the road and listened to "arriving at destination in five hundred yards," just as they all did, each, no doubt, having a different idea of what constituted five hundred yards. Bee sat in the backseat, the way she had as a child. In his Bilzerian suit, John sat more upright than usual, which was the way he responded to a perfectly tailored suit and a tie firmly tied. Jen was wearing her blue dress, which did indeed look lovely. She'd brought her pearl earrings he'd bought her in Paris years ago; she'd cleaned her rings before leaving the house, so they sparkled in the late-morning sunlight. "Arriving at destination on left," the GPS informed them, and Jen turned it off.

At the church there was a jumble of cars, and the minister stood leaning into a driver's window, then almost ran to the next car to poke his head in that window. They couldn't hear, with the windows up . . . something about parking elsewhere? But why was the minister himself running around like a headless chicken? A woman in a car exiting the grassy parking lot beside the church—not someone they knew—hollered to someone in a sports car, "Ruth fell in the shower and broke her ribs. It's horrible! Just horrible! She fell."

Through the windshield, John saw Belle, in a pink caftan and a picture-brim hat, running from the church with a huge vase of flowers. The minister hollered for Belle to wait for him—he was going to perform the ceremony at the hotel, the very hotel they'd just come from, but no one was invited, Ruth was in terrible pain, she had a concussion, it was all terrible, but he was needed to perform the ceremony anyway. "Who can pick up Ruth's son?" another man was asking, going from car to car. A line of cars sat empty, many of the drivers and passengers having hopped out to see what was the matter. People in suits and dresses threw their arms around each other and talked, and a small dog ran in circles on the church lawn.

Right, right: Ruth's son had flown back as a surprise for his mother, but he'd been in flight when her accident happened, and of course Dolph could not pick the boy up at the airport because he would be getting married, and the minister could not, and the lady in the purple dress with the tawny scarf could not because she didn't know where the Portland airport was. In any case, why was everyone so sure a transatlantic flight would land on time? But the boy did not have a cell phone, no one could leave a message so he would get it when the plane landed. Who was supposed to pick him up? Couldn't that person be located—or was that person en route to the airport, unaware of the situation? You kept hearing that everyone on earth had a cell phone, but none of these young people did. Shrieking at another woman, holding yet another, taller vase of flowers, Belle was saying that no matter what, she was not going to miss her sister's wedding; someone else called out to the minister to ask why the wedding couldn't be delayed until later in the day. He replied that he was certainly available, would do everything possible to still serve (as he put it), but as he understood it, Ruth and Randolph were awaiting his immediate presence. Some man did, at least, have Dolph on the phone. People cleared the way for Dolph's brother—Belle had screamed that was who John was—so he walked toward a man holding out a cell phone—truth was, he always called his brother's landline, he wouldn't have known how to contact him by cell. He thanked the man and tried to appear not as crazed and unreasonable as the other people, in or out of cars, standing around in suits and newly loosened ties and fancy dresses. The owner of the cell phone was the man who stacked wood, it seemed; the man had made that point very distinctly as he'd handed over the phone. Bee came to hover near John, but Jen was still in what looked like a bumper-car pileup. Someone with an SUV was behaving very rudely, though it seemed that person might not even be part of the wedding, but trying to drive down the road.

"Dolph, hello," John said, covering one ear from the crying baby in its mother's arms nearby, the mother holding her high heels in one hand and clasping her crying baby with her other arm.

"For once in your life, you've got to be helpful," his brother shouted. "Look, her son was coming back to surprise her. You've got to go to the airport and meet the plane. Let me give you the information."

"Dolph," he said, "why do you have to get married right this minute?"

"The minister's on his way!" Dolph said.

"No, he's not. He's running around yelling at cars like some L.A. valet who just had a psychotic break."

"Then send him! Tell him to get going," Dolph said.

"Dolph, do you understand what I'm saying? We'll go back to the airport, but do you have any way of knowing the plane is going to land on time?"

"It will be very meaningful to her to have her son here!" Dolph yelled. The volume might have been adjustable, but John didn't know where to look for the voice control, so he held the phone away from his ear. Bee lost interest in what he was saying to her uncle and scampered toward . . . well, damned if she wasn't heading toward Belle and some runt in a white tuxedo. A white tuxedo? "For once in your life, do me a real favor," Dolph said. "His name is Jack, and he's tall, six foot two, blond, how many tall blond seventeen-year-olds can there be on the plane? Try not to upset him, just get him to the hotel . . ."

"Okay, okay, what's the flight information? And why the hell do you keep saying 'for once in your life'? When did I ever let you down?"

"When I wanted to go to Colby, and you told Mom it was freezing cold and in the middle of nowhere, like I had to be on the streets of New Haven to be part of the real world—your real world."

"Dolph, Jesus, that was eons ago. I don't even know that I said that, but if I did—"

"What about the time we hitched and left the skateboard in that guy's car, and you said we'd been robbed while we were swimming? What about that?" John could almost hear Dolph spitting.

"You wanted me to say we'd been hitching and get in all kinds of trouble?" John said.

"You lie about everything. You lie all the time."

"What? I don't lie. That was kid stuff—trying to avoid being punished. So what if I wasn't always blubbering out the truth, the way you were? I got hit a lot less, didn't I?"

"Now you're trying to insult me and ruin my wedding, even though you'll say you aren't. You'll say this is clearing the air. If you can still fuck your wife, why does she say you can't?"

"What?"

"Bee told me. You live in a fantasy world, John. You always have. You live in a world where things go the way you say they go, for your convenience."

"Dolph, fuck you. If you want me to go get this kid, shut up immediately. What the hell would Bee say that for when it's not even true? I've fucked Jen twice since the radiation stopped. Get married and then come watch us, what do you think? We can check back in to the hotel. I can give you verifiable evidence."

The woodcutter's eyes were wide. Instead of pretending not to hear, he stood where he was, leaning as far forward as possible. In a minute, he'd be the perfect pantomime of a dowsing rod, having located water. Who else had heard?

John looked quickly around, but Bee—exasperating, full-of-opinions, wrongly assuming Bee—in fact, all the people around him had retreated; now everyone was leaving in a more orderly way. Screaming Belle had driven off, which he'd seen in his peripheral vision as he and Dolph argued. There were irises scattered like huge pickup sticks on the grass. The minister stood at Jen's car window, talking.

"American Airlines 662, arriving in twenty-five minutes. I'll get the airport to page him. I'll tell him to wait outside, you'll be there as fast as you can," Dolph said.

"Right. Your impotent brother will round him up because he's so terribly sorry he said you should go to Yale instead of some liberal-arts college where you read poetry and walk around through snow tunnels. Fine, Dolph. No problem—I'll race off to Portland International, ferry him back to the hotel. You have your wedding, I'll just drag my wife and daughter back to our house, where they can both pity me. It's turning out to be a great day." He snapped the phone closed. "And you," he said to the woodcutter. "Explain to me what you're doing chopping wood when there's no way to burn it."

"There's a Jøtul stove, potty mouth," the man said. "And life in the country isn't the sorry thing you think it is. Your brother is a gentleman. He would be the one to fix that house up, fix it so people from away, like you, could use it."

John got the woodcutter squarely in the jaw. The first man he'd hit in his entire life. So it was surprising the way the man grimaced as he sank to his knees, tossing his cell phone free as if it were a grenade. The few people on the lawn looked in their direction, too stunned or frightened to react. He saw Jen's narrowed eyes, peering around the minister's back, saw them clearly even though his distance vision wasn't great. There was going to be hell to pay. After which they'd make up, and he'd fuck her.

Why should he go to Portland airport after what Dolph had said to him, dragging up all that garbage from over thirty years ago? He'd be a chump to do it. Let the kid figure it out, let him figure out how to get where he wanted to go—just the way Bee's fine fellow had figured out things for himself—starting with paying to get a cab to the hotel, where he could be the human equivalent of a gift box, all tied up in shiny paper with a big ribbon as long as his umbilical cord. If the world belonged to the young, it was time for the kid to start coping.

ANECDOTES

"My husband and I were in Tivoli, and we went to the gardens at Villa d'Este. He'd been to Italy before, but it was my first trip. There were rails in front of the fountains because the water was so polluted, they wanted to keep you from being splashed."

"I went to Italy when they were almost giving shoes away—shoes made of leather as soft as gloves—and there were no tours being given of the Forum. I don't think there was one Japanese tourist in all of Rome. Maybe my trip was before cameras were invented."

Lucia and I were playing the Italy-One-Upmanship game in the backseat of a Carey car. I knew I was going to be the one to pay the fare. I was doing my friend Christine a favor. Lucia, her mother, had come in from Princeton on the train to hear Christine's talk at Columbia about Margaret Bourke-White. Christine would also be showing slides of newly discovered photographs, printed from Bourke-White negatives that had been mislabeled at *Life*. She was hoping to be hired full-time at Columbia, and this was one of several talks she would be giving there and elsewhere, aiming to impress.

Christine had hoped to be a model when she came to the city, but she'd been diagnosed with diabetes shortly thereafter and hadn't been able to keep up the pace. There were still problems with her energy; she felt like she was having what she'd heard were classic menopausal symptoms at thirty-four. She was pretty, though, as you'd imagine. I'd met her in college when we'd been two-timed by the same guy, who also happened to be our professor. I overheard the tantrum she threw, late one evening. I'd gone back to school because I'd forgotten my raincoat, and the forecast was for a weekend of rain. Arthur was in his office; Christine was yelling, and as I came up the stairs, I heard my name mentioned. Loudly. She and I went to a bar when she'd finished confronting him. He went home to his wife. Christine and I lost touch but met up several years later in New York, when she called to compliment me on an article I'd written for *The New York Times Magazine*.

Earlier in the week Christine had asked me to pick up her mother before she realized that my car was in the shop (hit from behind at a red light on West End Avenue), and she probably also called because I did better with her mother, generally, than she did.

"Let me ask you this, Anna," Lucia said. "Was there a moment when you knew your marriage wasn't going to work, or was it more gradual, the realization?"

"He took the puppy back to the breeder. That didn't help."

"You always say something unexpected. That's why you're a good writer, I guess. Let me ask this: Do you think Christine didn't marry Paul because all her women friends are independent, or do you think she just got tired of him? He sent me a Christmas card, and his heart is still broken."

I thought for a moment about poor brokenhearted Paul. Though ostensibly monogamous for the three-plus years he and Christine had lived together, he'd given her herpes. Another thing I knew about him was that he'd put a pillow over his head and stayed in bed the night she had food poisoning. I also thought that when she stopped wearing makeup and pulled her hair back in a French twist, the little tendrils that escaped still didn't make her feminine enough for him. He'd kept a picture from her modeling days in his wallet.

"Lucia," I said, "I don't think women break up with their boyfriends because other women are without boyfriends."

"But think: The diabetes made her angry, didn't it? She wanted somebody to take it away. I find significance in the fact that she started to go out with her doctor."

"You're as funny as I am," I said. "Shall I recommend you to my agent?"

"Funny? Nothing funny about that awful disease," she said, missing my point because she found it necessary to correct everyone.

"Which side?" the driver said.

"On the right," I said. "Far corner."

He gave me a quick look in the rearview mirror; the light had just turned red, and by the time he got to the far corner, cars in back of him would start honking the minute he stopped.

The young man setting up the slide projector looked up, assuming one of us must be the speaker. He held a clip-on

mike, awkwardly, as if courting someone with a little un-
wanted flower.

Lucia sat in a chair midway down the aisle. She looked
vaguely irritated, or simply tired. She had not wanted Christine to be a model, but neither had she wanted her to be in
the academic world, which Lucia felt was full of pseudo-
intellectuals hiding from society. As far as I could tell, Lucia
had some vague notion that her daughter should be working
outside the system, to save the world.

"Wasn't this scheduled for seven?" I said. "Where is
everybody?"

"I'm just here to set up," the young man said. "You've got
nothing to do with this?"

I shook my head. That was so often my situation with
Christine: She insisted I was indispensable, though I had
nothing directly to do with what was going on. In school,
I hadn't known she was seeing Arthur, but when I'd found
out, she'd insisted that we have a drink because only I could
fill in the pieces of the puzzle.

Lucia had taken off her enormous scarf—cashmere, certainly—and folded it on her lap, her hands clasped on top.
She looked at me with quiet attention, as if I might start
singing. Her hair, streaked with silver, was windblown. The
way the wind had messed up her part made her look less
austere. Where Christine had gotten her cheekbones, and her
lips, I couldn't imagine. (Her father had left before Christine
began school, and I'd seen him only once in a snapshot she
carried in her wallet.) Lucia was attractive but in a quite
ordinary way. Like many women her age, she diverted attention from her face by swirling scarves around her throat

and shoulders, wearing big necklaces or turtlenecks that seemed like perfect soufflés just lifted from the oven. I was rummaging in my bag, trying to find the piece of paper on which I'd written the time and place. Yes; the talk was taking place here—that's what I'd written down—at seven P.M.

Suddenly there were voices in the corridor, and students rushed in like horses spooked by firecrackers. There had been another lecture—this was part two of their evening. I stared into the crowd, hoping to see Christine. The person who'd set up the slide projector paced the aisle, talking on his cell phone. The microphone sat in a tangle of wires back on the table.

Lucia beckoned to me. I walked back a few rows, jostled by students—though I noticed none of them had disturbed the elderly lady who sat in the aisle seat, her garments piled in her lap. Lucia had slipped out of her coat, which was a shade somewhere between beige and butter.

"Listen: You have always been such a good friend to Christine that I want to tell you something. Will you sit?" She patted the chair next to her.

Almost none of the students seemed to be wearing winter clothes. A few had on unzipped jackets. I sat next to Lucia, carefully stepping over her elegant shoes.

"Here is what I want to talk about," Lucia said. "You remember Thanksgiving in Princeton? I pointed out my neighbor—the lady who had been so sweet on the visiting writer?"

"Vaguely," I said.

"Vaguely! I made an apple tart from scratch, with crème fraîche!"

"It was delicious. Your meals always are. I just couldn't

remember the face of the woman who'd—what? She'd written love notes to him or something? To the writer?"

"She wanted him to come live there. She said, 'Bring your wife, there is a whole separate house. Don't commute the way you do, it will wear you out. I love having young people around. I will teach your wife to cook—whatever she wants.' Which is true, by the way. Edwina cooks better than I do."

"I didn't know all that. I think you whispered to me who she was. That she'd made trouble by writing letters to him."

"She wrote letters, and he finally came over to have a drink. They hit it off, and he decided he and his wife should take her up on her offer."

"So what happened?" I said.

"His wife got on a small chartered plane in Michigan, and that was the end of her. It went down in a storm, the pilot killed, everybody. Two other people, I think. And he came over to Edwina's house and picked up bricks from the new walkway that was being laid and threw them through her picture window. The police were called. He was completely crazy. He couldn't ever go back to teach his classes. And Edwina was devastated."

Christine had come into the auditorium. From nowhere, the man with the tangled microphone charged up to her, getting much too close, so that before she understood who he was, she jumped back. She had a bulging bag slung over her shoulder, and carried another bag. It must have started raining, because her hair was matted to her head. A clump of it curved down her cheek like the top of a big question mark. Her earring stud might have been the point that completed the punctuation.

"Your friend shouldn't feel bad," I said. "You're right. It wasn't her fault, of course."

"Yes, but she thinks it was," Lucia said. She did not follow my eyes to Christine.

I waved. Christine didn't see me at first, but then she did. "There she is," I said to Lucia, wondering why she wasn't turning as I waved.

"What I understand of the situation is that he'd slept with Edwina once. She's old enough to be his mother! She was offering her home anyway, so I don't think he was calculating. . . ."

A girl and a boy pushed past us, trailing jackets. The girl had on pink UGGs.

I stood to walk toward Christine, who looked a little disoriented. When she saw me, she gave me a nervous smile. She said, "I washed my hair, and my dryer broke. Can you believe it?"

"That's awful," I said.

"Thanks for getting her," Christine said, squeezing my shoulder as she walked past, the microphone already clipped to her lapel, the receptor in her coat pocket. "Hi, Mom," she said, smiling but not bending to kiss her mother's cheek. They were more affectionate privately, I'd noticed. In public, there was some awkwardness.

The row Lucia sat in was almost full. She frowned as more students pushed past her seat. It was a small auditorium, but this was a good crowd.

Christine stood behind the podium, her coat tossed on a chair, the bags slumped beside it.

"The person who was going to introduce me has laryngitis,

so I'm just going to introduce myself—I'm Christine Liss, from the English department—and thank you for coming on such a cold night. There is exciting new work by the eminent photographer Margaret Bourke-White that I've gotten access to as it's being cataloged, some of which you'll see tonight. Ms. Bourke-White was a fearless photographer who did the first cover for *Life* magazine—a very influential picture magazine of its time, with a reputation that still elicits great respect. She worked downtown, in the then newly built Chrysler Building—a building with a terrace where she kept two small alligators she was given as gifts, until they grew large enough to devour the tortoise she had also been given. Some people wouldn't visit the studio. She was married twice, the last time to Erskine Caldwell, whose name might not be as recognizable to you now as he would have hoped. Her photographs can be seen many places in New York—currently at ICP Midtown. What you're going to see tonight are mostly aerial shots. . . ."

I probably should have returned to sit with Lucia, but I'd trailed Christine halfway down the aisle, and when the lights had begun to dim, I'd sat as if I'd been playing musical chairs. Down the row, someone was videotaping Christine, the little square of light distracting and mesmerizing. Rows back, a cell phone played music and was quickly turned off. The projection screen was filled with aerial views of destruction: Germany after the war.

Christine's hair had begun to dry, and she looked different with her hair down and her glasses on. Her earnestness made her look younger and took me back to the bar where we'd sat in Pennsylvania years ago. Christine cursing Arthur, pulling a necklace with a lapis stone out from under the neckline of her blouse, pulling so hard she broke the chain, the gold puddling on the tabletop, the little stone flashing in the fluorescent light. She had scooped it up and later addressed an envelope to Arthur's wife and mailed it to her without comment.

Slide after slide, when seen from a high vantage point, the world was transformed into abstract art. The photographs were pattern and shape before they became slowly distinguishable as the landscape—the wreckage—they depicted then; as you stared, they devolved into abstraction again, making your eyes skate figure eights. Margaret Bourke-White had no fear of heights, Christine told us, and couldn't have worried about being in a helicopter when she thought nothing of crawling out on the gargoyles atop the Chrysler Building to photograph the city. There she was, bent over her camera, high up, like a steelworker. She photographed machines. She photographed Stalin, who didn't give her an inch until she nervously dropped her flashbulbs, and then he laughed.

Christine talked about industry, mass production. She talked about photographs in black and white, about silver halide crystals and how photographs were processed. The images at the end of the talk were back in the world—dams and wheels, enormous things. When the lights came on, people applauded. Christine smiled, unclipping the mike, pushing her hair out of her eyes. A few people called out to each other; cell phones appeared immediately, hats and scarves were left behind, picked up by someone else who ran up behind them, like a relay race in reverse. I saw one of Christine's colleagues, whose name I couldn't remember, and said hello. He said, "God, Bourke-White photographed Stalin's *mother*, you know. I'd think *that* was a dangerous assignment—unless the guy didn't like his mother. And since he didn't like anybody . . ." He shook his head as he passed by to congratulate Christine. The person operating the slide projector was removing the tray, putting it in a box, his cell phone clamped between his chin and shoulder. Lucia stood, her row empty.

"Why do they wear those boots like horse hooves?" she said, looking at the departing students. "Pastel-pink horse hooves."

"Comfortable, I guess," I said. "Sort of like big bedroom slippers. They love pajama bottoms, too."

"It used to be that every generation had its style. I guess this generation's style is what you'd wear if you spent your day in the bedroom. In my day, that would have been a negligee and makeup, which is just as silly, I suppose."

"What a fascinating talk Christine gave," I said.

"Too many anecdotes," Lucia said.

I looked at her, surprised. She was often hard on Christine, but the talk had been so obviously good, I hadn't been expecting such a remark.

"It doesn't matter how many husbands a woman has or doesn't have. I don't know why she felt she had to mention that," she said. "I thought she was going to digress and tell us about the man she loved the most, a soldier she was going to reunite with except that he was in a military hospital in Italy, and they bombed his wing of the hospital. The other wing was intact, but he was killed instantly."

"You know about Margaret Bourke-White?" I said.

"I read autobiographies, Anna. It's all there in her book."

"Well, I thought Christine did a very good job, talking about how Bourke-White got into the workforce, and—"

"Getting the job done is what's important. Not how you got the job."

"You're too hard on her," I said.

She looked at me. "Do you think so? I just don't have much patience with anecdotes."

"She was explaining that Margaret Bourke-White had a lot of sadness in her life, just like the rest of us."

"Yes, I think we could assume that everyone experiences sadness," Lucia replied.

I thought: Why do you never offer to pay, like you're a princess? Why not arrange your own transportation in the city? Why don't you cook your own Thanksgiving dinner for fewer people, rather than having two Mexican women in the kitchen all day, and you making only your perfect apple tarts?

My face must have clouded over; she put her hand on my arm and said, "Sit down for a second. We're friends, you and I. I have something important to tell you."

I sank rather than sat. Was she going to tell me she was sick? She had seated herself one chair in, giving me the aisle, gesturing grandly, as if the seat were a gift. The last cluster of students stood talking to Christine.

"You're a writer. Writers have become celebrities, haven't they? Whether they want to be or not. Well, the visiting writer did want to be the center of attention, it seemed to me. Writers are so often insecure. So let me tell you: In my one conversation with him, it seems he'd never even heard that Bruce Chatwin hadn't told the whole truth and nothing but the truth. Didn't know Chatwin had made things up—including the information about what killed him, we now know. If I'd talked about James Frey, I suppose I could have made some of the same points. From what the visiting writer revealed about himself, I thought he was a literary lightweight. I wouldn't have offered him, and his wife, my house. But that's neither here nor there. Edwina, my friend, has been taking one of those mood-altering drugs, and she's calmer now, so she understands she isn't responsible, but you know, she'd gotten to the point where she imagined him and his wife in her house. She imagined them sitting by the fireplace, she looked at her window and saw the shattered glass even though it had been replaced, she saw the dead woman standing in the kitchen doing dishes—she didn't really *see* her, she's not crazy, but she imagined her. I told her, 'Come to my house. Get out of there; get out of that environment for a while.' I guess I did just what she did, didn't I, offering my house? But she was impulsive, and I was her friend of over twenty-five years. So it came as quite a surprise to both of us that we fell in love. We did. Your eyes are as big as saucers, Anna. If we did, we did."

I nodded, registering the beginning of a faint headache as I narrowed my eyes.

"Writers like to surprise readers, but they don't like to be surprised, I've found." She grasped my wrist. "Here is why I'm telling you: I'm going to tell Christine about it, and I think it's going to come as something of a shock for her, so I wanted you to know before we have our drink. You knew we were going to the Carlyle, where I'm staying tonight, the three of us, to have a drink?"

"I don't think she told me," I said, but as I spoke, I vaguely remembered Christine saying something. More as a possibility, though. Her phone call to me a couple of days before had been on the run, pleading: "I've got to teach, then run home and walk Walter, then get back to give the talk, so can you please, *please*, meet her train and see that she gets there okay?"

Lucia could book a room at an expensive hotel but not offer to pay for the car? She wanted . . . what? For me to be prepared in case her daughter became (improbably) a basket case when she told her? I wished she hadn't told me. I wasn't pleased about knowing this information before Christine did. It would make a liar of me if I pretended what I was hearing was news, and I'd be her mother's confidante if I let on that she'd already told me.

"This is private. It's between you and your daughter," I said. "I'm going to go home and let you two talk."

"No, Anna, you have to join us," she said.

"You want an audience, just like those writers you're so suspicious of," I said. "I'd wonder, if I were you, whether he ever slept with your friend, or whether that wasn't her imagination, too. You hear about it when a person has a reputation for sleeping around. I doubt that it's true."

I had met his wife at a fund-raiser. She'd quickly confessed that she felt out of place and didn't know what to talk about. Her pin had fallen on the floor, that was how we'd met. I'd bent to pick it up and had helped her refasten it to the collar of her silky black shirt. When her husband the writer saw us talking, he came up to us. I could tell by the way he put his arm around his wife's shoulders that he worried I might be too much for her in some way. They'd both grown up in the Midwest, and I'd grown up on the Upper West Side—which was no doubt why Pennsylvania had seemed like Siberia to me in my college days. I'd liked the writer's protectiveness, and I'd picked up on the fact that he wanted his wife to talk to people on her own, but the minute she did, he wanted to make sure she was comfortable. When he saw that we were giggling and talking about jewelry, he went away.

"Anna?" Lucia said. "You seem to have turned your attention inward. If I didn't know you so well, I might think I'd surprised you."

"I don't care who you have a relationship with," I said. "If you really care what I think about lesbianism, I approve of whatever relationship brings people happiness."

I walked away, up the aisle. When I was younger, I would have bought in to it, assumed I was involved just because someone older insisted I be. Now I thought how nice it would be to listen to music I wanted to listen to instead of the tinkling piano at the hotel. I wouldn't feel I had to offer to pay for my own drink, because I'd already paid earlier in the week, when I'd bought myself a bottle of Grey Goose I could pour from, into my favorite etched glass I'd bought at a stoop sale in Brooklyn. What would Christine think of me disappearing? Maybe that I was smart. I wondered how Lucia would lead in to the subject. By criticizing Christine for being "anecdotal," then zinging her with an important fact? Lucia was self-important and manipulative, and if Christine didn't know that by now, I could mention the obvious, by way of consolation, later.

Outside, I turned the corner and went into my favorite Chinese restaurant. There were only two tables, both taken, so I went to the counter for takeout. "Anna!" said Wang, the waiter, turning the paper menu toward him, pencil poised delicately, like a conductor's baton, to circle what I wanted.

"You don't know she wants shrimp fried rice?" said his brother, who was now known as James. James was taking night classes at NYU and sometimes asked me for help with his homework. "Once, twice a month she has chicken with broccoli, but tonight she doesn't want that. This is her look when she's in a hurry. In a hurry, always shrimp fried rice." He smiled a big smile and circled the correct item and handed the piece of paper through the opening into the kitchen. "Great reading in my course. The poetry of William Butler Yeats. Next time we'll talk," James said.

Wang had walked away from the counter and was standing at one of the tables, where a customer with his hands folded on top of his violin case on the shiny tabletop seemed to be giving him a bad time about the beer not being cold enough.

When I left, I held the paper bag away from my coat (I always worried I'd stain it). I'd splurged on the coat three years before, a midcalf cashmere I'd resolved I'd take good care of and wear for years. Every time I slipped into it, I felt like something good could happen.

In my apartment, no husband, no Walter the dog awaited me. Instead of a pet, I had a terrarium with small plastic knights inside, some on horseback, some felled, some still fighting on Astroturf sprinkled with red nail polish—a gift from a boyfriend who'd been a disaster, though he'd had a great sense of humor. I took off my coat, reached in the pocket, ripped up the receipt for the car, and threw it in the trash so I wouldn't be tempted to do something mean, like send it to Lucia. Christine was still my friend, though I was free of her mother now. I'd been without a family for almost ten years, and I didn't want a replacement, with all the inevitable surprises and secrets. The more I thought about it, the more sure I was that the writer hadn't slept with Lucia's friend, but that Lucia's neighbor/lover was on the make, and if she couldn't have the writer, she'd decided to move on to Lucia. I was glad he'd thrown a brick through her window, glad she'd had at least a moment of fear, that someone had created a little havoc in her so-well-intentioned Princeton life.

I sipped the vodka, admiring the glass, enjoying the taste. And then—though this is merely anecdotal—I picked up the phone, called information, and asked for Arthur's number in Pennsylvania from an operator who said, "Please hold," followed by an automated voice that gave me the number. He still lived in the same place. Imagine that: He was where he'd been all his adult life.

Arthur's wife answered on the second ring. She answered pleasantly, the way people did years ago, when there was no screening of calls, no answering machine to kick in. "Hello," she said, and I thought: She is completely, *completely* vulnerable. The winter landscape of the little town outside Pittsburgh where she lived came back to me: the whited-out sky; the frozen branches always about to snap. If I hung up, she probably wouldn't even know there was such a thing as hitting *69 to find out who the caller was. Or maybe she would, and she'd call back. Maybe she and I would talk and become fierce enemies or even best friends—why not, if neighbors in their sixties became lovers? But that couldn't really happen, because she and I were just two voices on the telephone. I didn't have anything against her. Back then all I'd had against her was that she had him.

"That necklace," I said, realizing immediately that I needed to raise my voice and speak clearly. "The one with the lapis lazuli. I was your husband's student—it doesn't matter who I am. I'm calling to explain. I returned it to you in 1994 because I found it on the floor of his office and knew it must be yours. He didn't see me pick it up. I was poor, and I wanted to keep it, but I figured it was yours, so I sent it back."

I hung up, crossed the floor, and reached into the terrarium. I bent the knees of one of the warriors and put him back in his saddle atop a shiny black plastic horse. I slipped a shield over another's head, inadvertently toppling him. I delicately stood the figure upright. I decided against a second vodka.

The phone did not ring. I got into bed, under the duvet, then spread my coat on top, the soft collar touching my chin, as I listened to jazz I wanted to hear, long into the night. When the storm started sometime after midnight, I imagined the sleet was hard little notes from a piano way across town that had come to pelt my window, telling me to come out. To come out and play, please.

OTHER PEOPLE'S BIRTHDAYS

Lawrence got on the plane in Charlottesville and flew to Dulles, a quick flight once airborne, but the reading light above the seat had only a slight inward glow, so no paperwork could be done. At Dulles, the board at her gate gave her the bad news: The flight to Boston was delayed, awaiting crew. The crew was probably trapped somewhere because of the side effects of the hurricane and general bad weather on the East Coast—but when were things much different? Whatever it took to make it an arduous trip, and you couldn't say the obvious, you had to smile and say there were worse problems blah blah blah. The mediocre glass of wine for thirteen dollars at the airport bar was one of them. The candy bar she'd eaten on top of that an hour later made her sick. Lawry, she had always been called. Her father had insisted the second and last child be named for him. People pronounced it Laurie, though she thought of herself as Lawrence. Her older sister was called Bett, for Bettina. Their late grandmother's name.

Finally, finally they boarded, the man with the tall toddler—

in a T-shirt, running shoes, and diapers—bemused by the boy's stomped excitement: "Yeah, we're going on a plane, that's what we're doing, buddy." Other children were crying or struggling, trying to break free of the hands of parents gripping their wrists. Lawrence knew about that, though she wasn't a mother. She could easily predict the tantrums about to erupt, as if she were mercury rising in a thermometer.

Which dated her. They were digital now.

She had her purse in one hand, a Tumi bag with ingenious inside compartments that meant she could never find anything she reached in for. Why were so many of them narrow? She didn't smoke cigars. She'd managed to fit her Mac into the bag, though that meant she had to leave it unzipped. In her other hand she carried a canvas L.L.Bean bag embossed with an old ex-boyfriend's name, Lincoln. She and Lincoln had once been on the verge of moving in together, though she'd refused to look at apartments with him, and when he'd found one he thought was perfect, she'd gotten cold feet and told him it would be better if he completed his first year of medical school before they lived together. Then she'd seen him talking to a pretty girl at a party—talking in a way that made her nervous. "Exactly what gesture did I make? What gesture?" he'd asked afterward as they got in the car. "Do you want to make me inhibited about using my hands in a particular way when I talk? Are you serious?" Maybe she was insecure, but she also trusted her instincts. Would she be in for a lifetime of watching him gesture in that way with pretty women, with nothing she could ever articulate any better than she'd been able to in the parked car?

Now, waiting in the airport, she saw that there was a

missed call from John, her newer ex-boyfriend, which must have come in while she was drinking her sour Italian white wine. He was a lawyer who worked twelve hours a day, minimum, except for Saturdays shopping for groceries, then on to the racquetball court, followed by a massage and a quiet evening reading a mystery on his Kindle. It had been one, but only one, of the reasons they'd parted company a year and a half ago.

Which also dated her. They had not passively "parted company." He had screamed at her, standing by the Tidal Basin, "You think you have the hardest life, the worst luck, the only problems worth considering. I'm a so-called workaholic because I'm dedicated to something, and I don't expect the world to wipe away my tears. It would be one thing if we were in our twenties, but we're in our forties. Are you ever going to be capable of understanding or even, God forbid, empathy? Or are you just going to protect every minute of your precious time and bounce back and forth from D.C. to Newton to remain the perfect daughter to people who will never thank you for it, who'll always think you're the unimportant one?" The ugliness of that night (she had answered back) had been one of the deciding factors: She'd moved from Washington to Charlottesville, where she'd made a couple of friends, and where people treated her more kindly, and to her surprise, she never visited John in Washington anymore, except for one time she'd driven there to be his date at a fund-raiser at the Corcoran. They'd sat at a big round table with his friends, acquaintances, and colleagues, and she'd felt sure all of them knew what a handful she was (according to John). An hour or so into the evening, she'd taken one very pink rose from the centerpiece as she excused herself to go to the restroom, a rose with no thorns. She'd carried it there, leaving it by the sink while she peed, then carried it Olympic-victory-style to the parking garage, only to forget it overnight in her car. Back in Virginia, the head hung limply, like a dead bird's, when she noticed the rose the next day on the passenger seat.

Starting about the time she'd walked off without saying goodbye, John had called her cell phone, hours later her landline, even her monstrous parents, because for some paranoid reason he'd assumed they'd contacted her and she'd rushed "home" to Newton. All her anger at herself about letting the beautiful flower die had been misplaced in the letter she wrote him, snail mail, saying their relationship was over. He'd continued to call her home phone and her cell, but he'd left her parents out of it, at least. Never once had she called him back, but a few times she'd responded to one of his e-mails. Was that so hard? No, it wasn't, she admitted, but she'd stuck to answering his questions and not even offering some pleasantry. He certainly did not deserve an apology, because to be honest, at the Tidal Basin he had shoved her, hard, as he raged.

She called her father on his cell phone when she disembarked, telling him she was at Terminal C. He was waiting in a nearby area reserved for just that; with luck, they'd be at the house in under half an hour. She wondered if her mother might be along for the ride, or even Bett. The next day would be Bett's forty-third birthday, and they would be driving to Bett's favorite place in the world, Barnacle Billy's, in Perkins Cove in Ogunquit, Maine, where their father had appeared at the playhouse in several roles, years before he became a father. It was where he'd met Johanna forty-five years ago. She'd been taking a year off from nursing school, living with her aunt in Wells, waitressing during the summer and ushering two days a week at the Ogunquit Playhouse in exchange for sitting in the back row and seeing performances. In her father's opinion, Philip Seymour Hoffman was the greatest American actor. He'd taken the Acela to New York to see him in *Death of a Salesman*, and he still talked about little else. Had the play's run been longer, he would have gone a second time. Come to think of it, he liked to repeat experiences. She herself was the repeat of his experience of fatherhood: Bett; Lawrence. Johanna was his second wife (he'd married his first wife at twenty, been divorced at twenty-five). He always bought Volvos.

The new dark-blue Volvo was now coasting to the curb, her father flashing his lights even though she'd raised a hand to let him know she saw him. From inside the car, he popped the trunk, though she only tapped it closed and opened the door on the passenger side, dragging her purse and her L.L.Bean bag in after her, dropping them in the ample room to either side of her feet, leaning toward her father for a wordless peck on the cheek.

"Did you buy the perfect present? Is there a bicycle folded up in that big bag, or a dehydrated horse, maybe?"

"You'll see tomorrow. But I'll give you a hint: You won't have to teach her how to ride a bike or provide any hay."

"Your boyfriend called tonight," he said.

She was startled. After months of silence, he'd called her father? "Why?" she asked, surprised at the childlike petulance in her voice.

"How would I know? I kept waiting to find out. Just a coincidence, it seems. At least he didn't mention knowing you'd be coming in, and I didn't say anything about that, either. He wouldn't know when your sister's birthday is and put two and two together, would he?"

"What did he talk to you about?" she asked. There was no chance he would know the date of her sister's birthday.

"The election. He'd heard what some of Clinton's talking points were going to be and was passing them on. He said it had been the hottest, most humid summer he could remember. We talked about Nora Ephron's death. He met her once in New York, you must know about that? No? At a movie premiere, he said. She gave him the name of a good moving company in Washington, agreed with him that he should live in New York if he was going to be putting up with big-city hassle in the first place. Who wouldn't prefer New York, except maybe for the impossibility of parking. Well, you can do it. You just have to be a millionaire."

"He claims he's moving?" Lawrence asked.

"No, I didn't get that," her father said. "It was something he once thought about." He nodded to himself.

"I can't tell you who to talk to," she said, "but I don't talk to him anymore."

"You're hard-hearted, we all know that."

"Maybe I'll call your ex-wife and shoot the shit about the heat in the Midwest versus the heat in the South."

"She's not in the Midwest anymore. She kept up with

one of Uncle Earle's kids, to my surprise. Nathan. He told me when we saw him last Christmas that she'd moved. She's in Santa Monica."

"Really?" she asked, but her surprise was that he'd seen Nathan. She'd had a huge crush on her cousin when she was a teenager. "What is Nathan doing?"

"Bankrupt," he said. "Lives in Florida, which is one of those states where they can't take your house. He's trying to open an organic nursery there. I sent him a little something, I admit it. I hope he can climb out of the hole."

"Did you know I had a crush on him when I was sixteen or seventeen?"

"You were fifteen when you met Nathan, and yes, I did. He's a nice boy, always was. I look back and think he had a breakdown when he was in college, and nobody in the family reacted to it as seriously as they should have. He was self-medicating all that time he was at Berkeley, is the way I see it now. Maybe it was just the times, the fact that he was overshadowed by his brilliant sister. But this latest reversal isn't going to do him in, I could tell that. He and Bella are still married. They have a rescued greyhound. He sounded pretty good, considering."

"I suppose you and Johanna will be visiting, come winter?"

"You've always been inhabited by the green-eyed monster, Lawrence. What if we did visit? Do you think that would mean we care about Nathan more than we care about our own daughter?" A slight pause. "Daughters."

"Bankrupt!" she said. "Wow. Nathan with that 160 IQ and that long, curly hair."

"Yeah, and some dog racing around looking like a harp

with a big nose. He got my e-mail and sent me a picture of the dog by attachment."

There was little traffic, at least for Boston. When was he going to thank her for coming? Her father had such good manners. He seemed a little preoccupied by something. She asked outright if that might be so.

"Lawrence," he said, a tinge of regret in his voice. He removed one hand from the wheel and took her hand. He held it silently until someone cut them off on the right, and his hands automatically flew back to three o'clock and nine o'clock. Oh, that: life, itself.

Back at the house, Johanna was waiting in the rocker on the porch. The entire vast porch had been an anniversary present to themselves, covering the front of the house and wrapping around one side. A bit of stage decoration: an enormous fern in a Victorian urn. A historically correct light glowed from either side of the front door. Though her father had been the actor, it was her mother who had a flair for the dramatic. "Lawrence, my most wonderful daughter!" she said, enfolding Lawrence in her arms. "Thank you for coming. It's a pick-me-up just to see you."

"Love you," Lawrence whispered as she and her mother embraced. A big moth fluttered against the light, making a sound so loud, it sounded amplified.

"I'll take these things inside. Your sister went to bed early with a headache. But she's so looking forward to tomorrow. Her best friend returned, and a drive to Barnacle Billy's."

She watched her mother's smile instantly subside. Johanna might be able to set stages, but she didn't have her husband's ability to act.

"It's just a regular headache? Not a migraine?"

"She hasn't had a migraine for ages. Knock on wood," her mother said, knocking on the arm of the rocker. She'd sat down. Lawrence handed her canvas bag to her father, indicating with a slight gesture that she'd keep her purse. He took the bag inside. There were three other chairs on the porch, but only one rocker.

Lawrence collapsed into a comfortably cushioned wicker chair. "Everything okay?" she asked.

"We're luckier than most," her mother said, avoiding the question, clearly trying to determine a mood of grateful acceptance. She was really at her best at Thanksgiving, but in recent years, because of the difficulty of air travel, Lawrence hadn't come for Thanksgiving.

"You don't look like a person who's been traveling for hours," her mother said. "Are those new boots? I'm afraid you'll be hot in them here, but you can wear any of my shoes you want." Lawrence smiled, acknowledging all of it: They should be grateful for what they had; the Cole Haan boots were new, and she loved them so much that she'd worn them even though she'd known they'd be too warm; she and her mother had worn the same size shoe for years.

"Vanity," Lawrence said, crossing her legs, showing the boot from its buckled side.

"Have whatever you want," her mother said. "You work hard for your money. You're a wonderful person."

"But you missed your guess about my marrying John, didn't you?"

"I never thought you had to marry at all, unless you were entirely sure you'd found the right one. I just lucked in to your father. I do sometimes regret not going back to school, though."

"And he regrets not being Philip Seymour Hoffman."

"But your father is so inherently *handsome*," Johanna said. She looked up just in time to smile at him as he came out, carrying a tray with three iced teas, big slices of lemon stuck to the rims. None of them took sugar. The sterling-silver iced-tea spoons had belonged to their grandmother and were monogrammed W. As a child, Bett had been spanked for digging in the dirt with one. It was the only time Lawrence could ever remember her mother spanking either of them. But through the years, the spanking had been discussed, and discussed, and discussed. She wished her father had just brought the iced teas without the spoons.

"I'm here, too!" Bett hollered, descending the stairs. She was carrying a big flashlight, like the ones cops use when they stop your car and come to your window. She shone it in their eyes for painful seconds, first Lawrence's, then Johanna's. Their father had escaped the blinding light when she sideswiped him and walked onto the porch in her pink nightgown and navy-blue UGGs that she wore everywhere, in every season. Her braid was lopsided and a lot of hair escaped it. She insisted on doing her own hair.

"So how about a hug for your sis," Lawrence said, arm over her eyes, rising.

"No more hugs, because touching is socially inappropriate," Bett said. "It's a hot topic."

"Don't be ridiculous," Lawrence said, going toward her. But she could tell from her sister's expression that a hug was unwelcome. She held out her hand. Bett shook it and seemed to throw it down, as if it were a pancake she was flipping from the spatula. Lawrence did have rather small, light hands. She knew to grip firmly, and did, but still you could often see the other person surprised at the inherent lightness of her hands.

"Did you know that tomorrow is my birthday?" Bett asked.

"Yes, I did, and your present is in the bag Larry just put inside," Lawrence said. "Two hints: not a bicycle and not a horse."

"Two hints," Bett echoed. "Not a clown and not a corpse."

It was always possible she was joking. Lawrence considered this interpretation more often than she thought their parents did. "Corpse" more or less rhymed with "horse." Maybe just a bit of wordplay. Bett hated clowns; she wasn't afraid of them, she hated them, as well as anything that reminded her of them, such as marionettes or children in face paint, or certain mannequins. She'd once had a meltdown on Newbury Street. Belatedly, Lawrence realized that a bicycle, or a unicycle, really, might indeed conjure up some clown at the circus. She was pretty good at getting inside her sister's head. But why would Bett happily watch motorcyclists? Why did children on bicycles not bother her, though she sometimes shuddered if an adult passed by on a bicycle?

"I'm afraid we're out of decaf tea," Larry said, lowering the tray onto a table, "but would you like something else to drink? Orange juice or seltzer?"

"Tomorrow's my birthday, so maybe champagne!" Bett said.

Alcohol could not be mixed with Bett's medicine. She was also to avoid caffeine, which meant no chocolate, and chocolate was one of her favorite things. A life without chocolate was impossible, so sometimes Bett enjoyed a bit. What could you do?

"Orange juice, seltzer?" her father repeated.

"Harpoon, weather," Bett said. She took the slice of lemon from the rim of her mother's glass and raised her eyebrows, sucked it, cried, "Ew!," and threw it over the railing.

"At least it wasn't a container of Chinese food," Johanna said dully.

Larry said nothing. The family counselor, who had lived with the three of them for a weekend several years ago, had made the point to Larry that whatever his wife said was her business, and he helped nothing by correcting her in front of their daughter. Otherwise, Larry would have spoken to Johanna as if she'd been another of their children and instructed her not to be sarcastic, because it "wasn't attractive." That was what both daughters had been taught as they were growing up. Not to fidget; not to put a used Kleenex anywhere but in their pocket; not to be ironic or mocking or sarcastic. But still, in her own lame way, Bett had gone on and on and on. For a while, before college, and before she got out into the world more, Lawrence had been so well mannered, she'd seemed like someone out of an Edith Wharton novel. That ended courtesy of weed and cocaine, and resulted in the eventual loosening of a sharp tongue that could make people gasp. Lincoln had thought one day she'd burst through the shell of her body and attack with the frenzy of a comic-book viper.

"I could use help with openin' my presents tonight, ma'am," Bett said. Her sister was addicted to old TV westerns (*Gunsmoke* being her favorite) and to *Deadwood*. Whenever she wanted to be emphatic, she turned her hand sideways and made a gun with her thumb and first finger. She did not, however, point her gun in her parents' direction any longer. A lot of invisible bullets were fired into the carpet or the porch or even the mattress.

Larry sang, "I'm an old cowhand, from the Rio Grande . . ." between sips of iced tea. He'd given his lemon to his wife. Lawrence found herself staring at the squeezed lemon floating in her mother's iced tea, exactly lit by the outdoor light until her mother lifted the glass to drink from it. Her parents were stuck with Bett for the rest of their lives. Still, they had friends, they'd recently found another sitter whom Bett seemed to like (a gay man who was back living with his parents until he began his new job in Buffalo), so they'd resumed going out one night a week. On the other nights, her father attended a book discussion group on Mondays, and her mother volunteered to help the activity director of a local nursing home. The previous Christmas, Larry had been recruited to play an elf who went mad in Santa's workshop in a play written by the activity director. It had been a huge success. As one of the activities, those who could still write had written him thank-you notes, and they'd *wanted* to do it. A few notes were attached by funny magnets to the refrigerator, as if it were still the sort of home where the children came back from school with stars on their papers. Make that *with a star on her paper.* Bett had gone to several schools before the one in Connecticut was found. For those two years, Larry and Johanna had lived alone. They'd joined a gym, gone to the theater in London, Johanna had lost the ten or fifteen pounds she'd gained since her wedding and had bought some beautiful new clothes on Newbury Street. Then the answering machine caught up with them: The school was always calling. Were things appreciably worse, or for some reason did the convenience of the machine, and the quick response they'd get, result in their being called more often? Who knew? But that had been the signal, like the whistle blown at the end of a race, that it was over. School ended, Bett graduated (because everyone did), Bett returned to her old bedroom in the house in Newton.

"Why don't you have cowboy boots, if you're going to wear boots?" Bett asked Lawrence. "They're much cooler."

"I like soft leather," Lawrence said. "These are the sort of boots you can wear in the evening, too, with a black dress."

"Well, I wouldn't have boots like that, I'd have cowboy boots, and then you could kick your toe at people, and cowboy boots are worn more and more now. Who would want to be in a stupid evening dress, anyhow?"

Lawrence shrugged. The last time she'd worn an evening dress had been at the Corcoran—a Priscilla of Boston knee-length dress that had probably once been some bridal attendant's, in the most beautiful shade of sea-glass green. She had gotten it for thirty-five dollars on eBay.

"Mom has corns!" Bett said, pointing to their mother's black clogs.

"Mom has a sore toe from running to catch the train in tennis shoes without socks," Johanna said. She slipped her foot out of her shoe to prove it. There was a small Band-Aid wrapped around her second toe. She'd gotten a pedicure; her toenails sparkled and had been expertly painted pale pink.

"If you'll excuse me, I need to check to see if I got a

message I'm waiting for," Larry said. He left his empty glass on the tray. He'd carried it out; one of them could carry it in. From Johanna's perspective, he was always making a mess (though even she would not have criticized the tray of glasses of iced tea), and she was always having to clean up after him. From his perspective, and he often cited his source (Malcolm Gladwell), people formed first impressions within the first few seconds of meeting you. Why, then, do anything but be yourself? And he was lazy, he did throw his clothes on the floor. Johanna had tried to reason with him: Would he come out onto the stage and act well for the first fifteen seconds, then just wander around, doing any old thing? What did it mean to "be yourself"? But they'd been married for over forty years, and they adored each other. There was that. He kissed the top of his wife's head as he walked, empty-handed, toward the house.

"Bring out my present!" Bett called.

"That's for tomorrow," he said.

"No, bring it NOW!" she said, pointing her finger gun at his back. He turned. The gun was still pointed. He shaped his own hand into a gun and said, with no inflection, "Pow."

And then Bett went crazy. She knocked over the little table when she jumped forward, waving her arms as she stomped toward him, Johanna cringing and raising her hand to her mouth before she recovered herself and also got to her feet. "Bett! Bett!" she screamed, though Larry said nothing, only used his arms to shield his face from the blows. He'd been spat on! By his daughter! A first (he would later tell Lawrence). "Stop it immediately!" Johanna said, raising her own arm as she spoke, in case Bett whirled in her direction.

Which she did. She didn't whirl, but she did turn slowly, and look at her mother with incomprehension. "You don't want it to be my birthday," she finally said. "There are no plans except the trip tomorrow."

"Bett," Larry said in his super-reasonable voice, "what do you think happens on people's birthdays? Your sister has come with presents. Your mother and I have a gift for you. We're taking you to Maine, to your favorite restaurant, for a lobster roll. For ten lobster rolls, if that's what you want. What do you think happens on other people's birthdays?"

"They get cakes made with killer sugar," she said. "They get ten cakes if they want, and it's full of sugar and it doesn't make them crazy, they eat their cake and have it, too."

This produced an undisguised look of surprise between Johanna and Lawrence, who now stood at her mother's side in a show of support. Not in time to have been helpful, but when she'd recovered from the sheer shock of Bett's attack, she'd gone to her mother's side as fast as she could.

"We try to do what's best for you. You've had the conversation about alcohol and sugar and caffeine with the doctor many times yourself, Bett. I repeat: We try to do what's best for you, even if we are not always right."

In the way he said Bett's name, Lawrence understood that he despised his older daughter. Don't take it back and say she can have a piece of cake, please don't, she thought silently. Her wish was granted. He said nothing more, pulled his rumpled but still-tucked-in shirt out of his pants rather than trying to figure out how to neatly retuck it, turned his back, and went into the house. Next, Lawrence thought: Please don't leave me alone on the porch with the two of them. But it was apparent that Bett was through and their mother unhurt.

"May I suggest that we forget that happened and sit here and enjoy the lovely weather and hear what's new with your sister, Bett? Unless there is anything more you feel you must say?" Johanna asked.

"I feel I must say that she only came to see you, not to see me," Bett said. "But now we can hear from the important daughter."

"Bett, I'm serious. I want you to avoid that tone of voice," Johanna said.

"And I want to go to bed. I'll see you in the morning," Lawrence said. She was thinking that she'd go upstairs, find her father at his desk, at his computer, wordlessly squeeze his hand for a few seconds, perhaps bend to touch her forehead to his, all the silent signals they had. That night she might even crawl into her mother's bed and do spoons. In recent years her mother had taken over the spare bedroom, and now the bed again had its canopy, and the sheets were amazingly white and soft. Larry had been diagnosed with sleep apnea and had to sleep with a breathing mask at night.

Upstairs, Larry sat with his head on his arms. He heard her footsteps, the upstairs floorboards creaking, but didn't look up. He was mumbling when she came into the room— then he did look up, red-eyed—and he was saying, "In Greek tragedy, all the battles are summarized, we don't have to see them onstage: Here's the way it happened, here's what the violence consisted of, who fought hardest, who screamed loudest, who died. We exist in our suburban idyll, where everything can also be summarized: We've had pretty good fortune, pretty good health; we've been married for longer than we've known any of our mutual friends; we have a daughter we call 'troubled.' No attention must be paid. In fact, please don't. Those are the facts, sir. Ma'am. Now the action resumes."

"You left out your other daughter," she said, hands planted on his shoulders. She felt suddenly exhausted: the outburst; the travel; maybe going back further than that, her lousy romances; her bad decisions.

"My other daughter is named for me. I'm really a Larry, though, not a Lawrence. I didn't inhabit that name even before she was born. I was always a pretty good actor, never a great one. No loss to the stage that that career didn't work out."

"Philip Seymour Hoffman," she said tiredly. "Spare me."

The last word wasn't out of her mouth when they heard the crash. Larry ran for the stairs and, coward that she was, Lawrence went to the window. At first it seemed like strobe lights were flashing on the porch, but no, it was her mother and sister, engaged in a struggle. The bag with the prettily wrapped present inside was swinging back and forth and finally became airborne, Bett getting it long enough to throw it over her shoulder as she continued to wrestle with Johanna, who'd sunk to her knees. Lawrence raced down the steps, thinking, I only wasted ten seconds looking, I'm getting there now as fast as I can, I'm sorry, I'm sorry, I'm running downstairs. All she could do, more or less, was throw herself onto the heap, her father pinning Bett's hands behind her back in spite of her screaming protests; Johanna, bleeding from a cut on her cheekbone, running inside the house to call the ambulance, or the doctor, or whomever she'd be calling—Johanna, the tail of her torn blouse pressed to her face, scrambling for the phone, as Lawrence tugged silently on her father's shirt as if to get his attention, as if she were a desperate child, as desperate as Bett, who was trying to shake off her father's hands. It was no time until they heard the ambulance siren. So little time that Lawrence thought it must be responding to another call, but it was coming to this house, an ambulance full of what already looked like a lot of people, their eyes searching but their faces rearranged into neutral expressions, everything indicating that this was just another thing to deal with competently, they'd seen it all before, they recognized everything, including the sad trickle of blood, they'd get on those restraints as quickly and painlessly as possible.

An hour later, a bit more, Lawrence and Johanna sat in the same chairs on the porch, having a glass of white wine. "I knew it the minute she was put in my arms in the delivery room. She looked me right in the eye, and I knew I was in for it. You're our bonus, you're our present. Do you hate us for bringing you into it? How could you not? But I didn't understand that at the time. I think I thought Bett would be fine, that she was just prone to tantrums, a strong-willed child intent on getting her way. Hey, what's in the box, by the way? Anything breakable?" It was clear that if it was breakable, her mother didn't care.

"Cowboy boots," Lawrence said. "Lucchese. eBay, in the box, never worn. Size ten, brown snakeskin. I didn't think

about that before: snakeskin. But since they don't make us
see shrinks anymore, I guess that doesn't need to be noted.
It was un-con-scious." She pronounced all three syllables of
the last word, mocking only herself.

"Can you bear to pick up the box from the lawn?" her
mother asked.

"Yes. You go take a shower, and when you get into bed,
I'll come rub your shoulders."

"Thank you. That's a good idea."

"What was the play Larry was in—the one where you
first met in the lobby, after the performance?"

"What? Oh. It was *Our Town*. He was the Stage Manager. Do you know the play? A bunch of dead people sitting
around at the end, your father gesturing and saying how they
all died. It does choke you up, however corny it is. It would
have been a low joke to point to one of them and say that
so-and-so died of boredom."

"Did he gesture with the gun pointed?"

"I'm sure he didn't," Johanna said. "I'm sure it would have
been subtle, the way your father is. Most of the time."

"I'll get the box, but only after you go inside," she said.

"Well, far be it from me to have a disagreement with one
of my daughters," Johanna said. She rose and went inside
without saying anything else. When Lawrence finally went
down the steps and looked back at the house, the light was
on in the bathroom. Not like her mother to have forgotten
to drop the blind, but she had. And she was standing there
looking out the window. She waved, naked. She was a sixty-
five-year-old woman, looking beyond Lawrence to the moon.

Lawrence went over to the big box and picked it up, no

differently than if it had been a dropped flower or someone's litter. Then she did a double take and looked at her hand. She hadn't realized she had the strength, or the finger spread, to hold such a heavy cardboard box one-handed. She wrapped her other arm around it and brought it in to her body: her present; her shield. In the mode of her father, she gestured to the squirrel running across the telephone wires and said, "And that fellow, in his prime, electrocuted." The squirrel ran quickly to the end of the wire, jumped into a high bush, and was gone. "Upstairs? That naked lady? She filled the tub full of water and drowned, and on the same night, it turned out her husband was deeply depressed. All kidding aside, he had a real gun, and he used it on himself. The survivor, the so-called normal daughter? She took out her cell phone before she went inside, full of contempt for the idea of birthdays, angry instead of proud of herself that she'd returned 'home' for her sister's birthday, and she did something uncharacteristic, but you don't see her sitting here, because it didn't kill her. She called the man she missed most, Lincoln, as nice a man as his namesake, who'd freed the slaves, and in that way she freed herself, and they lived happily ever after."

She stopped to look at some feathery green leaves barely illuminated by moonlight and the porch lights. She would not have known what they were, except that her mother had impaled the seed envelope beside them—it would be her mother who'd put the chopstick in the ground, piercing the seed packet like a big needle taking a stitch, wouldn't it? Of all unlikely things, next to the front steps her mother had planted "Red Cored Chantenay Carrots," though there was no other garden, and to her knowledge her mother never grew anything, though she did pick from the spreading patch of mint along the fence every now and then and stick a sprig between ice cubes in the iced tea, or she sometimes pulled apart a bit to flavor a fruit salad. It was September, and her mother was growing a patch of carrots. Lawrence ruffled their tops, found them sturdier than they looked but fragile at their tips, and faintly ticklish. They were pretty enough to put in a bouquet.

She thought she would remember that.

COMPANY

Henry Siddis, by the time he turned sixty-two, felt that the difference in ages between himself and those he taught no longer mattered, and that therefore they should call him Henry. When he'd started teaching long ago, only five or six years had separated him from his students, but these days, with the fashion for shaved heads the second the hairline began to recede, and everyone's hair turning white so much earlier (what was that about?), he sometimes looked more youthful than his students. Quite a few had become real friends, and they appreciated being asked to their professor's summer house in Maine. "Should I worry?" his wife, Dana, had asked him recently—meaning that the student-friends were exclusively male, except for Shannon Ryan. He supposed he could have interpreted Dana's kidding in two ways. It was a standing joke in the house that there were at least three possibilities about everything, though that particular comment seemed open to only two interpretations, neither of which his wife would have truly meant. Watching *Bruno* on DVD the night before, she'd turned to him with alarm when one of the actors—it was not entirely clear sometimes when a real person was being set up and when someone was an actor—said that women jumped all over the place, switching from one topic to another. "I'd forgotten the stereotype!" she'd said. "My God! Do you think that lingers on? It probably does, doesn't it?"

At Lobster Lou's, adjacent to the gym, he was given, for the same price, pound-and-a-half lobsters instead of the pound-and-a-quarters he had ordered because (1) they were probably more plentiful; (2) he had bought a pound of extremely high-priced picked lobster meat the week before; (3) he liked the new clerk, and the new clerk knew it. This was his friend Raymond's nephew, who had just finished his first year at Harvard. Jasper, the nephew, also worked as a personal trainer at the local gym; in high school, he'd volunteered his time to a physical therapist in need of assistance with clients who presented particular problems, such as being obese. Jasper was useful in hauling them to their feet, after which she could take over. Jasper was thinking about going into medicine, but Henry had his doubts. Perhaps, as Dana had implied with her nervous question about female stereotypes, it was because the usual reasons for things were never stated anymore, as if they were all part of the collective unconscious. He just thought Jasper would want to do something that put him more out in the world than being a doctor. He could also read the young man's mind as he wrapped up the lobsters: These things are full of cholesterol. It's not just the butter, either.

The brown bag squirmed on the passenger seat, and he lowered it out of the sun onto the floor on the passenger side not so much out of respect for the lobster but because he feared spoilage. Two sets of former students would be visiting this evening, Jackson and his fiancée (which made her not really his former student) driving from Portland and arriving at five, and Benoit and Cara around six, assuming their plane got in to Logan on schedule. Dana would have time to show Daphne around the garden, and if he knew Daphne, she'd be coming with a package of seeds and teasing that there was still time in mid-July to plant them. Benoit liked to sit and smoke his pipe on the back porch and bring up topics that were sure to be slightly provocative but would also no doubt elicit a thoughtful response from Henry that was often—as Benoit had told him more than once in e-mails—very helpful in his sorting out certain things. "No advice!" was Henry's motto, but he supposed that from the way he discussed things, Benoit could extrapolate where he stood. Wasn't it funny sometimes? The young women were more intense than their young men, more adventurous: mountain climbers, white-water rafters. The men seemed to fade faster. One day they were full of vigor and humor, and a year later—most certainly they did not turn on a dime—but a year later, sometimes a bit more, they'd often be retreating. From their adamant notions; from their aversion to marriage; away from communing with nature and suddenly more inclined to have a lobster and a glass of prosecco on the back porch. Though he had never discussed this directly with Dana, he felt sure she'd noticed it, too. Which made him wonder what she thought of it, what she thought of him. He was still table-thumping and wide-eyed about the fate of the country, the Supreme Court, the threat of Romney—though he, too, went on fewer long walks (four hours was what he meant by "long") and often sat silently rocking, with *The New York Times*, if nobody was visiting. One of the many things he appreciated about his wife was that she trusted her perceptions. Even if she found something puzzling or problematic, she wouldn't think of asking him to explain it to her. To his regret, he had been married three times, though he and Dana had been married now for twenty years and were very happy together. The first marriage had been forced on him—on them—by his college girlfriend's parents when they found out she was pregnant. A month after being married by a justice of the peace (who was now a fishing buddy), she had miscarried and told him that she did not want to remain married. His second wife had been nine years older, a woman he'd met in Italy who'd wanted to escape her terrible marriage and make a good home for herself and her two-year-old daughter. She had come to his hotel with welts on her legs and begged him to take her back to the United States with him (he'd stayed involved with the agency through Bill Clinton's presidency) so that she could live with a cousin in Brooklyn and start over. The cousin was real (a nice guy); the child was real, but not her child (to this day, he did not know how she'd seemed to be living in the apartment in Trastevere with the neighbor's child, presenting herself as the child's mother). No different than if a gypsy had robbed him outside Termini, he'd been hoodwinked, bought her a ticket to New York City, spent the first night in Cobble Hill with her and the child (he had already met Dana before his trip), then agreed to marry her, thereby making her a legal citizen. They'd flown to Las Vegas, the child left behind with the cousin's girlfriend, the cousin—his name was Luca—alternating between happiness, gaiety, and a more serious mode in which he twice took Henry aside to ask if he was sure about what he intended to do. It was all over in less than three months, Luca stuck with the problem, a Russian boyfriend suddenly on the scene, the child returned to her family in Rome, and—back in the days when such things still existed—he had called Dana from a phone booth in a little town in Virginia where he was en route to interview for the job in the business school at UVA—somehow it had been decided that she would take a plane to meet him for the weekend, though they'd never officially dated. He rarely pulled rank or asked a favor, but he'd called his friend Peter in New York and asked if Dana could hop aboard his private plane, and so she had, flying in to Dulles, where he'd gone, carrying an armload of daisies, and that was that. To this day, she had little knowledge of his relationship with his second wife. He'd been surprised once, when someone was questioning Dana more than they should have, that she'd said something, however she had put it, suggesting she thought the relationship had been quite long, years and years. How could he possibly correct her and retain any self-respect? Her impression was, in a way, less troubling than the truth.

These were not usually his thoughts, they certainly were not, but traffic was heavy and slow on Friday afternoon on Route 1, and something about the animated brown bag on the floor and his slight worry that the Allegra seemed not to be working effectively, so that he often had to swallow a few times before he recovered easy breathing . . . well, he was not about to die, he worked out with Jasper for an hour and a half every week and exercised once or twice in the gym in addition, he was not at all overweight, and he knew that the summer heat and humidity affected everyone. But to be honest, what he'd started to think was that he was going to die. As simple as that. He'd done so well in his job because his hunches were usually right on, his instincts reliable.

Cars were pouring off the exit from 95. He sharpened his senses to make it through the yellow light, neither obviously speeding nor failing to clear the intersection by the time it turned red. To the left was Stonewall Kitchen, impassable in the aisles during the summer, few shoppers having any idea whatsoever why the business was named as it was, and to further obfuscate the issue, there was a stone wall parallel to the road with lovely gardens in front of it. He had an image of the lobsters set free among the plants, some prank, some video that would be shown on one of the late-night talk shows, lobsters crawling through bristling cleome! The audience would laugh and laugh. He, too, could tell the story for laughs, flipping burgers on the grill: *I was only releasing them to another form of death, probably better to have boiled them alive.* His devoted—the ones who were devoted were so devoted—students, willing to laugh, nowhere near as skeptical as they should be, even if his odd remark became pillow talk among couples at the end of the night.

Let me try this out, he thought, pulling into the driveway with its bottom-scraping incline, the one Dana always said would eventually force her to get out of the car and walk when she'd piled on the pounds as an old lady. I'll try this out: I instinctively know I'm sick, I suspect I'm dying, but in a way not remotely heroic, I will nonetheless carry this bag into the house and greet my wife if she's anywhere nearby, but I will start seeing everything from the point of view of someone looking down on all of it from above (he did not believe in the afterlife, but he did believe in perspective), and perhaps there is solace, even freedom, in seeing everything as if it's already over. It was like some crazy mental exercise they would have been given in Virginia, one of those what-ifs that turned out to be a nursery rhyme compared to what happened in the real world.

"Henry," Dana called from upstairs. He looked up. She had on her white cotton bathrobe that made her look like a big vertical anemic waffle. "Honey, no surprise, they're caught at the airport in Charlotte and the ETA is seven o'clock, just for Logan. So let's cook all the lobsters, because who minds cold lobster? We can render more fat when they get here. Poor things," she added, turning.

It took him a second to realize that she'd been saying they could melt more butter.

He looked at the large pot of water on the stove. Earlier in the summer they'd looked up the cold-water-versus-hot-water controversy on the Internet, although no one truly believed there could be any difference if you set the pot to boil with cold or hot water. He picked up a potholder and lifted the lid. The water was simmering. She was so organized, she'd started it heating before her shower. He put the brown bag in the refrigerator, feeling something hard knock against his knuckle as he shoved it onto the top shelf. He looked at the knuckle as if it had, itself, offended him.

"Dana!" he called upstairs. "I'm sick of doing errands and spending the rest of my life readjusting to normal life to atone for my pathetic patriotic feelings. From now on, it's hamburgers on the grill, and I'm not going to round up the cows."

He could hear the water pounding down in the shower above the kitchen ceiling. It was a very noisy shower. She loved the new showerhead, which approximated a rainstorm that would fall with enough force to blind frogs.

He poured himself a glass of wine from the already open bottle of Viognier. It was her favorite, his less so. Less by a factor of 75 percent. Still, it was cold, and he could see that if this was the sort of wine you liked, this would be the sort of wine you liked. He approved his resistance to being civilized by sipping it from a pottery mug. "I only knew that Italian woman for a couple of months, what do you think of that?" he hollered at the ceiling. A cobweb hung from the light above the kitchen island. He looked at his hands. They were trembling slightly. Oh, what chaos his impending death was about to cause, with the rivulets merging together (Cara and Benoit; Jackson and Daphne) to flow into the great sea of regret, and Dana on the shore, Mrs. Ramsay–like in her benign good intentions. He sipped the wine, thinking that wine was never as cold as the water at the beach, which seemed ridiculous but was true. He lived in a town where there was frigid water. As had been observed, its intermittent slight warming had nothing to do with air temperature but rather with the tide. You might drive by the beach below the Stage Neck Inn and see adults in the water, inexplicably, in early June, and then not at all in August. Received wisdom: It had to do with the currents. It was also generally agreed upon that children, whether because of their enthusiasm or blunted nervous systems, could tolerate water no grown-up would wade into.

He heard a car pulling into the driveway. Silently, he said: You are coming to see a dead man. You will find him upright and talkative. You will embrace him without hesitation. He will hug you in return. You will go on to do whatever you do with your lives, with a 50 percent chance of divorce. Thirty years from now, when you, too, are old, something sniffed for a second in the breeze will take you back to this moment of your arrival, and you will remember the feel of loose gravel underneath your sandals and the sight of your dead teacher in his doorway, and then the memory will not so much evaporate as flick some little particle into your eye, which will make you wince. That feeling, conventionally called pain, will take you elsewhere, your feet without feeling, your hair unstirred. That somewhere will be the exit ramp or the detour or the alternate route to the rest of your lives, which will also continue to be interrupted by divorce, appendicitis, mice in your basement, and random prosecution by the IRS because of your political beliefs.

Dana, damp-haired, was embracing him from behind. "Jackson!" he called. "And the beautiful Daphne!" He could feel Dana's head peeking around from behind his sweaty striped shirt. He smiled as the couple approached, but he couldn't snap out of it. He was dead. She was his devoted life-mate, refreshingly showered and ready for an evening of good discussions and laughter (she'd already made her potato salad with garden sage), yet he was not, as she thought, her personal Velcro, but rather an already unraveled spool of thread. He could feel his spine like a wooden spool, his body hastily reassembled to approximate an ordinary cylinder of thread.

"We're Mr. and Mrs. Wilburn!" Jackson called. "We eloped!" Of course, he had no sense that he was stepping on every ant on the brick walkway, their feet crushing every sprouting blade of grass, wisteria blossoms sprinkled in their hair like the rice they'd foregone.

"*Are* you?" he heard Dana squeal.

He turned to look at her, his face too numb for his brain to name its expression. She looked at him quizzically. He'd forgotten that word. When would you ever use it, "quizzically"? He didn't think, any longer, that he was dead—that had been speculative, a moment's morbid game—but whatever she saw stilled her so that she seemed like a puppet dangling from lax strings as she was embraced by their visitors. Did they sense the discombobulation, her posture, his inability to make his eyes coordinate with his smile? Too many questions! The way to proceed was not to pose them, even silently. If they'd trained him in anything, they'd trained him in this. So what exactly had shattered that nugget of certainty inside him? The lobster's banded claw had knocked against his knuckle, advantage Henry, and without even seeing it, because of course it was only a split-second's feeling, the lobster was in the bag . . . but touch had become recognition, and the hard thing, the resolve, the sure thing, had crumbled like an oyster cracker, expected to remain crisp in spite of being floated in soup. In the soup, he thought wryly.

"We have to go on a tour of the house and find you the most wonderful wedding present," Dana was saying. Beside him, Jackson was smiling tentatively. Anything would do if he could only form the words. "Old bean!" he said, and to his great relief Jackson laughed instantly, clapped him on the back, and that was enough to mobilize him, several paces behind the giggling women with their arms around each other's waists. "You never know," he heard himself saying to Jackson, who smiled broadly, thinking he'd gotten Henry's drift, or that he'd missed the beginning of the sentence. The comment had come out with a tone of complete goodwill. He was very relieved to know that was so. He smiled at Jackson.

In the kitchen, Henry's great-aunt's silver ice bucket was thrust into Daphne's arms. Oh, she would hold so many more precious things, but in this moment the heavy, dented ice bucket totally mesmerized her. They had only three chairs in their apartment in McLean! Protests, counterarguments, "You never know!" he heard himself exploding again, like some bizarre grenade configured to blow up twice. This time Jackson smiled with a little more reserve, but when their eyes met—thank God, that worked—Jackson's eyes widened, and unless Henry was wrong, he almost, though not quite, clapped him on the back again, each realizing at the last second that two such moments would be too much.

The boiled lobster was lifted with big tongs from its salted water, put into deep soup bowls, their rims decorated with tiny crosshatching that looked disconcertingly like barbed wire. Lights that shone on the garden, dimly or well, depending on the day's absorption of sunlight, bordered the porch. Medium tonight, but enough to illuminate the rubrum lilies and the almost-blackened purple flower cones of the butterfly bush. "Don't let me," Henry heard himself saying. As all heads turned toward him, he continued this already begun sentence: "Don't let me fail to raise a glass, if these so-called flutes can be considered a proper glass, rather than a musical instrument best tapped by the beaks of songbirds. Anyway: I raise a toast to the happiness of our friends Jackson and Daphne, and wish them good luck. May they always be as happy as they are tonight. We share in your joy," he said. It was such a classy toast, Dana looked at him with admiration. He coordinated his eyes with his smile and was so effective that she put her hand in his.

"Tell us how you do it. What's the secret to a long and happy marriage, since pretty much no one has one anymore?" Daphne said.

"Oh, Daphne, you can just transform yourself into a tree if there's ever a bad moment. Just disguise yourself and wait it out, isn't that what Henry would say? Stand still and just be someone or something else, and then the earth will rotate on its axis and everything will come around and be all right again," Dana said.

Daphne frowned. "No. I'm serious," she said.

"Oh, I am, too," Dana said, smoothing Daphne's hair. "Forgive me for playing on your name, which is as beautiful as you are, and not only because of your *looks*. Just don't be angry, wait things out; remember that stillness, like meditation, can give you those few moments to ride something out, during which time you're sure to remember you really love the other person."

"That's amazing!" Daphne said.

"Are you guys being serious?" Jackson said. "You're bound to disagree, but it's kind of a waiting game or something?"

"What do you want to do, say something you'll regret or don't even half believe?"

"Oh. Okay. You mean it," Jackson said. "Sorry. It just sounded so practical that—well, I'm only digging myself in deeper. Thank you for the good advice. I'll try to remember it."

"And try not to be solemn," Henry added. "It's always right there, because we're serious people, but though we might seriously disagree from time to time, solemnity is the enemy of compromise."

"Henry—are you serious?" Jackson said. He looked at Henry across the table, over the bowl mounded high with lobster carcasses, butter thickly gelled in everyone's little individual dishes that surrounded the big aluminum bowl like devotional candles flickering around the pedestal of a saint. The hurricane globe allowed the candle to burn evenly. It was now half gone.

"I was imagining myself dead," Henry said.

A rabbit. A rabbit dashed across the lawn.

"What did you say?" Daphne asked after a few moments had elapsed in silence.

"Purely speculative. If I could speak to my two dear young friends from beyond life itself, should I mind that my advice is conventional and think that because of that, because they're so intelligent, both of them, they can't hear it? No, in answer to my own question. Go ahead and tell them that disagreements aren't the end of the world, and that sometimes the less said, the better."

In his peripheral vision, Dana nodded. He was aware that

Jackson's knee touched Daphne's beneath the table, perhaps unintentionally, perhaps not.

"We're so happy for you," Dana said in her usual calm, sincere voice. "Sudden marriages always come as a surprise, of course. But in this case, an excellent surprise." She drained the last of her prosecco. "I hate to think what's happened to their plane," she said, looking at her watch. "We can always just leave the door unlocked."

"I'll wait up," Jackson said. "I want to tell Benoit and Cara."

"And I will wait with you. Which means that we're hinting that the women clear the table," Henry said.

"He's hinting. But I happen to know there's one more bottle of prosecco, and if you carry a couple of plates into the kitchen with me, we can open it," Dana said to Daphne.

Henry looked at her approvingly. He was her second husband. What had happened to her first husband was terrible and never discussed. Of course, if the man hadn't died, Henry would not be married to Dana. Had he ever mentioned any of that to Jackson? Probably not, since he rarely brought it up, even the fact that she'd been married before.

Dana, in her cropped pants and blue gauzy top, and Daphne, in her summer dress that looked like marbleized paper, walked barefoot into the kitchen. They did not return for the other plates. The candle flickered and went out.

"Are there matches?" Jackson finally said.

"Are you following in my footsteps?" Henry said. "The screens don't have ears. Neither do the petunias. That's why we summer in Maine."

Jackson knitted his brow. He reached beyond the pepper grinder and picked up a book of matches, removed the hurricane globe, set it aside, struck a match, lit the candle, replaced the globe. "As you've said, one doesn't say," Jackson replied.

Henry nodded. His heart had just taken a complete, speeded-up roller-coaster ride. By saying so little, he'd taught Jackson very well. Good boy. So this was a celebratory night in other major ways as well. Jackson would live a long time until he, too, unexpectedly died, like any other soldier who always knew the risk, in theory, but who had to believe he'd be the exception. One day he'd also be driving down Route 1 with a bag on the floor, and he would start to die. By that time, there might be monorails instead of highways, they'd been around forever, but with the exploding population, they might be quickly built to transport people, carrying their groceries, carrying out their routines. Or people might have little rockets on their ankles, like spurs, that would move them through the universe, allow them to zoom into black holes (*fatally* attractive) and out again. Whatever was coming was coming. But the human brain, so far, hadn't been co-opted. You couldn't lie to it, though it could still lie to you. Things might very well change in the future, in the days before global warming fried the planet: Men might be kinder to other men; Mussolini might be resurrected to do his much discussed routine of making the trains arrive on time; but at this odd limbo moment, this bend-backward-and-shimmy-under-the-pole limbo moment, with porch lights glowing and solar spotlights allowing the stamens of flowers to puncture the night like so many silent tongues, he and Jackson were just two men—you know, any two men—passing time on the back porch.

THE DEBT

The plane landed in Fort Lauderdale, and Dick and Royce (Royal) were picked up by a pretty young woman wearing a tank top, shorts, and silver antlers and driven to Hertz. Royal's brother, Brandt, arranged such things—or his secretary, Jacki, did ("Bag claim F. Laud surprise," she'd texted). When things like the Lexus Reindeer unexpectedly appeared, the secretary knew it made Royal's day. It took his friends—it took *him*—a short while to sort it out: Jacki's kindness, perfectly paired with her taste for the absurd.

"Donna," the reindeer said when Dick asked her name. Their bags, one each, were in the trunk. When she'd hopped out of the silver Lexus, they'd both been impressed with her extremely short shorts.

"Donner? Your name's Donner, and you've got a friend named Blitzen?" Royal teased.

"Donner?" she said. "Like that guy that got everybody stuck out on the ice?"

He cocked his head and wondered whether she was kidding.

She fumbled a piece of paper out of her pocket and read: " 'My bro the traveler have a good rest / Enjoy those breezes, partake of life's zest / When reindeer depart, you still have your bro / And his goodwill forever, I'm sure you know.'" She smiled and hopped back in the car.

"Thank you," he said as seriously as he would have thanked a mourner at a funeral. "Thank you very much, Donna."

It had not always been a pleasure for Royal to be Brandt's brother. Brainy Brandt, a lush in his teens, now a teetotaler: jogged five miles minimum, daily, in Central Park before work. Lived in a penthouse rented from some Saudi's daughter, and one wall of the bathroom was a waterfall. Brandt had changed when his high school sweetheart left him fifteen years before, after a year of marriage. His best friend was English—a former boyfriend of the late Princess Di. Brandt spent a couple of weeks every couple of months in London, playing polo and seeing plays, and said repeatedly that friendship was all that mattered; he'd never marry again. He and Royal talked on the phone every few weeks. In Royal's opinion, Brandt became kinder every year—so much so that Royal wondered if he took notes during their calls, or whether he taped them and just gave the recording to his secretary, who understood she should do anything possible to facilitate . . . well, to call in the reindeer, if that was what she thought best.

Royal drove. Dick slid the passenger seat all the way back, tugged the brim of his cap toward his nose. On the radio, Elvis was dreaming of a blue Christmas. But Elvis wasn't alive, and now, when the tourist ladies went weeping to Graceland, their faces were more immobile every year, their ages increasing along with the number of Botox injections. He wondered if Graceland were decorated, if there were a Christmas tree to enthrall the people touring the low-ceilinged rooms as they stared solemnly at the pool-table deity. What strange creatures their generation's gods had turned out to be.

They stopped for a microbrew at Second Sunset, a bar that overlooked the channel, with a thatched roof and seagulls walking the rails like prissy prison guards. "We're outta Gotham, man," Dick said, locking thumbs with his buddy. By which, of course, he meant New York City. He was proud of himself for having found cheap flights to Florida that landed in Fort Lauderdale, adding a little time to the trip but allowing them to avoid the usual hectic, expensive Miami mess, and to save half the price of a ticket.

The bartender was bare-chested, wearing a leather vest. His head was shaved. He wore jeans with holes here and there, like stars that didn't quite fit the celestial grid. A gold chain necklace dangling a shell. Gay or just a Florida dude? Hard to tell in the Keys. No earring. Maybe straight. Especially if the holes in his jeans hadn't been frayed with a razor. A few seats down, on barstools, two women talked animatedly about the size of the rats outside some restaurant. Neither seemed at all squeamish; it was more like talk about "the one that got away." The fatter woman kept flexing her foot, slapping her sandal against her heel. As Royal watched, trying not to appear to be looking, a muscular arm pushed something past his peripheral vision: a shot of tequila each, "on the house." Did that mean they didn't look like tourists, that the bartender thought they might come back? If so, did that make the bartender straight, a guy who bonded with his bros, or gay, thinking about how the night might go? Dick left a big tip.

"Good luck with the holidays!" the bartender called before he even saw the amount of the tip. "Good luck with the holidays"? No clue about his sexuality there.

About five-thirty, as the sky was lightening to pink and clouds were darkening to gray, Royal pulled into the breakdown lane and checked the MapQuest directions. "We're a mile away," he said to Dick, but Dick was sleeping. "You think the bartender was gay?" he asked, testing. No answer. "Would you sleep through the night if some cop didn't pull up and hassle us, do you think, sitting there like a ventriloquist's dummy playing I'm a Tourist in Florida?"

Dick's lips parted stickily. He touched the rim of his cap. He said, "You've always got to give yourself the most important role, notice that? You're Edgar Bergen, I'm Charlie McCarthy. If you're so smart, why don't you know whether the guy was gay?"

They were headed for Kegan's house, empty of Kegan's longtime girlfriend, Sarah, though her daughter, Belle, who was either Kegan's child or wasn't, still lived there with him. She spent all her time on her Mac, writing and revising personal statements to apply to colleges, though college was three years away, *if* she could get a scholarship or some sort of financial aid. Sarah and her new boyfriend (an absolute jackass who signed his name "Second Papa" in the letters he and Sarah wrote Belle, Kegan had complained to Royal) sent money to the girl every month; how much, Kegan didn't know, because Belle had informed him that this was "a personal question." Belle, who'd inherited Kegan's distrust of banks, had bought a safe he'd grudgingly bolted into the floor of her closet, joking that the termites would take it down in a matter of months no matter what he did.

"Say wha?" Dick said, leaning forward to lower the radio volume while simultaneously listening to Royal's rather long paraphrase of the situation they'd be walking into. Dick's lips were chapped from winter. His nostrils looked like wood that had been sanded down, the result of a recent cold. "She's practicing writing personal statements? What the hell are personal statements?"

"She helps old ladies in the community shop for groceries or something."

"Okay, Sarah raised a nice child, we've always known that," Dick said, missing the point entirely.

Who knew Kegan had a dog? All he ever talked about was how little money he had, and about Sarah, who was gone for good, anybody understood that. He also talked about Belle and her preoccupation with getting in to a good college. Leave it to Kegan not to even mention he had a year-old dog mottled like an ugly neo-Expressionist painting, a mutt with a blue eye and a brown eye and one ear up, one that dangled like a limp leaf, as it had ever since Kegan picked the dog up on the side of the highway and carried it into his house in his palm. He'd gone out to the mailbox, and there in the gravel had been the half-dead, panting puppy. Which he had named—big joke—"Royal." The dog loved him. He loved everybody. Kegan mixed canned tuna into his dry food. Every Sunday, Belle made the dog the same cooked-in-butter omelet she and Kegan ate—the one meal a week she was responsible for. The time she'd cut up green pepper and put it into the omelet, the dog had spit out every piece, then rolled in the little collection of soggy green cubes. It was Kegan's opinion that the dog had better sense than humans. In all ways, Kegan was impressed with the dog. He told them that—including the fact that he'd also personally stopped eating green peppers—in the first five minutes they were in the house.

Kegan popped open three Coronas, and the three Zetes ceremonially blew into the bottles before taking the first sip (and none of that piece-of-lime shit, either) the way they'd done in the old days. Now, over thirty years down the line, they stood outside on Kegan's spongy deck, where every so often the silence was punctured by the buzzing of the electric mosquito catcher. Belle came out to say hello—taller than the last time Royal had seen her, or maybe it was just the platform shoes she wore (apparently she epitomized Florida style)—then quickly retreated into her room. The dog looked at her with great interest but stayed at Kegan's side.

"So our road trip's still on?" Kegan said. "You made the hotel reservation?"

"Yeah, hotel prices down there are extortion," Royal said, "and I'm not a cheap guy. I took a room with a king and a rollout. It's on me. *And* I've bought you Christmas presents."

"Presents? What are they?" Kegan said.

"You don't tell what presents are. You give them and they're opened."

"So give me my present. I'm dying of curiosity," Kegan said.

To their surprise—to Dick's, at least—Royal jumped down from where he'd been sitting on the railing and went into the house and unzipped his suitcase. He came back with three boxes wrapped in Christmas paper and handed one to their host.

"Does it explode when I remove the top?" Kegan asked—a reference to a prank they'd pulled years ago. The present was an old-fashioned-looking telephone receiver with a long cord, the kind you saw all over New York now, in the same shade of green that had appeared for the first time in the seventies when pink was "shocking pink," so maybe the green was "violent green." You plugged them in to your cell phone, and the reception was much better, and also you were participating in a joke. Kegan had never seen one and really liked it. "You next," Royal said to Dick, holding out a smaller box wrapped in shiny red paper. It contained a red-and-green-striped satin thong edged on top with white feathers. Dick put it on his head. "Santa to tower, we're coming in for a crash landing!" he yelled. Everybody exploded with laughter. "And here's something for Belle to make her take her face out of a book," Royal said. "It's the entire series of *The Wire*. It'll make her grateful she grew up in the Keys." He tossed the box, wrapped in shiny blue paper, on the cushion of a redwood chair. "And for myself," Royal said, reaching in his shirt pocket and taking out a small transparent Ziploc bag, "an antique diamond solitaire ring, one and a half carats, rose gold, with channel-set diamonds, that may be offered to another woman—one I have yet to meet—because Sharon said that nothing would be worse than marrying an under-achiever, unless it was marrying a materialistic underachiever, which was not where I thought our relationship was going when I won this 1920s beauty in an eBay auction that got pretty out of control in the last thirty seconds. She kept the tufted box with the little pearl button because keeping that wouldn't be materialistic, but I understand that without the box, the value of the ring may be less."

"You're just telling us now, when I spent the whole day with you?" Dick asked.

"Hey, *he* didn't tell us he had a dog," Royal said, pointing to the dog that lay securely wedged between their host's size-fourteen sandals.

"I'm sorry to hear Sharon reacted that way," Kegan said. "She was all over you the time I met you two at that place near Washington Square."

"She said that to you?" Dick said. "I mean, how exactly did she ask for the *box*?"

"She just said could she keep the box. I shouldn't have given it to her. I think she took me aback, if that's the correct way to say it."

"Yeah, well, we can make her sorry for dissing you, the same way we're going to make—"

"Shut up, Dick. She's got her AC off and her window open," Kegan said, jutting his chin in the direction of Belle's room.

"Some people are just crazy, you know? We're supposed to bend over backward not to say women are crazy, but refusing a *marriage proposal* from Royal, there you go. Crazy."

"I appreciate your vote of confidence," Royal said to Dick. "I didn't realize you thought I'd be such a good husband."

"Well, I mean, *I'd* turn you down."

"I got stone crab for dinner," Kegan said. "Made a deal with my dentist, who's got a dozen traps or so. Deal was, I'd bite the bullet about this expensive implant he wants me to do if he gave me enough stone crabs for me and my friends. Belle doesn't like them. And my other friend, here, is always happy with his tuna fish." Kegan rubbed his big feet over the dog's sides. The dog snorted, rearranged itself, and flopped onto its back. Its ears looked like someone had given up while folding origami. "You weary travelers hungry? Like to catch the news on the flat-screen, have a shot of Cuervo and a few chips before dinner?" When nobody answered, Kegan said, "You know, it's unusual, not having any women around. It used to be us outside, and Sharon and Sarah in the kitchen, and that one time at the fireworks, Dick, your very nice girlfriend who had us up to the roof—"

"Beth Anne," Dick said. "Remarried her first husband."

"I thought he was sent to military prison."

"That was the second husband."

"The one that was younger?" Kegan asked.

"Yeah. Her Ashton Kutcher. Except I don't think Ashton went out and strangled a guitar player in a bar."

"We've become sort of ridiculous," Royal said. "Standing around in Florida bouncing rings in our pockets instead of change, with girlfriends who go back to first base like they're human boomerangs, and *Sarah*, for God's sake, going to Vegas to work at some hotel with fake dragons breathing fire outside, some Donald Trump wet dream or something, with some guy she meets at Bikram yoga, for God's sake, in Florida, where it's hot as hell to begin with."

"Thirteen years," Kegan said.

"My point is, this somehow makes us ridiculous," Royal said. "I could have left the ring back in New York. Why the hell did I bring it?

"Good pawnshop in Marathon. Guy in the witness-protection program runs it. One week he's got a beak like a parrot, next week the nose is bandaged, hair dyed brown, bandage comes off, he's got a snub nose half the size of the original honker. I heard he had his pierced ear closed up and airbrushed or whatever the hell. Something to cover the hole." Kegan shrugged.

"You know, the more I think about it, the more I really want to get a good answer from John about what the hell he thought he was doing when he screwed us out of that money," Dick said. "Motherfucker."

"Keep it down. She's right behind those blinds, she can hear anything we say. Voices carry out here like we're talking across water."

"Kegan, it's not like she's in a cloister," Royal said, frowning deeply.

"It *is* like she's in a cloister, and she put herself there, but I respect that, I do," Kegan said. "She doesn't drink or do drugs, she doesn't even go out with guys. She maybe goes out with a group occasionally. It's too bad some of that maturity didn't rub off on her mother."

"I could use some dinner," Dick said. "If we all crack our teeth eating crab, maybe we can work out another deal with your dentist. I never heard of any doctor striking a deal. Must say something about our present health insurance situation. And excuse me, Royal, but is this a comment on our new world without women you're making, pissing off the deck?"

"Jesus, what if Belle comes out?" Kegan said. "There's as many bathrooms inside as bedrooms. Go figure. Selling point of houses here. Everywhere you turn, another john."

Royal the dog, who'd been sniffing a bug walking along the bottom of the railing, disdained it and walked over to his owner and flopped down. Again, Kegan's big feet toed the dog's ribs. "You know, he used to sleep in my hair. I let him in the bed, and he'd work his way onto the pillow and fall asleep curled around the top of my head like a puppy yarmulke."

"I wouldn't have figured you for a dog person," Dick said.

"Or a father. Or a volunteer fireman. Somebody who sings in the choir."

"You sing in a choir?" Royal said, zipping his fly, walking back toward them.

"Yeah, I'm a soprano," Kegan said. "You should hear me on the Hallelujah Chorus."

"'For the Lord God om-ni-po-tent reigneth,'" Royal baritoned.

"Your shirt's caught in your fly," Kegan said.

"HA-llelujah! Hallelujah! Hallelujah!" Dick sang in shrill falsetto as Royal unzipped his fly and tucked his shirt down his pants again, then rezipped his fly.

"And Prince Philip, what's the deal with him? We heard on the radio he had a stent put in or something?"

"All those years, trailing after Her Majesty," Kegan said. "Prince Philip and the corgis. Royal, how about some dinner? You can pretend the stone crabs' claws are Sharon's neck."

"Listen to you, and you want everything nice-nice and hush-hush, so the nun can concentrate on her devotions!" Royal said.

"I just need to make the sauce," Kegan said. "It's Hellman's mayonnaise with two key limes squirted into it, a half teaspoon of coarse salt, and a couple tablespoons of horseradish."

"Lead the way," Dick said.

"What happened to your tooth that you need an implant?" Royal said, heading into the house behind Kegan.

"Bit down on a sandwich at Bojangle Bill's with a rock or something in the lettuce and it broke my tooth," Kegan said. "If I'd eaten lunch at home that day, it wouldn't have happened. I wash my lettuce. Wouldn't have been worth it, hearing Sarah bitch if I didn't. 'Wash the lettuce, wash the lettuce.' Then you have to spin it dry for about five minutes, which at least builds your biceps, then you have to dry the lettuce spinner and pick out the stuff that always gets stuck in the top. Now I wash the lettuce under the faucet, shake it over the floor—it's tile, anyway—dry it on a dish towel. Times change, bros. Times change." He handed Royal the mayonnaise jar. He handed Dick the key limes and pointed to the cutting board, which was made of multicolored wood in the shape of the state of Florida.

This was three nights before Christmas, two nights before they drove south to confront John Reynolds in Key West about screwing them over, two nights before Yuliana, the Moldovan girl Royal picked up after a private lap dance on Truman Avenue, got the best Christmas present she ever received, which also fit her finger *perfectly*, two nights before Kegan took off on his own and, as they'd later learn, put down one ice-cold Stoli shot after another, served by a bartender in an elf costume at a beach bar, from which he was ejected when he commented on the elf's cleavage, after which he apparently wandered down to Dick Dock, stepped out of his Bermuda shorts, Lacoste shirt, and Tevas, and dove into the Atlantic. Three Japanese tourists came upon his body at dawn. Tonight, though, as they stood pouring drinks and mixing mayonnaise with horseradish, it was five nights before Kegan's funeral, five nights before Royal and Dick rented a car and headed back to New York with Kegan's dog in the backseat, each trying to manipulate the other into keeping him. Belle didn't want him. She was, however, tentatively happy to see her mother again—even happier because the boyfriend stayed behind in Las Vegas. Sarah kept insisting that it was all her fault; neither her daughter nor Dick and Royal could reason with her. After the funeral at Christ by the Sea Church (which Kegan had always called "Christ, Chicken of the Sea"), attended by a smattering of people, including Kegan's dentist (who went around afterward giving out business cards that said he was a member of the VFW), Belle explained to Dick and Royal back at the house, while Sarah sobbed in the bedroom she'd shared with Kegan, that Kegan had been joking with them: The dog's name was Loyal, not Royal, but her father loved stupid jokes, didn't he? Like getting drunk and drowning—was that a stupid enough joke for everybody? And her mother's grief—wasn't that inevitable, too? One parent in the desert, the other one going as far south as possible in the continental United States to drown in the Atlantic when she still had three years of high school to go before she could go to college. Maybe that information could be shaped into a good "personal statement." How many people applied to Ivy League schools and could say that? Or was irony not appreciated in such circumstances? That was what Belle demanded to know, a little hysterically, standing on the deck in the same platform shoes, rhinestone-studded jeans, and black T-shirt she'd worn the night they'd first arrived.

"Your dad sure did love you, no doubt about that," Dick said to Belle, not having any idea what to say in response to her outburst. Royal echoed those words. It had been Royal who'd identified Kegan's body. That was him: the onetime president of their fraternity at the University of Virginia, the one who'd lived most on the edge, or at least the one who'd made the most sincere retreat from real life. The one with the blue veins on the bulb of his nose from drinking too much. The one starting to get a paunch in spite of kayaking, basketball, and twice-weekly tennis. Just another guy who, like so many others, had been left by his woman. He'd been wearing black Jockeys, nothing else. In India they could have started the bonfire on the beach, but as unpredictable as Key West was, Higgs Beach cremations had not yet become a custom. Instead, Kegan was carried away on a stretcher, pushed into an ambulance as some weedy Rastas suspended their badminton game to stare at the sad, bloated, soggy mess that was what remained of him at dawn. He'd gone to Key West to confront John Reynolds and had ended up confronting vodka shots and a Christmas elf—an elf who'd handed over the guy's keys and his cell phone to the bouncer, because she'd had enough of him and was sure he'd come back. Royal's number was the first to pop up—the last name with its double A's had helped or hurt him all his life—when the cops went to the beach bar to inquire about whether "the deceased" might have been there the previous night. They made the call to the hotel where Royal, still asleep, fumbled for the cell phone on the table a little before noon, expecting it to be Reynolds, enraged, or Yuliana—that was right; her name had been Yuliana. The autopsy found no trace of Kegan's daily heart medicine (who knew he took it?), which led the coroner to conjecture that because of Kegan's seriously low blood pressure and no presence of the drugs that should have been in his system, several factors might have contributed— along with alcohol, of course—to the heart attack.

Before Dick, Royal, and Kegan had gone their separate ways when they left Titters that night, they'd had a pretty nasty encounter with Reynolds. They had walked through the un- locked front door of Reynolds's house on Catholic Lane—the one he was renting after he'd had to short-sell the big house on Eaton—and strong-armed him into a chair while they told him in detail what a devious, self-serving shit he was. He'd certainly neglected to tell them he was on the verge of bankruptcy, and that if he declared it, they'd be low on the totem pole of creditors, which meant he had his own little pyramid scheme going. He'd known when he'd borrowed their money that the bank was about to repossess his house, which meant he could get no further loans against it, which meant he wouldn't have his promised 50 percent to put down on the old schoolhouse conversion project, which meant he'd have had to appeal to them for even more money if the schoolhouse investors had accepted his offer. Cowering in the chair in his cutoff jeans and Mile O tank top with the white-painted O crumbling like dandruff, his tennis shoes and his big fat diver's watch, he'd tried to convince them all over again that he was a good businessman. But he wasn't. He only pretended to have access to cash, to loans, to know the way to grease the palms of the code-enforcement guys. They made him turn over his wallet: All that was in it was a driver's license and a five-dollar bill and a rubber, which Dick opened and stretched over Reynolds's head as he screamed they were tearing out his hair. "Who cares, Reynolds! We lose a shitload of money, you lose your fucking hair?" Dick had hollered in his face, then he'd gone into the kitchen and returned with kitchen shears and, as Royal pinned Reynolds's shoulders to the back of the chair, cut off gobs of hair, pushing so hard with the tips of the shears that Reynolds bled. On the table was a silver Christmas tree with fake snow on the branches. Dick cut two boughs and returned to the chair and punctured the stretched prophylactic so that two green antennae protruded from either side above Reynolds's ears, as little rivulets of blood ran down his face. They turned on Christmas music, loud, and tied him to the chair with bungee cords triple-knotted behind the chair, and walked out. They walked down the street to the gated cemetery, where young women in halters and little skirts steered their bikes around the speed bumps, calling, "Merry Christmas!" to them. Kegan, who knew Key West pretty well, led Dick and Royal down an alleyway that led to the back parking lot of a strip joint beside a liquor store. That was where Dick met Anja, who lured him into a private room for a lap dance. Kegan—still fuming about all the money down the drain—said no thanks to both girls who approached him—he didn't want to be tricked anymore; he wanted his fucking money back from

Reynolds, that was what he wanted—and sat back gloomily with his beer bottle, waiting for the pole dancer to begin her routine again. Royal bought a Moldovan girl champagne, which had about as much resemblance to champagne as Royal had to royalty. Several expensive plastic flutes later, she sneaked him her number and whispered when she'd be off work. Oh, right—to be mugged by her brothers, no doubt. He left Dick and Kegan in Titters and walked to the hotel, watched TV for a few minutes—Jon Stewart, what was with that guy and his perfect silver hair and his twirling pencil?—then flipped through a guide to Key West that offered pizza delivery, biplane rides, windsurfing, an all-night pharmacy, and transgender counseling. Maybe all in one day would be fun, he thought. He channel-surfed, did not do much of anything but stare at the TV for a half hour or so, wondering why his mood was so bad. He had been thinking about the terrible falling-out he'd had with Dick back, what, twenty-five years ago, when he'd dared to date Dick's girlfriend after they'd separated, and Dick had thrown a punch at him. He'd ducked it, grabbing Dick's hand, and then Dick had started to cry, which was what he really held against him, wasn't that it? In the intervening years, neither of them had ever mentioned the incident.

Royal took a deep breath and exhaled, looked around the room where their suitcases sat—did Kegan putting his duffel on the sofa mean he was claiming the foldout, and Dick and Royal could share the king? Royal suddenly decided what the hell and took out his cell phone and called the number Yuliana had given him. Good she'd written her name: Who'd know how to spell that?

An hour later, after he'd showered and bought a pack of American Spirits and smoked two, Yuliana—as arranged—came out the unmarked back door of Titters and led him by the hand (bony fingers!) around the corner, opening a side door of the hotel there and turning on the lights, then leading him through the laundry room (what the fuck!) to a Murphy-bed sort of contraption: a converted closet with a mattress on some sort of platform shoved three quarters of the way inside it, and dusty navy-blue curtains stretching over the mattress from ceiling to floor, held down by hooks in the concrete. Inside the weird bed/tent, she told him to lie down, then unfastened her bra, a cheap purple lace thing that did nothing for him, zero, then she sat on his stomach and told him about her family (her "famblee"): her brother; the violent father (of course). All the while, laundry machines shook and rattled, and every so often someone slammed a door and Yuliana held her breath, though it didn't seem like anyone entered the laundry room. He told her about his family—the truth, even. That his girlfriend had left him. His mother had died of bone cancer. His older brother ran a corporation in New York and was a big success: He kept his distance, Brandt was in A.A. and thought much social contact with anybody who wasn't—with the exception of Brits, for some reason Royal couldn't fathom—was potentially dangerous, but he looked out for Royal and was generous, and even if his brother didn't have a great sense of humor, his secretary Jacki did. The only lie he told Yuliana was that he'd come to the Keys to go fishing.

"When I first get here," she said, "I'm thinking dolphin are fish like Flipper, and I can't understand who would eat

Flipper. But they just call this fish that, you know, as fisherman. Nobody is eating the nice guy from the movie." He asked why they didn't go to her place instead of some closet in a hotel laundry room. It depressed him to be on the dirty, uncomfortable little bed when anybody might walk in. Also, she hadn't yet mentioned money. "I don't have bed until six A.M.," she said. "You know warm bed? Three people share bed, everybody eight hours." He'd never heard of such a thing, but it had the ring of truth to it. He suggested they leave the closet and go to his hotel room, figuring he could leave a note on the door for Kegan or Dick to get lost for an hour or so, if they even came back while he was going at it with Yuliana. The idea didn't much excite him, though: She seemed young and asexual. He suspected that she, too, might enjoy a pizza and a biplane ride more.

"You know the Hallelujah Chorus?" he asked her. He was making a point not to touch her in this ridiculous setup; his hands folded below his collarbones grasped only each other. "Okay," she said reluctantly. At first he thought that she hadn't understood but was afraid to say so, but then she said: "Not knowing it by heart. You can hear that at some churches here."

"How old are you?" he said.

"Twenty," she said, too quickly, he thought.

"And how much is my night with you going to cost me?" She shrugged.

"You don't have a price?"

"I have prices, but I like you."

"That really isn't possible, Yuliana. I'm a fifty-two-year-old guy with love handles, and I stink five minutes after taking a shower. I didn't shave today. It's been a stressful day of roughing up, *tying up*, a former friend who cheated my partners and me out of some money." He suddenly had an idea that did excite him. "Would you be up for going to his house, maybe you and me putting on a little show for him? After I duct-tape his mouth?"

"You are criminal?" she asked.

"Who's going to admit to being a criminal?" he said. "I'm an executive. I work in New York City."

"Then I charge more, because I never see you again," she pouted. The cheap brassiere dangled loosely in front of her breasts.

"What if you don't charge me anything, and I give you a really beautiful piece of jewelry?"

"Crap jewelry," she shot back.

He smiled. "Maybe you should look at it first," he said. "Let's get out of here, take a stroll, check out how my former frat brother's doing, the former head of the IFC, you know what that is? I didn't think so. Fraternity council. A Jefferson Scholar in his youth, now a loser tied up in a La-Z-Boy. Maybe the two of us can interject some fun into his life, put on a little show."

"I only do private," she said.

"Let's get out of here," he said, shifting his weight onto one hip to stand up. "You see what you think of my crap ring, and if you like it, it's yours. Then maybe we'll talk about your moving to New York."

"Why did you say about Hallelujah Chorus?" she asked, standing, the blue curtain hanging just behind her. One of the washing machines clicked off loudly, sending a vibration through his legs.

"Because I think that should be our special song, Yuliana. Because if you stay in this country, you're going to hear it at Christmas for the rest of your life."

"Not hear it just in this country," she said.

"True," he said, "wherever you go, every time you hear it, you'll think of me. You'll tell your grandchildren: Once, when Grandma was an exotic dancer in Key West, she had sex with a man from New York who gave her a beautiful ring and, being a materialistic girl, she fell in love with him, and their special song was the Hallelujah Chorus."

"You think I am that kind of girl?"

"Wait till you see the ring," he said, fingering his pants pocket, where he'd thought to drop it, since that pocket seemed safer than his shirt's. "Allow me to introduce myself, Yuliana. I'm a man of wealth and taste."

She frowned, dropping her long thin legs to the floor as if dropping oars into water, then leaning forward and standing. He said, "You don't know what that is, do you? It's another song, almost as famous as the Hallelujah Chorus. But it was certainly before your time. It was the soundtrack in another lifetime of mine. Back when I was young and never thought I'd have money to lose, let alone tie up a guy who fucked me out of my money, who once walked half the Appalachian Trail with me, which was a considerable distance, and who tutored me in History of Diplomacy, and who used to be one of my best friends. And if you don't mind, I'd really like to get out of the laundry room now."

"Okay, follow me," she said. He watched her walking. She had a very nice ass. She went to the back door, unbolted it, then turned to him. "Let's see so beautiful ring," she said suddenly.

He looked at her and wondered if she was as old as twenty. He'd be in big trouble if she was Belle's age. The room they'd been in smelled of detergent, and the fumes caught up with them as the door opened, its smell even more overpowering as it was diluted with the salt air. She locked the door from the outside. He reached in his pocket and withdrew the little bag, carefully removed the ring, and held it out to her under the ugly yellowish overhead lights in the parking lot. He held it upright, between thumb and first finger. "My God," she said.

He said, "Try it on. We'll walk over to my former friend's place. I think you and I can work something out."

Dick left Titters last, after the second lap dance by the same girl, who had a fire-breathing dragon blowing down a tree or something on her thigh, wandering Duval Street for a while, then going to a movie at the Tropic Cinema, an art deco place with a statue of Marilyn Monroe outside and a concession stand where he bought a bag of popcorn and a glass of wine. The movie was about some guy who went crazy, an ordinary sort of guy in some nowhere place who got fixated on building a bomb shelter to protect himself and his family from whatever coming disaster he feared. As he watched, he thought: Imagine being Reynolds. Imagine losing your house, your friends, being on the verge of bankruptcy. There was no excuse for what he'd done, but what if he might still be sitting in the chair? They really couldn't leave him tied up and just drive away the next day. It wasn't like his housekeeper was going to find him or anything. He'd looked so wretched, with the prophylactic on his head like one of those infant caps, a buttercup or something, a big rubber nipple pointing up at the ceiling. Nothing that had happened had been motivated by his desire to screw them. Or not directly. What he'd done was wrong, but his own life was more of a mess than any punishment they could dole out. And, after all, it was almost Christmas. In the movie, the nice-guy-crazy-man was climbing out of a big hole that had been bulldozed outside his house. His shocked wife and deaf kid stared in amazement. The problems people had were awful. Reynolds himself had been hospitalized for depression twice that Dick knew of, once during their school years, when he had his choice of either being suspended for a semester or going into a substance abuse program, though they didn't call it anything so lofty back then. Another time after he seemed to be doing well, building strip malls in upstate New York, where his parents lived. He'd been in his thirties then, with two failed marriages behind him. Dick remembered Mrs. Reynolds's face, her eyes narrowed with worry, asking him in the corridor of the university hospital if he thought her son was going to be all right. Then, as ever, lying came easily to him: he'd told Mrs. Reynolds that her son would be fine, and her eyes had opened just enough that he could see their color. Their color, he remembered all these years later, had been green. It was wrong to leave Reynolds tied up, Dick thought—even if he felt more charitable toward the world only because of the fifty-dollar blow job he'd gotten in the backseat of a parked car with painted windows from a German girl who was going off work at Titters. Reynolds didn't have the money to give them. From the look of his crappy rental, he didn't have the money for much, though about now he might really be regretting bringing in the one big comfortable chair.

Dick pushed his empty plastic glass under his seat, along with the empty popcorn bag, and walked out of the movie and back to the rental car, pushed a few buttons that eventually opened the door. He got in, turned on the overhead light, and consulted a map of Key West on a place mat they'd gotten at the bar they'd stopped at on the way to Kegan's that for some reason he'd folded and taken with them.

Dick drove back toward Catholic Lane. He arrived at Reynolds's house to see it all lit up, the only house on the street that wasn't dark: A single strand of red Christmas lights wound around the big cactus outside, but the house itself was eerily aglow, like some Thomas Kinkade nightmare. So Reynolds had made his escape. Of course he had. What was he going to do, sit there forever or struggle free? Dick was proud of Reynolds for slipping the bungee cords. He continued toward the front door, prepared to apologize, to hope something could be worked out about the lost money in the New Year.

The music from inside vibrated the walkway. Behind him, two people on bikes rang their bells and waved as if they knew him. Seasonal goodwill! He smiled. Then he walked a bit farther and looked into the house through the front window, assuming that what he saw must be Reynolds and some other people dancing. A *party*, after being berated and tied up, humiliated? But no: He was looking at Royal, naked, who looked like he was doing an impersonation of a Jerry Lewis telethon. Reynolds was still tied to the chair, his eyes widening as they connected with Dick's, the bottom half of Reynolds's face silver, which Dick realized must be duct tape. It was the Hallelujah Chorus—"For unto us a child is born," the glass panes vibrating in the window—and Royal was chasing some scrawny naked girl around the room, shrieking as he feinted and sprang forward, arms waving madly, every bit as energetic as he'd been back when he played basketball at UVA, and it was so strange, there was no other way to describe it, it was so strange. Here the two of them were, down from New York City, Royal naked and roaring, some woman trying to escape him or, it seemed pretty obvious, *pretending* to be trying to get away, so that when they collided and fell to the floor, it seemed like part of their game, all of it choreographed. Reynolds's head, as his neck twisted from side to side, seemed like a metronome helping Royal keep up the frantic tempo. Dick had seen plenty of weird shit before, *plenty* of it, but now he felt implicated, implicated at the same time he was excluded, so that when Reynolds's wild eyes met his again, he closed his own. The image that appeared behind his eyes was of Reynolds's mother, back when he and her son were undergraduates, a woman that, at the time, he'd assumed must be the generic age of all grown-ups, but who he now thought must have been only in her forties, asking whether her son would be all right.

What was he supposed to do? Go in?

When Royal came back to the hotel room, fumbling his key in the lock sometime after three in the morning, Dick sprang

up from bed and tackled him without even thinking. Royal
stank of sweat and alcohol and sex. He toppled easily. As
he went down, cursing, Dick had a flash-forward in which
he was fighting Royal, on top of him on the floor, pounding
him. Which would be a different version of what he'd seen
through the window, but if he did that, he'd be as debased
as Royal. When was there ever going to be any sanity? Why
would he fly at his friend like a mountain lion jumping on
its prey? He scared himself. But action preceded conscious
thought, and he'd been asleep, or passed out after the two
double whiskey sours he'd drunk in a bar after he'd slunk
away from Reynolds's place. Where was Kegan? And was
Reynolds at least untied, for God's sake? Dick felt humiliated at their excess. What exactly were they trying to prove?
That they could recover money that didn't exist anymore?
Kegan's insistent calls from Islamorada to both of them in
New York had gotten them to Florida, all right—but now,
in the middle of the night, almost dawn, Dick had come
close to punching out his best friend, and Kegan—where was
he? Why wasn't he leading the battle, if he was so hungry
for revenge?

He was dead, but Dick and Royal had no way of knowing
that. Royal's own thoughts had entirely to do with why
his old frat buddy had tackled him that way when all he'd
been doing was coming back to their hotel room after a
night of animated but very mediocre sex, though it had
been pretty interesting being observed by the guy who had
fucked them over: Reynolds being forced to close his eyes

or watch Royal fucking Yuliana, some random whore who now had what should have been Sharon's ring—because, hey, he wasn't a liar. Yuliana was going to turn out to be the liar. She wasn't going to call him in New York, no way. Did he believe what she'd said as she'd put on her ugly underwear, pulled on her dress, fastened her belt? He'd offered to walk her home, wherever home might be, back to her warm bed. This mediocre lay, this person with whom he had nothing in common, might move to New York, with its piles of dirty snow, the freezing winds off the Hudson whipping between buildings? No. She'd stay amid palm trees, in what was called by the tourist board "Paradise," wearing her not-at-all-hard-won sparkler.

The Japanese tourists on Dick Dock called the police when they saw the body facedown, slapping against a pylon. They wouldn't have been there themselves except that they'd gotten lost searching for the Southernmost Point.

Half inch by half inch, Reynolds bumped the chair to the front window and knocked his head against the glass so hard when the mail lady finally arrived the next day, it took seventeen stitches to close the gash.

Yuliana, who was eighteen, moved to New York, studied English in night school, went to Pilates class, renamed herself Julie, and became a well-paid hostess at a restaurant with an unlisted number in the Meatpacking District. On her nineteenth birthday, she married Royal in a wedding paid for by his brother that took place atop the Gramercy Park Hotel. It was the first time Royal met the famous Jacki, who was plump and fortyish, with hair conventionally called "highlighted" that made her look like a jack-o'-lantern, if a jack-o'-lantern had hair. Kegan's dog, renamed Islamorada and called Isle, attended the ceremony and the reception. A leash was never necessary; the dog instantly obeyed a firm verbal command. Jacki, by previous agreement, would be taking the dog while Royal and Julie honeymooned on Mustique: A two-week honeymoon, paid for by Brandt, but when the honeymoon couple went to the airport at the end of their two weeks in a beach house with French doors that opened onto a private patio with a hot tub and a keyboard and bench, they were approached by a dark-skinned person in a clown suit that didn't quite cover his forearms, his features made antic with white face paint, who ran up to Royal and unrolled a scroll saying that Brandt (called "Mr. Brandt" throughout) had rented the house they'd been staying in for another week—they should continue to enjoy their honeymoon. He and Julie laughed and laughed. Two hundred white orchids at the reception, six brass cages of white doves, now this! A year and a half later they had twin boys, and the year after that, Julie left him. A private detective found her immediately, crammed into some other Moldovan's one-bedroom Hell's Kitchen apartment with their babies and the other Moldovan's daughter, but Royal didn't ask her to come back. Jacki took care of the details of the divorce—Jacki, who now lived with Kegan's dog in her

Park Slope apartment, renamed, after her favorite movie actor, Penn. Of course, this was no ordinary dog and never had been. In his adaptability, he had proved to be flexible, intelligent, empathetic. What human being could hope to be more? His story follows.

Do you finally get it, that guys who graduated from college can still be pigs, that "human" is just a vague, general term? I don't know the educational background of the other people who wrung the necks of my brothers and somehow overlooked mine when they threw us out the car window like so many cigarette butts. It was a time of intense pain, but I had no real concept of "past" or "future" and also no idea how such pain could be endured, let alone a notion that it might end. Then Kegan walked out of his house, flopping along in his big sandals, talking on his cell to some woman he was flirting with, and stopped dead, stunned, reaching down for all that was left of the litter: me. I was at the vet's, wrapped in a towel, in half an hour. They did some things to me, but it was all an agony of pain, just more. If I'd known only one word, it might have been "more." They set my broken back legs, sutured my eye, put in an IV drip. I was put on a heated cushion on the first tier of cages—since I couldn't move, the door was left open—so people came by and reached in and smoothed the area between my eyes with their thumbs and spoke to me quietly. Belle cried and cried. I spent over a week there, but since this was all some bizarre fairy tale, Kegan worked out a payment plan with the vet and visited every day, though once he explained to

me that he absolutely couldn't come on Wednesday, only
to show up as usual, which came as a relief. I tried to make
the kind of eye contact that would let him know how much
I appreciated everything. He bought me my first DQ Bliz-
zard on the ride home, where I was held in Belle's lap on a
pillow, though he drank all of it but the one small nibble I
was able to take when he removed the lid. I don't remember
that, but I overheard the story so many times, about how
my face lit up and how Kegan was immediately convinced
I was going to live, that it became my reality. I remember
when the casts came off, my lying on the pillow above his
head. It made him laugh. He'd reach up a big hand and
sort of slap/pat me, but whatever that touch meant, it was
pure affection. That was the way we went to sleep until it
got a little too twisted up for both of us as I grew, and then
we started sleeping spoon-style. He had a lot of anger, but
not toward me. Not much toward Belle, either, though
sometimes she caught it. It was always about her mother,
which was not a good thing to reproach her with. She was
cautious about getting attached to anybody, but he mistook
that, understandably enough, for her being bookish and
private. Still, he gave her a new Mac for Christmas and
never teased her in front of her friends, and always encour-
aged her, especially once you figured out how to interpret
some of his vague comments, or once you got the Zeta
Psi mythology down and understood the allusions. Belle
got the fact that he cared, even if she didn't always know
exactly what he was talking about. You pick up emotions,
you register the essence of things, even if you don't always
understand exactly what's being said. You also absorb the

smells of certain places, and sometimes, when you least expect it, you get a whiff of where you used to live, and it takes you back. A little mystical, I realize. But things you can't see, like breeze, music, sensory memories there are no words for—though I'm trying my best, here—my belief is that not only do you exist on the planet, but the planet exists inside you, its stars behind your eyes, its retained sunshine warming you from the inside out, as many times as it does from the outside in. I understand why Belle didn't want any reminders when he died: She would have thought of him every time she saw me. He had a much easier time relating to me than to her. Of course, I was just a dog, with no way to express anything except maybe with a sparkle in my eye or with my jaw hanging open. Even though she gave me away to a not bad person—though I notice I was handed off again at the first opportunity—I'll never get over losing the person I loved most. By the time Belle said, "His name's Loyal, not Royal, it was just one of his jokes," and sent me to New York with Royal and Dick, I'd already become a part of her. Now it's not just Belle applying to colleges but me, curled up small inside her brain the way I once was when I slept over her father's head. I'm thinking along with her, having experienced a lot of the same things she did, though she can put them down on paper, I can't. Because the talking-dog joke is just that: a joke. You think anybody is going to believe a dog writes *essays*? Good luck to her with the college thing: If education might make the world a better place, a place of more kindness and awareness, I'm all for it. As much good as I've experienced, along with having had more than the usual share of good luck, the damage that's done to you when you're young—abandonment being one of the worst things—can never be entirely undone, so I'm not of the opinion that the world is a very nice place. If you agree with me, it makes more sense if you take from it what you can: the breeze, the stars, all that.

LADY NEPTUNE

Mrs. Edward R. was pushed into the building in a wheelchair with a half-sized seat, several straps pulled not exactly tightly, but tightly enough, over her lap. She loved, loved those skirts from several years ago, weighted at the bottom and voluminous, with ruched sides billowing below the stitches into parachutes—so comfortable, so (as is said) forgiving.

But of course, with a real parachute you'd be up in the air, dangling above the Atlantic. Blowing right past the condos overlooking the water, such as 1800 Atlantic, where her son, Darryl, lived with the nicer of his twin sons following an abominable stroke when he was fifty-six: a nonsmoker; a jogger; okay—a few too many recreational drugs in his youth. Darryl spent many days on the balcony, staring at the water. She didn't do that—she wasn't in that sort of shape, thank God—but she did sometimes cross her eyes and look at nothing as a way of introspecting.

She was being carried into the building's private elevator, key-activated so that everyone else coming to the party would have to climb the stairs, regardless of age, infirmity, fame. That, or they'd already know better than to come. Only for her, only for Alva, did the host admit to having the key. "Alvie," he'd said to her years ago, "it's our little secret." Among their other little secrets was that they sent the cook away and had a flute of champagne with lunch, and that they'd found an accountant who had ingenious ways for his clients to cheat on their taxes. Her husband, R. (that was their nasty nickname for him; he'd read too many Russian novels), had never particularly liked Duncan Oswald, though he, too, had usually gone to Duncan's annual Christmas party. It was a small community, and one didn't want to give offense by not attending. Still, one year R. had sent Alva along without him—back when she simply walked places—and sent flowers the next day with a note of apology about his ostensible last-minute nausea, but the florist had gotten the orders mixed up, so Duncan—who always did like R., or at least appreciated that he was often, wittingly or not, the occasion for fun—received a bouquet of tulips and a dirty note about how their dowsing heads wanted to be you-know-where. It was Key West, so of course the florist had just written down whatever message the caller gave. Though he had nothing to do with the mix-up, obviously, R. resented Duncan for the amount of kidding he'd had to endure: Duncan had spread this story around.

Ned, the less nice of her grandsons, was accompanying her. At this very moment, he was squeezing into the little elevator, placing a hand on her shoulder. The elevator's slowness made him nervous. "Here we go," he said tensely. He had nothing else to say as they ascended. She plucked up a bit of fabric so that it fell even lower on her leg—she hoped low enough to obscure the bruise. She couldn't get into panty hose anymore, and she detested those stockings that ended just at the knee. That scam was always somehow humiliatingly revealed, and then you felt worse, and the person seeing felt worse.

Less-Nice Ned (she and Duncan had agreed on this, over a little Taittinger) was on best behavior tonight, for whatever reason. Duncan's cook (who had previously been a burglar in Miami; he got early parole because it was a first offense, and the prison was filled to bursting) almost collided with her grandson as the elevator door opened, in his haste to be helpful. Less-Nice Ned rolled her forward as the cook swept away imaginary obstacles, including a full-body block of a potted hibiscus at least eight feet away from the wheelchair.

Christmas lights twinkled around the pot. They twinkled from the ceiling beams, hanging like little glittering stalactites. Soon Gay Santa would appear, to change into his faux-edgy costume and perform the annual ritual of handing out small wrapped presents. You could really end up on the short end of the stick sometimes. The previous year, one guest had received a package of airplane peanuts.

Her present, though, was a promissory note: "My devotion forever, and my cook for your birthday, who will prepare dinner for up to ten friends." Very generous! And yes—she had ten friends. Especially if you counted her son and his two boys, though her son would not attend, even if he said he would, and if Less-Nice Ned got a better offer, he'd probably cancel at the last minute. Her accountant and his wife would be there. Her psychiatrist. Jeannelle, who walked her dog every night (somebody not worth inviting walked the dog in the morning and midafternoon). Marie and Harry would be there. Maybe the Perrys. The cook himself. Shouldn't she include the cook and, of course, the gift-giver? Was that ten, or more than ten?

She settled on the sofa this way: The narrow wheelchair was turned sideways, with the cook fanning dust out of the air, as if its settling might somehow interfere with the transfer. (There was no dust; the cook also cleaned.) Next she slid one-two-three (moving prematurely on two) with her grandson's hand lightly curled under her armpit, guiding her along what even she could see was a short sideways bump onto the Naugahyde sectional sofa. Under the cushion, she knew, were books. Duncan put them there because otherwise the cushion sank down too much, and rising would be difficult. Three decorative pillows in varying shades of green were available to be placed behind her back, if she might want to sit a little farther forward. She wasn't sure about that; it made a person look too eager, too truly on the edge of the chair.

Ah! It was very comfortable, but books or not, she was not pleased about the amount of armpit pressure that would have to be applied at the end of the evening. Still, she looked up and gave a small smile and nodded. "Everything comfortable?" the cook said. He always spoke with bravado. He had found God while in jail, but had given Him up the second he was paroled. Also, he knew they drank champagne—she'd seen him peeking once, before he left—but what did he care? What might the cook truly care about? He was not a person she would have known in her youth. Old people couldn't meet anyone new—other people looked right through you. And her friends—she didn't want to know any more about them.

"If you could have anything in the world, what might that be?" she said to the cook.

He looked momentarily confused, as if someone might be standing behind his back. "A lot of money," he said.

She considered this. It seemed an honest answer. Also, just because she was old and in not very good shape, why should she be allowed a follow-up question? So she didn't ask it. It would be taking advantage of his position. Making a monkey of him. You could talk about a zebra's stripes only because it didn't speak. Now, it was turning out that if you said something about a monkey, the monkey would probably understand entirely and even consider an ironic reply. Or was that gorillas? What was Koko?

"My husband was a great believer in mutual funds. In diversifying. But I do understand that you have to have money in order to 'grow your money.' Even grass doesn't grow on its own. Or at least you have to water it and not let anyone walk on it and then worry about it for the rest of your life, those times it does take."

"Ma'am," he said.

"Well, that's enough of *that* conversation," Less-Nice Ned said.

Duncan had given her her present the day before the party, delivered by messenger. Of course, the cook had been the messenger, coming with the little wrapped box in his bike basket, crossing paths with Olinda the Boring Dog Walker, flirting with her, in her deep-cut tank shirt and shorts with the peace sign on the back pockets. Still, she'd never considered the possibility that the cook might have replied, "Olinda."

"You stop hovering like bees around the hive and get

yourselves something to drink," Duncan said to all the people suddenly grouped in front of them. Then he plopped down beside her. Duncan was eighty. He went to the gym two days a week and power-walked on the sidewalk by the beach another couple of nights. He had a droopy eye, but nothing was going to fix that. It wasn't even entirely age-related. When the bees scattered, he patted her knee lightly, through peaks and gulleys of fabric. "And if you could have anything you wanted, what would it be?"

"Are you mad that I asked him?" she said.

"No, dear. He's not quite at the cutoff age where it would only be condescending. He's turned his life around since his incarceration, we see that. If he doesn't kill me in my sleep. I've promised him money when I die, and he doesn't want to go back to prison, and he doesn't seem violent, anyway. You know, they caught him because he peed a little during the robbery. How they cross-match pee, I don't know. Or maybe it was a hair that finally did him in."

She started laughing. Her eyes darted to the cook, who was standing talking to her grandson and another man who'd entered the party but not come over to say hello. No, wait: It was Olinda. Olinda, in one of those trilbies everybody wore, pulled down low, and black leather motorcycle pants and black boots, her eyebrows drawn on darkly, her hair jaggedly cut off. As short a haircut as a man would have! And a black leather jacket to complete the outfit. Olinda raised a Heineken bottle in greeting.

Then, because it was the same every year, an even larger crowd of people rushed in like a huge wave that would grow more and more threatening, more frightening, the higher it rose. You'd expect unwavering, nearly naked men and women, with their feet spread for perfect balance, to be riding it on surfboards until the enormous wave crested (which would have to be at the ceiling beams) and propelled everyone in her direction all at once, like so many grains of sand, toward where she sat like Neptune without a scepter (without even a drink, publicly) on a throne propped up with the Yellow Pages and hardback dictionaries you couldn't give away anymore. She was their destination, no different than arriving at the Pyramids, hardly distinguishable (except for her age) from the Fountain of Youth.

She crossed her legs. Her calves were gnarled varicose veins of seaweed. She'd started out the proud sandcastle fortress; she'd become the unlovely sun-bleached towel; she'd been so, so long ago the little shoe left behind; her finger was now the remaining claw of the crab that had already been pecked apart by seagulls.

"Merry Christmas, Merry Christmas!"

An echo or just a lot of identical thoughts? Impossible to tell, underwater, when you'd lost your sense of hearing and the sound inside your head was a roar.

Was it true that if you went under for the third time, that was it? Were only bird feathers—there! What about bird feathers, didn't they repel water and float?

But too many garments . . . too much material . . . like shoes, they'd drag you down.

The word "money" popped up like a bit of the ocean's detritus riding in on a wave, but her lips formed the words "Merry Christmas."

THE CATERER

M oira the cake maker had a broken toe, and Caitlin Lee was recovering from an appendectomy, so Janet recruited her daughter, Blair, and Blair's boyfriend, Steven, to help her load the Subaru wagon with trays of food, serving implements, and enormous bunches of peonies from her garden, along with a pile of nice tablecloths and some sparkly stars to scatter here and there, and oh, how many times had people's corkscrews broken during a party? As well as the one in her Swiss Army knife, she put in a Cuisinart corkscrew that her clients always fell in love with once they'd used it and—really last-minute—dipped in to the bucket on the front porch and took out a handful of shells, carefully rinsed by Blair and Steven, because those might be nice, too.

It had been a rainy summer in Maine, but finally it was almost July and sunny. Everything was very green; Janet had to duck to get under the wisteria growing on the arbor at the end of the walkway, amazed at the amount of lavender petals scattered prettily over the path. No doubt some would be in her hair. "Get a move on," she called back toward the house. The only response was from the cat, who darted up the stairs and went through the cat door into the house.

Blair opened the door, holding the cat in her arms. Blair had just graduated as a journalism major from Northwestern, and she was entirely too skinny and pale. She needed some meals instead of snacks, and to be out in the sun soaking up vitamin D. It hadn't helped that she'd gotten sick in Mexico, even though she'd drunk only bottled water and brushed her teeth with it, too.

"Mom, Grandpa Gerald just called, but I didn't pick up because I knew you had to get going."

Janet hated caller ID, which had simply materialized after she'd had to replace the old phone. To her dismay, after living alone for almost twenty years, she'd developed the habit of running for the phone only to look sadly at the phone even if she was happy to get the call, because seeing the caller's name made it seem as if they'd already spoken: The name signified an end rather than a beginning.

"I guess that's the right thing to have done," she said. "Where is Steven?"

"He's doing what you told him and putting the cake frosting in a plastic container."

"We have fifteen minutes to get there, and there might be construction on the bridge again," Janet said.

Her daughter lowered the cat to the porch. It ran through its door. Steven came out of the house carrying one of her vinyl bags that seemed handbag-small in his big hands, wearing a white linen shirt, linen Bermuda shorts, and flip-flops, looking harried, as he always did. He had given up smoking for the second time in three months, found that the nicotine patch made him woozy, after which he'd adopted the motions of smoking without a cigarette in his hand. The hand not carrying the bag gripped an imaginary cigarette between the first and second fingers.

"We're all packed. Flowers, yes; tablecloths; decorations; extra corkscrew. Okay. You can just put that bag with the cake stuff on the floor, Steven. Ready to roll?"

Janet's cell phone rang. She pulled it out of her pants pocket: black linen pants with a sharp crease—her catering pants, with the deep pockets so hard to find in women's clothes these days. "Hello," she said without looking at who was calling. Of course it was her father; he had just tried the house phone and moved on to plan B. "Honey," he said, "I want you to take a deep breath and listen to what I have to say, because I can only say it once."

"What's the matter, Dad?" she said.

"Law and order got in the way," he said. "I guess that's the best way to say it. I was going to Kmart to get your mother's prescription, and three kids with a bucket came up and wanted to wash my car—why, there was no rinse water there in the middle of the parking lot. But one of 'em wouldn't take no for an answer, so I put out my arm and told him when I saw a hose, then maybe we could talk, but then the other one, one of the other ones, started dumping sudsy water on the hood of the Chevy, and I saw red. I don't know exactly what happened, but I grabbed the bucket outta his hand and threw it at him, then sure enough, his father or some adult showed up, and before you know it, there I was in a police cruiser, my car still unlocked, and don't think those three boys weren't inside it the second the cops pulled away, but it took a minute to get the police to listen to me, and then they said, 'Well, we can't go back now, we'll get somebody over there to lock your car.' The handle scraped this kid's wrist when I grabbed the bucket. What do we need now? Security guards to protect customers going into Kmart to pick up a prescription? If they'd wanted to cut my hair, should I have sat on the hood and let 'em do that, too? So I'm going to have to tell my story to the judge, but right now your mother's got Doris Miller coming to pick me up and the policeman gave me a cell phone and a doughnut and a mug of coffee, and says his father fought in the Pacific during the war. If your mother calls you, I don't want you misunderstanding the situation, because as you know, your mother never could keep a story straight, so I only gave her the basic outline."

"Dad, no—this is awful. Were you hurt?"

"I'm not hurt, I'm a six-foot man, or maybe I'm a raging bull, I don't know, but the only one hurt was the aggressor, even though you and I know that's not going to make him change his ways."

"That's terrible, just terrible. It's hard to believe. I really wish you lived closer."

"Even with the class of people we've got here, it's a better place to live than that climate you live in, where it's winter except for three months a year. It would kill your mother."

"So, Dad, you're okay, and you're having coffee, and everything's going to work out?"

"Nothing's easy. Going on a five-minute errand's not easy.

It makes me so mad, when I get out of here, I'm going to go sit at that new sports bar and watch the game and have a beer, and the hell with everything."

"What's wrong, Mom?" Blair said.

The cat had come out of the house again and pounced successfully on a field mouse. "Eww," Blair squealed, seeing it, too. One of Steven's big hands covered her face, giving her peek room between the fingers. Janet's phone beeped to signal a low battery.

"Dad, I'm on my way to a job, but just as soon as I get home, I'm going to call you. Are you sure you're okay?"

"Next I'm going to read the sports section. One of the officers has been very accommodating, bringing me the coffee and the sports pages. If I was one of those kids, I would have taken the coffee and thrown it in his face and scalded him. I guess it's clear I'm not that class of person."

"Okay, and Mom is okay? This was just routine, your filling—"

"They think she's got a headache because she's going to have to have a root canal, but there's worry about that because of the heart situation she had the other time, you know? So the doctor phoned in a pain pill prescription, and on Monday this'll all get sorted out with the cardiologist or the dentist and so forth."

"She's in bed without medicine?"

"I see Doris now, coming through the door. She looks plenty glad to see me. Well, we'll get that prescription from somewhere other than Kmart. I'm sure they can switch it over to someplace where you don't take your life in your hands going to get it."

"Dad, I'm glad you're okay. This will all work out. We'll talk as soon as—"

The phone beeped again and she snapped it shut, letting him think they'd been cut off. "Why has Steven gone back in the house?" Janet said to Blair.

"To pee."

"Well, please go get him. We're supposed to be there now, not standing in the driveway."

"I hardly think I should tell him to hurry up. He's just peeing."

"Steven!" Janet called loudly. While Blair looked at her as if she'd turned into Stanley Kowalski in *A Streetcar Named Desire*, Janet loudly closed the trunk. In a couple of minutes Steven sauntered out of the house, eating a Fudgsicle.

This client was the second wife of some stockbroker disgraced by the SEC, now in "early retirement." Both of them had had plastic surgery, which, instead of making them look youthful, made their faces look rosy, with high unlined foreheads that seemed oddly blank, like a street sign not imprinted with a word or an image. He was the difficult one; she was only neurotic. He thought Costco frozen appetizers cooked and smothered in expensive and recognizable Stonewall Kitchen sauces were perfectly fine. He put out bottles of homemade seltzer because "everyone wants to cut down on drinking." (Which he told the guests repeatedly as he circulated among them.) This was the third occasion Janet had catered for them and would probably be the last, since Jeff, the husband, had called after her bedtime to say that they had plenty of toothpicks and plastic glasses. Her food did not need toothpicks, and she had explained to his wife that she did not provide plates, glasses, or flatware—information that was also written in bold type inside the folder she'd left with them.

The occasion of the party was the next day's sentencing of Bernie Madoff. As they pulled in, Janet saw a Madoff dartboard leaning on an easel in the yard and their dog peeing against a horseshoe stand that had been altered by the insertion of a short pole with a magazine cover photo of Madoff atop it.

"Don't eat anything we're bringing, even if they offer. Say no to seltzer. Absolutely nothing but 'No, thank you,' and we leave the minute we've finished setting up, is that clear? We are not their guests, and we are providing the food, we are not circulating."

"You're unbelievable," Blair said. "Why don't you lighten up?"

"Because these people would suck us all into their vortex, where we would stay, answering questions and trying to calm them until the first guests showed up, and then we'd be blocked in and never get out of their driveway."

Blair snorted a little laugh. Steven tried to stay out of it, but Janet could see from his expression that he was surprised by the Madoff effigies.

Dee Dee, the blank-faced, surgery-enhanced wife, came toward Janet, wearing a bizarre costume that looked more like a fancy hat than a dress, with the shoulders squared and crinkly pieces of plastic shooting out beneath the waist like damaged chopsticks. Manolos, what else? "I am frantic!" she said. "The oven won't turn on. We can't heat anything. This is going to be a disaster. Do you have a lot of crackers? Maybe we could put some of the hors d'oeuvres in the blender and eat them room-temperature on crackers? Why the fuck won't the oven heat up?"

"Let me take a look at it," Steven said, stepping into her lair, beginning to get sucked in. Suddenly even Blair looked horrified. The back of Dee Dee's dress was an enormous butterfly, its wings divided by the raised material covering the zipper. Janet did not dare exchange glances with her daughter.

"Almost nothing needs heating. You could use a pan on top of the stove to heat just . . ."

Jeff stood in the kitchen, watching the oven's digital display register 300, 310, 320.

"You fixed it. You fixed it!" Dee Dee squealed, so excited that her flapping hand knocked Steven's shoulder and toppled him lightly into her husband, who reached out his own big hand to say, "Whoa! Whoa! Anybody want a slug of seltzer to celebrate?"

"No, thanks," they murmured in unison.

"Dee Dee," Janet said decisively, "we are going to set the tables and get out of your way. All I need are a few vases for peonies. You just relax."

"Vases?" repeated Dee Dee. Janet might as well have said cauldrons or pieces of abstract sculpture. "Vases," she intoned, looking into the distance and narrowing her eyes, as if the vases might call to her from wherever they were hiding.

"They are very, very pretty no matter what you put them in. Short stems. Long. No stems at all, floating. Shall I delegate this task to my daughter, Dee Dee?"

"How did you fix the oven?" Dee Dee suddenly said to Jeff.

"I pressed 'cook,'" he said.

Blair preceded Janet out of the room onto the porch, where the buffet tables were set up. Steven raced past her to help Janet unload the car. "Does she die at midnight?" Steven said as Janet opened the trunk.

"Excuse me?"

"Butterflies. Don't they only live one day?"

"Don't make me laugh. Please."

There were ants moving around the trunk, though she'd left the peonies out overnight and shaken them thoroughly to avoid just that problem. Steven and Janet flicked them away quickly, without comment. Fortunately, the foil on top of the trays was on tightly. Janet picked up the biggest tray and draped the tablecloths over her arm, the small bag containing the corkscrew and other little things dangling from her wrist. Steven followed, a tray in each hand. Blair, they saw through the window, was in the kitchen with Dee Dee, selecting vases. There were probably fifteen or twenty cut-crystal vases, Janet saw as she poked her head in the kitchen. "No," Dee Dee was murmuring, "no, no." The currents of air from the ceiling fan flapped her wings behind her. Mercifully, her husband had disappeared. Outside, the dog was trying to break the neck of his neon-green stuffed barbell, while the big blowup of the as yet unpunctured face of Bernie Madoff looked down on them like Dr. T. J. Eckleburg from his billboard.

"They're really celebrating Madoff going to jail? Did he, like, know the guy?"

"Steven and Blair, please do not talk among yourselves, in case you are overheard. Please get the cake and ask her for a knife to frost it, Blair, and Steven, you could take the cake into the kitchen, please."

"I feel like I'm six," Blair said. She held open the screen door. Unpleasant instrumental music—bagpipes?—played quietly somewhere inside the house. Blair pulled a dead leaf off a hanging geranium, then looked nervously at her mother. "It's not like I'm already in the Peace Corps and I'm doing something to upset the natives," she said. Silently, she smoothed the tablecloth with Janet. She reached into the little bag, saw the shells, and polished one on the side of her pants leg. She placed it tentatively on the table.

"Please get the peonies," Janet said.

"Where'd everybody go all of a sudden?"

"Give thanks," she said quietly. "And if Steven is having any trouble frosting the cake, help him."

"Mom. He worked in a bakery last summer. He knows how to frost cakes. Cupcakes, at least."

"Small problem," Steven said, coming out of the kitchen. "Jeff isn't feeling good. He wants to see you, Janet."

"What? Where is he?"

"Lying on the sofa. There's a sofa thing in the pantry. A futon."

"Well, where is his wife?"

"I don't know. He's sweating."

"He's sweating? That's the problem?" But she was already following Steven into the house, through the kitchen, into a side room where, sitting slumped on a pink futon on a frame with quite a few dog toys at his feet, Jeff stared ahead, clenching his teeth.

"It's my arm. Pain all up and down my arm."

"Where's your wife? Steven, dial 911 and say you think someone's having a heart attack. Do you know where your wife is?"

"Taking off her dress, putting on another one. Can you just . . . can you help me stand up a bit here?"

"I think you should stay seated, don't exert yourself. Here's a pillow"—she thought it was a pillow, but it was a dog toy that squeaked when she wedged it under his shoulder—"here's, okay, you're fine, but this could be a heart attack, Jeff."

"Cosmic punishment for trashing Bernie," he said. "I'm going to be really upset if I die on the dog's bed. Can you help me stand up?"

"Absolutely not. Move as little as possible. Pain radiating down your arm is a classic symptom of a heart attack, you know that, don't you?"

"I don't know what she'd do without me. She doesn't even know how to turn on the oven. Now my jaw is getting numb."

"Sir, I don't think there'd be any problem if you took some aspirin, right?" Steven said, but his eyes shot to Janet. He held two white pills in his palm. Blair stood behind him, holding an ornate cut glass vase half filled with water. Everything in the house seemed to be cut glass. "I'm going upstairs to get Dee Dee," Janet said, "but promise me you won't stand up. How long did they say, Steven?"

The sirens in the distance answered her question. Jeff said, "You have to push 'bake' and 'cook.' Maybe that's confusing. I try not to lord it over her."

"You're going to be fine," Janet said, trying to sound reassuring. "Dee Dee?" she called ahead of her.

She had never been upstairs, but this was where the music was coming from. "Dee Dee, something important," Janet called. A tiny woman with black hair in a braid and white tennis shoes and a black dress stepped out of a doorway. She looked startled. *"No hablo inglés,"* she said, averting her eyes.

"Where's Dee Dee?" Janet asked, gesturing at the many doorways, sweating profusely herself. The sirens were right outside. There was a clunk she feared might mean her car had been hit. The woman in the hallway gestured to a door at the end of the corridor. Inside, Dee Dee sat with earphones clamped to her ears, humming, wearing a fuchsia lace slip and odd gold gladiator sandals that laced up her calves. A boom box on the windowsill was playing music. Dee Dee actually had a huge perfume bottle she was using like a crazed exterminator, spritzing the air. Her life was about to change profoundly, and this was what she was doing. Janet faltered, unable to begin. The tiny woman hovered in the doorway.

"Dee Dee," she said, stepping forward. "Something has happened. Take off the earphones."

Dee Dee pulled them off, and they rested like enormous parentheses around her neck. "The house is on fire, isn't it?" she said. "Isn't that what it is?"

"No, it's an ambulance. Jeff was having trouble breathing. He's probably had a heart attack. You need to come right away."

Dee Dee scrambled off the green velvet ladies' chair she was sitting on, stumbling over one of her kicked-off ankle boots. The butterfly dress was facedown on the bed. Frowning deeply, the little brown-skinned woman—could this be an apparition?—opened the closet and walked in, pulling the door shut silently behind her. There was a mirror on the door. Janet looked at herself, stunned: Her hair was wild, bits of wisteria dotting it like confetti in a bride's hair. From downstairs came sounds of shock and surprise as Dee Dee screamed her husband's name over and over.

There was not going to be any party. This was also hardly a circumstance in which she could ask the client to pay the bill. How awful even to think such a thing, but there it was, she had thought it. She checked her watch. If anyone in the world was punctual, there would have been a guest at the house, but no doubt there were at least fifteen minutes to go before anyone besides the ambulance pulled into the driveway. How really awful, Janet thought, that it all struck her as business, or as the degraded version of business, going through the motions; Jeff had had a heart attack, and all she could think of was a checkoff list: Well, we called the ambulance, told his wife. She stared at the closet. The door did not open. She thought about gently tapping on it, reassuring the woman inside that whatever the circumstances, she was not . . . what? Going to report her to the police? Not going to get her into any trouble. But it did not seem the woman spoke English, so how . . . The music reached a paradoxically faint climax; it was the part of the dance where people would have been dancing frantically. On the floor Janet saw again the pair of soft leather ankle-high black boots, very fashionable, near the chair where Dee Dee—now wailing downstairs—had been sitting.

She walked over to the chair, stepped out of one clog, unzipped a boot, and slipped her bare foot in. The lining was so soft, it felt like poking into a powder puff. Her size. She did not even need to stand up to know that. She looked and looked at her foot, elegant and riveting, the other one clumsy in its clog. Then she stepped out of the boot, pushed it aside without bothering to rezip it or even to stand it upright. Ashamed, she slipped her foot into her old shoe and went downstairs as quickly as she could.

Blair, her kind daughter, was embracing Dee Dee, who was crying on her shoulder. Janet saw Jeff on the gurney, being put into the ambulance. Steven—good boy—was signing paperwork, then gesturing to Blair, letting her know that Dee Dee just needed to take the pen and sign in one place. Blair had grown up. She did perfectly fine in any situation. This was her third serious boyfriend, and every one of them had been handsome, liberal, conscientious, smitten.

There was a shower of pink peony petals on the counter, and the cake sat untouched, unfrosted. Without its siren, the ambulance streaked away, with Dee Dee still moaning in Blair's arms. Did anyone suggest she go in the ambulance? Janet asked Blair with her eyes; Blair let her mother know by her expression that yes, she'd been asked. Janet watched a large black ant—theirs? hers?—move quickly down the kitchen counter and run behind a sponge. An SUV that was waiting for the ambulance to exit came into the driveway, and a man and a woman, both in summer suits, got out and walked quickly toward the house, all the while looking over their shoulders. The dog stood atop the fallen poster board, scratching Bernie Madoff's face as if digging down to find a little mole.

Her mother and father. Janet had forgotten them. She went into the kitchen and picked up the telephone, dialed their number. Dee Dee left Blair's arms, and Blair began talking to the woman in the pale-yellow suit as the man embraced Dee Dee. The dog had decided the poster board was carrion and had begun wiggling against it. The dog consistently kept itself amused. "Dad?" Janet said shakily. "You're home okay? Mom has her medicine?"

"Bottom line, yes, but the pills already made her upchuck, so we're waiting for the doctor's call. Everything was stolen out of my car, and that includes my golf bag and clubs, my ESPN jacket, my favorite cap, and approximately ten dollars' worth of quarters for parking meters, along with your mother's cashmere shawl so the air-conditioning won't kill her. So that's how smart our police are, picking the human scum off the car like barnacles on a ship, then leaving the ship wide open for pirates. What can you do? Hard to blame them. At first they thought I was some old codger who didn't know what he was talking about, so why listen to him? Your mother —"

"Yes! Is she able to talk on the phone, Dad? Do you think you should get an ambulance if she's throwing up, and take her to the emergency room?"

"You take care of yourself, my baby," Janet's mother said in the faintest voice imaginable. "Everything works out for the best. Daddy is safely home."

"Mom, do you think—"

The phone dropped. "Mom!" Janet shouted. "Dad, pick up the phone. Dad?"

Steven appeared at Janet's side and put an arm around her shoulders. "Okay, let's not involve a lot of people in this situation," he said. "Big excitement, but things are going to work out and"—he lowered his voice—"not our problem."

Janet was listening to a dial tone.

Dee Dee suddenly came up behind Steven. She said, "What happened to Jeff was revenge, pure and simple. Why didn't he just let it go? He blames Madoff for everything, Madoff ruined the country, made fools of everybody, Madoff, Madoff, Madoff. He was going to have a funeral pyre, throw his poster-board artwork on the fire for a grand finale. Now you see where all his anger and bitterness got him."

"Oh, Dee Dee, I don't think this happened because of his feelings about Madoff, do you really think that?" the man in the suit said. "Has Jeff been that upset?"

"I think we'll just leave things as they are and pick up whatever's left tomorrow," Blair said. Dee Dee was running her fingers through her hair, looking dazed. The woman in the yellow suit murmured agreement with what Blair had said, shooting the man warning glances that he shouldn't say anything more. Another car pulled into the drive.

"This isn't America! It's not the America I grew up in, it's a joke," Dee Dee cried, "it's a big joke controlled by evildoers, and that's what they are, whether people want to laugh at George Bush or not, they are evil, and they do want us to be driven into the ground, everybody ruined, let the pirates ride the high seas. I agree with Jeff: I could take Madoff's head and push it under the water, and then push it under again, and then . . ." Another car bumped up the driveway.

"Okay, tomorrow, be back tomorrow, don't worry about this—" Steven gestured. His gesture seemed to encompass a lot; it was a very big house.

"Fuck him, fuck him," Dee Dee said. When she returned

to railing against America, it was clear she'd been talking about Madoff, not Jeff.

Everything had happened so quickly. All of it had happened in ten or fifteen minutes. Janet was breathing heavily. It seemed important to go upstairs, on any pretext, to open the closet door and make sure that there was indeed a small person in Dee Dee's closet. Just that: Open; close; confirm. Then, as smart, sane Steven had said, they'd be off.

No one said a thing as Janet turned and walked quickly upstairs. This won't be definitive, she told herself. The little woman easily could have stepped out of the closet; she could be in any of that long row of bedrooms—and even if Janet found her, what would that mean? Some illegal immigrant, someone without a green card, she'd decided. Maybe it would be the wrong thing to do, to open the door and frighten her, if she'd stayed inside the closet.

Instead Janet stood in the darkening room. The woman must have closed the curtains because Janet remembered the windows being open when she'd first entered the room. She decided that the woman was waiting in her hiding place, immobile, as if about to go onstage, or as if she were in a lineup and had been told to stand where she was: Show us your profile; take two steps forward. The woman had done both things earlier, excruciatingly slowly, fear in her eyes. Janet dropped her eyes, ashamed, and on the rug she saw her Swiss Army knife and quickly snatched it up. There! She'd had every reason to sense the need to return, subconsciously registering the loss of something. She dropped the knife in her pocket and turned when she sensed she was being watched.

The woman stood in the doorway, holding out a slightly lumpy package, neatly wrapped in brown paper. The woman said, *"Por favor,"* then gestured for Janet to shove it down her waistband.

Which she did, numb. The dark-skinned woman was most certainly real, and although it was upsetting that the person was probably Dee Dee's frightened servant, Janet wanted to communicate that she meant no harm. Janet knew her hair was frenzied, and she was panting like a beast while the woman standing across from her barely breathed. Janet smiled and nodded, seeing flower petals fall in her peripheral vision, gestured to the closet, pointing to her heart, shaking her head. The little woman watched; then, moving gently across the floor, she passed by and walked into the closet, once again pulling the door closed soundlessly behind her.

Janet was talking to herself, muttering consolations, reassurances, whatever it was she was saying, until she'd moved through the gathering crowd—another car was driving in, passing her Subaru halfway down the drive. She ran to get into her car. Steven was sitting behind the wheel. "You holler for *me* when I take three minutes to pee?" he said. "Let's get outta here."

"I have this horrible feeling something bad is happening with Dad and Mom," Janet said, raising her hand to smooth her hair. "They say a parent always knows when a child is in trouble, but it goes the other way, too: A child knows when a parent—when a parent might not make it."

"That's what's been going on long-distance?" Steven said.

"What if she dies? I don't think I convinced him to call an ambulance, and she's in pain, vomiting. They're hundreds of miles away. This is horrible. Horrible."

"Take it easy, Mom," Blair said from the front seat. "They're old, and there are bound to be a lot of false alarms. We'll go home and call the neighbor, make her call an ambulance. She loves Grandmom—she'd be over there anyway if she was sick, wouldn't she?"

It was just what Janet wanted to believe. The answer was yes. Yes, she would. Someone would be taking control.

"I sort of can't believe what just happened," Steven said. "Not even getting in the ambulance. I mean, the bottom line has to be that she doesn't care very much about the guy."

Blair looked over her shoulder and peered into the backseat. "Do you have a stomachache?" she asked.

"No. Just—" Janet didn't want to say she was clutching something tightly under her tunic and didn't even know what it was. She'd been weird enough with them; they'd done a good job of being mature, while she'd pretty much run away like a child.

That night she opened the package, the ends of the brown paper bag folded at the corners and neatly taped, paper towel padding inside, to find the black boots she'd tried on in the bedroom. There were two possibilities: that the woman had instinctually known what was going on in the room, or that there'd been a tiny crack between the door and the frame or some other peephole through which she'd seen Janet trying on the boot. There was, however, only one explanation of why the woman had done it: to buy Janet's silence. There'd been no long-term thinking about any question that might have arisen regarding where the boots were. The woman had done it because it was exactly the thing to do in the moment, and that knowledge had overwhelmed her, made what she did absolutely necessary.

Janet put on the boots and walked through the house, her daughter and her boyfriend asleep in Blair's old bedroom. She walked onto the porch, then out the door and down the steps, standing in the dewy grass, under starlight, imagining the rest of herself coordinated with the beautiful, audacious boots. Instead of the stretched-out, oversize T-shirt, she'd be wearing clingy satin lingerie. Then what did she think? That she'd be a bride again, Blair's age, but because of the magic boots, her husband would love her forever and not leave her for another woman? Or that whatever happened in her life, she'd still be standing ramrod-straight, the sexy boots making her tall, powerful, risky?

At her feet lay the corpse of a half-eaten field mouse. Though the proud cat had not dropped it at her feet, she had found her way to the gift.

THE GYPSY CHOOSES THE
WHATEVER CARD

Pru Silowicz has listed me on her CV (not that I would have known what that was, if she hadn't told me in plain English) as the recipient of her "Volunteer activity: Interacting with older community member needing help." This CV situation has them thinking all the time—really thinking hard, like Nixon in his last days at the White House. She showed the piece of paper to me proudly, the way Edith, my next-door neighbor back in the day, used to post her son's crayon drawings of the family, even when her husband was identified as "Fat Dad Frank."

Who knows what my own husband, Donny, would have made of it, if he'd lived to see the way the world changed.

Pru usually comes on Tuesday afternoon after lunch, though recently she's been rearranging the time—calling on her cell phone, shouting over hectic background noise. I can only hope she isn't calling while driving. She's a nice girl. She's rather ordinary-looking, with her eyes, predictably, her nicest feature. She will be twenty-one in September. Last year she made her own birthday cake, as she tells me she's done for years, so she can have exactly what she wants. In this case, a slightly lopsided cake that almost made me faint when she cut into it: mahogany-red layers of "red velvet cake" with a gooey marshmallow frosting that looked like a caterpillar tent.

My best friend, Edith, now lives in an assisted-living facility. ("Facility" automatically follows "assisted-living." You would not, for example, say, "She lives in assisted-living limbo.") Anyway, Edith met her when Pru and some of her sorority sisters went visiting with their dogs to cheer the ladies. It was assumed that a pet, staring a lady right in the eye, would both engage her and also make her feel in command, since the dog would eventually deferentially drop its eyes. The pets gave the ladies the opportunity to touch fur again—even if it wasn't a beloved fur coat now probably moldering in some great-niece's closet—without being spit on by PETA. For some reason Edith didn't understand, they'd also brought an assortment of barrettes and headbands in case anyone wanted them. When one of the dogs jumped for a headband and tried to run away with it—minimalist Frisbee!—everyone almost died laughing. Truth be told, Edith was more taken with that particular dog than with the visitors, but only Pru and one other girl returned the following week, without their dogs (Pru's had been borrowed), and then Edith, being Edith, decided on her favorite among the girls and had a private word with Pru to ask if she could use a little extra income doing some errands and helping out at the home of an old friend (me).

Today Pru will be bringing another sorority sister with

her—the reason being not what I suspected at first (dumping me; introducing me to her replacement) but still something to cause wariness: The girl's mother is an Avon salesperson whose house may soon be in foreclosure. Like Lady Macbeth, I feel that all the perfume in Arabia—all her perfume sales, that is—could not alter her situation, but because Pru greatly esteems reciprocity, I will accompany Pru and her friend Carrie to a coffee shop where the mother will be waiting to pounce. I will buy a few Avon products to help out.

Pru comes into the house in her usual rush. She always has a topic, the way people at war always move forward with a weapon. She earnestly wants to know what I think of double-dating. Does it more or less ensure that the couples will swap partners "somewhere down the line"? (This is one of Pru's favorite expressions; she often uses it when discussing a potential romantic relationship.) I tell her honestly that although it was common for groups of people to go out together in my youth, I never double-dated.

She says: "What would be something a group of people did back then?"

"Well, in the summertime there were always musicians down by the Tidal Basin who got together and played, never for money, they would have been mortified by such a thought, but often someone would have found out that so-and-so was going to be playing his banjo that night, and someone else's visiting cousin would turn out to be a good singer, so we'd pack a picnic and go sit by the water and listen to them play. Almost everyone knew the same songs, and people would just chime in if they knew the words, or someone might bring out his harmonica."

"Got it. And you weren't afraid of getting mugged, right? And you didn't make sandwiches with mayonnaise because it would spoil and poison you."

She has integrated these important life lessons. I wonder if she also knows that Napoleon was said to have lost Waterloo because of his painful hemorrhoids, but I decide against asking. I do like to tease her, though. "I would take my parasol, of course. And swirl it three times 'round to signal my best friend if I liked the boy I was sitting next to."

"Really?" she squeals.

"No," I say. "Don't make yourself miserable thinking life was easier. It was always complicated."

"My grandfather bought my grandmother—I told you I was named after her, right?—a heart-shaped aquamarine ring and wrote her a poem to propose, but she burst into tears because she was in love with his brother. As an example of something that was complicated, I mean," she says. "Tic Tac?"

"No, thank you," I say. All flavors of Tic Tac are so intense they could bore a hole in my tongue. "But she married your grandfather anyway?"

"No. She married his older brother, who gave her a ruby ring made of white gold."

"Wasn't that a little awkward for everyone involved?"

"He enlisted in the army and never came back. Like that old song—the Boston guy on the MTA? You know that song, right?"

Damned if I'll tell her I do. "Faintly," I say.

"Riding forever, or whatever," she says.

At my request, she has taken down the bowls from the top shelf of a cabinet where I can't reach them and put them on the counter. Nowadays, it's usual for people to have all sorts of mundane things sitting around, so I'll just leave the bowls on the kitchen counter. Pru folds the stepstool and puts it back behind the kitchen door. Now I am to be taken to the coffee shop to meet the destitute Avon lady. Apparently her husband left her and their daughter and also gave her an STD. (This had to be explained to me. Not the concept but the abbreviation.)

"I used to make coffee in a percolator," I tell her. "It was delicious, we thought. But now coffee tastes like a fine wine. Some things do improve."

"Thanks for meeting her," Pru says. "Coffee's on me. And don't feel like you have to buy hydrating skin masks or anything really expensive to try to save her from the poorhouse. Just if there might be something you could really use, like blush or lipstick."

"I don't think my purchases can solve her problems, Pru."

"Bonding with women—it's got to help, right?"

"What is helped if two women turn out to like each other?"

"Well, I mean—" (I've thrown her.) "It's a sisterhood and everything. You don't feel alone. It's, like, somebody shares with you and you share with them and you're friends. So everything has got to be a little better, right?"

"What can friendship matter if you're being put out of your house?"

"I know. Her only backup plan if the bank takes it is to go live with her sister-in-law in Buffalo and work the night shift at the drugstore, because the sister-in-law has some connection to a druggist or something. Imagine having to start over, with your kid, in some really cold place, and you didn't get an education because you quit school when you got pregnant and you just couldn't hack anthropology anymore, and then you had the baby and it had colic. The sister-in-law has a husband, but they're estranged, so I guess she might move in to her house."

"It's a terrible situation, but at least the woman has somewhere to go."

"She does, but if she meets a guy—what? She has to tell him she's got this STD? Most guys never call again."

"First things first, Pru. First she has to get to Buffalo, then she has to settle in and get a job. If she's selling Avon products, maybe she can do the same thing in Buffalo. She doesn't have to think about men right away."

"She's definitely not going to sell blush there," Pru says. "Who needs it, when the wind chill is ten below?"

"You have a good sense of humor. That's always an asset."

"Right, like I can be a stand-up comic or something if I never get a job. They all turn out to be bipolar."

This time I laugh out loud. "Is this your way of telling me you have a medical problem?"

"Jeez, no, except for menstrual cramps that make me feel like I'm constantly trying to pry stuck lids off jars. I pop Midol like Junior Mints."

"Pru, you're going to do fine. I know these sad stories that people tell you affect you more than you let on. It's a good deed to introduce me to the woman, and you've spent the morning doing good deeds at my house, and goodness still does get rewarded. You're going to graduate and find your way in the world."

"I appreciate your optimism," she says.

"Tell me her name again?"

"Allison, but to be honest, she had this awakening experience, so she's going to ask you to call her Bonobo."

I look at her questioningly.

"Right. Well, there was some chimp that got discovered—really; this isn't a joke—and it turned out to be a new species or something, and it got its name because the Belgian people who discovered it called it Bonobo, which they thought meant 'chimp' in Zaire. Except that they got the wrong word. So—you know."

"What on earth are you talking about?"

"Just wait for Allison to ask you to call her Bonobo. She can explain it."

"In my experience, it's usually a sign that people are troubled when they assign themselves nicknames or change their name as an adult."

"My dad called me Sugar Diaper, but that wasn't exactly a nickname you'd want anybody to know about. He used to call me 'sugar,' and my first word was 'diaper.'"

"Can't be too careful these days."

"No, like, can you imagine?"

"I do a lot of imagining when I'm with you, Pru. You live in a world that would be completely closed to me."

"Yeah, well, three twirls of the umbrella if you two really hit it off," she says, pulling into the lot and nosing into a parking place, turning off the ignition.

Bonobo—could I have expected otherwise?—is a strange woman. She is quite thin except for sturdy shoulders, which she must consider a good feature because she is wearing a tube top, a silver necklace dangling a palm tree and a tiny monkey with its hands over its eyes (I have to lean in to see; my close-up vision is bad; my long-distance vision is perfectly fine), and her makeup is lovely: sheer foundation; glistening, ever so slightly coral lips; mascara and a little subtly applied eye shadow that accentuates her blue eyes. She tells me to call her Bonobo. She does not explain; she spells the name, so I understand. Her daughter, Carrie, shakes my hand formally. Bonobo's backpack is enormous and seems to have a life of its own. For a second I wonder if two tiny animals are fighting inside, so many things continue to shift when she lowers it onto an empty chair. Pru knows the young woman working behind the counter, so, she has already informed me, there will be a 50 percent discount on four lattes.

"Maybe the girls could sit at that table, and you and I could have a few moments to talk privately?" Bonobo says. "Not that I want to pressure you at all. Pru said you were interested in a beauty update, though, and I do have a few items that are quite easy to use that I can show you."

I half expect her to pull out a banana.

"Lattes all around?" Pru asks. "We'll bring them back, and you can put in your own sugar from that counter over there. Okay?"

We nod. Both girls immediately walk to the counter, looking at the pastries in front of them and laughing as if the muffins and slices of cake have merrily animated themselves for a special show inside the glass case. Bonobo leans toward me. She says, "I don't have anywhere to turn. You don't even know me, but I assume Pru filled you in, and that you know my life is a wreck and these cosmetics might as well be lint in my pocket for all the good they're going to do me. But I'm certainly not asking you to co-sign a loan so my house isn't auctioned off."

I raise my eyebrows.

"Pru says you have soul. It's the first thing she told me. Not just some old lady, somebody with soul. We can be honest. You are old, and I am a middle-aged failure. Pru is my favorite of Carrie's friends. Pru has soul. She thinks if you buy a lipstick and a bottle of perfume, I'm helped. I'm not. There are two private investigators failing every day to find my husband. I drove past your house last night. It's perfectly located for an Avon presentation. So what I'm wondering is if I could borrow your house for an afternoon?"

"I don't see how I could refuse."

"You'd do that for me?"

"I wouldn't mind. I can invite a few friends. I know some people who are still mobile."

"I knew you had good karma the minute you walked in. Isn't it cute how the roles are reversed and they're buying us coffee and trying to make everything better? Doesn't it make you feel more optimistic about the future?"

"Obama more so," I say.

The girls bring our drinks. It is not until Bonobo stands up that I realize she is wearing blowsy chef's pants made of fabric printed with chili peppers. She has on pink flip-flops and a woven ankle bracelet. None of this goes with her makeup. She and I walk to the counter where the milk and sugar are. Her hand shakes as she adds sugar. The sides of her hair are combed, but the back is a tangled mess. I am not even sure how something like that could be untangled. As I stir my drink, I think of my husband and how very many years he has been gone. Gone meaning dead, not enlisted in the army or being sought by investigators for collection of child-support payments. Gone meaning he'll never know about the proliferation of coffee shops, or the collapse of the financial system, or that we have our first African-American president, or that his wife has turned gray (me—not Michelle Obama), and that every time she sticks out her tongue privately, it's because her life often leaves a bitter taste, which is her most tactile sense of the twenty-first century.

"Bonobo is an unusual name," I say as we resettle ourselves.

"Scientists found a chimp with a skull much smaller than usual and realized they'd discovered a new species," she says. "Ironically, they named it the wrong thing because of a misunderstanding. So I like both qualities: small head; wrong identity. That's me." She sips her coffee. "Do you have a nickname?" she asks.

"Pookie," I say.

"Pookie," she repeats. "A childhood nickname?"

"My late husband's name for me," I say. Lying is easy. Which reminds me: Didn't some poet write that "dying is easy"? It wasn't, in my husband's case: First came kidney dialysis, then a stroke.

"Do friends call you Pookie?" she asks.

"My minister does," I say, although I do not have a minister.

The potential for inventing a whole new self is beginning to interest me. The girls have returned to the counter and are in a huddle with their friend. Bizarre music, a flute rising above beating drums as people chant, plays loudly on the sound system. Today is a sunny summer day in Alexandria, Virginia. I, Pookie, am going to open my house so that a near-stranger can sell Avon cosmetics there. I sip my latte. It feels like drinking a big shrug. It occurs to me that maybe this is a version of what happened to her—to Bonobo. She conjured up one lie, her marriage, then she conjured up another, the ongoing ability to afford their house payments. Aren't they all necessary stories that one tells oneself: Wall Street stories (until they change); Oprah stories?

"I have to be honest and say that I prefer OPI products because of the names," I say. "A nail polish called MacArthur Park After Dark! OPI nail polish and whatever pianist is playing at the Carlyle are the last expressions of wit in our society. In my life, wit has disappeared, and the by-product is irony."

She frowns. She has to like me, even if I'm stranger than she realized: There's my house; her future.

"When will you hold your gathering?" I ask.

"Forgive me for asking, but exactly . . ." She looks at me intently. "What age are you?" she asks, her voice teetering on reverence.

"Eighty, and proud of it," I say, reverting to honesty. "And you?"

"Forty-two. I don't want to take advantage, in any way. You don't mind my hosting this event at your house?"

"Not a bit, though I'm afraid I don't see how it can help much."

"I suspect you're right," she says, "though I'd feel better

knowing that I did absolutely everything I could. You know how good that feels, when you're sure you tried every last thing."

I certainly do. At eighty, your life becomes nothing but improvisation, whether you want it to or not. You'll do the craziest things, desperate to triumph in something as ordinary as changing a lightbulb.

"Tell me your darkest secrets, and I'll tell you mine," I hear myself blurting out. It is a line from the Gypsy at Glen Echo Park, where my husband and I used to go in the summer. The Gypsy was a life-size plaster figure who sat in a glass cubicle and sorted cards with her chipped fingers. You activated her by pushing a button, and she asked one of three things. Donny and I almost died laughing over "Tell me your darkest secrets, and I'll tell you mine." But she never kept her part of the bargain. Whatever you replied, she'd laugh and put her cards down, then look upward as if receiving inspiration, then move her broken fingers over the deck of cards and pretend to select one just for you. She'd send the card out to you in the retractable tray. They were playing cards, but the back was imprinted with your special message—the equivalent of today's ubiquitous "whatever."

"Darkest secrets?" Bonobo says.

"We'll have a bond. We'll have the same sort of secrets the girls share—secrets that bind us forever."

She fingers her necklace and frowns. Just as I'm about to explain the in-joke to her, she says, "I killed the neighbor's cat. The cat pounced on a blue jay and I ran for the shovel and ran out into the yard, and the cat turned toward me and made a little leap into the air, and the bird hobbled off—it couldn't fly—and before I knew it, the shovel made contact, and the cat went flying. There were signs all over the neighborhood the next day. I thought I'd be found out because I'd managed to get the blue jay into a box and I'd taken it to the vet. I drove like a bat out of hell, but all they did was euthanize it. I went home and dug a hole and buried the cat. I thought somebody at the vet's would tell somebody else about the bird, and figured that would lead to everyone knowing I'd killed the cat, but that was years ago, and my neighbor still says hello every time we run into each other."

The dance music has reached a crescendo. Two men and a woman in high heels, wearing a power suit (I know what these are now), stand in line for coffee. The girls are sitting at a table, sipping their drinks. I am thinking about the worst thing I ever did, not sure what that would be, when a man in a ski mask and a gun bursts into the store and yells at us to drop to the floor. At first I think it must be a joke—this is a coffee shop, not a bank. It isn't even a Starbucks. A small coffee costs a dollar. "Get down! Now!" he shouts. "Cash. Hurry up," he says to the girl behind the counter. The stainless-steel steamer continues to hiss. Whoever stands behind it has as much protection as someone at the Alamo, but still a woman screams. She is the only one who does. The girl behind the counter reaches for the plastic bag that the man with the gun is handing over the counter. She opens the cash register, and it rings—an antique cash resister; of course it rings! The man points his gun at the drawer, frightening the girl, causing her to stumble backward. She recovers and steps forward, snatching up money.

Bonobo has tugged so long on my arm that—to my

amazement—I am kneeling on the floor. I can't think of the last time I knelt. The floor is very cold and hard. What exactly is the worst thing I ever did in my life? Next to me, Bonobo grits her teeth and fingers her necklace, as if each dangling charm is a sore tooth. Her other hand remains clamped on my arm. The woman in the suit, missing one of her high heels, lies sprawled on her stomach. One man lies on his side with his legs drawn up, his hands covering his face. The other man lies on his stomach, his head closer to the woman's buttocks than it could have been in his wildest dreams. I look right at Mr. Ski Mask, and he looks at me, and it seems from the look in his eyes that he is posing a question. A thought pops into my head: the time I rammed my husband's Chevy into a tree after his secretary called to tell me they'd been having an affair. I just marched out the kitchen door—he was sitting in the living room, but I had nothing to say to him—I snatched up the keys and marched out and started the car, drove it to the end of the driveway, looked both ways, then drove it into a tree. Not one second of that incident ever became even slightly amusing to either of us, though suddenly it does strike me as funny. Or maybe I'm just congratulating myself for having a little gumption— always better than tears—and doing exactly what I felt like doing. I envy that former self and her spontaneity; as you get older, spontaneity disappears as an option.

"Oh God, oh God," Bonobo's tremulous voice wails over and over—though why she is so upset, I can't understand. The man has run from the store. Sirens? Can't we expect to hear sirens? The counter girl is talking on her cell phone. Our girls—Pru isn't mine, but it more or less feels that way—dash out from under their table. I look up just as Pru misjudges her distance from the top and bangs her head, hard. She lets out a yelp. My knee is cut, but not badly—though the Coumadin makes me bruise easily, so I can imagine what it will look like in a few hours. One of the men who'd been waiting to order is staring at a knife with several blades protruding in different directions—examining it closely, as if it wasn't in his pocket all along but has magically appeared. He really stares at the knife as everyone else fumbles forward, groping for one another like first-timers at a square dance.

Not with that music! That's no square-dance music.

I am going to have quite the story to tell Edith about how her nice young friend took me out for coffee and a man with a gun came in and robbed the store. But what I don't anticipate is the rest of it: that Bonobo and Carrie will return to my house with me, so concerned are they that I might suffer bad aftereffects (they call this potential trauma PTSD). Pru's mother will call and demand to speak to me; then, inexplicably, she will cry and stop just short of accusing me of leading her daughter into disaster.

That night in bed, it comes to me: I never had to tell. Donny's transgression and the car mashed into the tree and my moment of revenge slip back into the past like a body tucking itself under covers in a dark room where all is quiet again.

Go to sleep, I tell myself. The pain in your knee is fate, coming up behind you. A madman whacking you with a hatchet? Every fairy tale tells you he will get his comeuppance. The gunman will be arrested. The Avon party will be a success, but more important, Bonobo's husband will return and beg her forgiveness; Pru will be accepted at her first choice for graduate school. In the darkness of my room, I walk in the forest and gradually realize that each tree is a beautiful lady. I am looking for a specific one, though. I walk in deeper, as the place I came from vanishes. Something stops me. One tree has a design on the tree bark: a heart with my husband's initials inside, along with those of his lady friend. I suppose that as long as there are people, they will stop to carve their initials, along with their beloved's, into bark, oblivious to the passage of time and to the way those initials are sure to fade as they expand, changing from letters into abstract marks, joining the confluence of the wood. I almost pass by, but then, by instinct, I narrow my eyes and grab a low-lying branch and twist hard. Then I reach up and break a higher one, my hand scrambling through the limbs. Each bone of the lovely lady that breaks, breaks separately, because we were young, and every moment was distinct.

THE CLOUD

B ack in the town where she'd graduated from the university five years before, Candace waited at the inn to be picked up by Uncle Sterling. This was a business trip, paid for by her company in D.C., and they were amenable to putting her somewhere other than the DoubleTree out on the highway. Sterling was able to drive his car again, after finishing the last round of chemo three weeks earlier. The prognosis was good, but Candace's mother, Claire, still wept about it on the phone, and Candace was worried herself. Sterling was her favorite relative, even if he did maintain contact with her father. *For sure* he understood that Hank was an untrustworthy liar, but the two former brothers-in-law still occasionally golfed together, belonged to the same gym— not that Sterling had been seeing much of that place lately. *For sure* Claire deserved better than a dry-drunk ex who'd married a woman barely older than his daughter. Hank lived in Keswick now, courtesy of his buyout and early retirement, with his newly acquired young wife with whom he had twin boys. Candace had seen them once, about a year before, on

Saturday at the City Market, her father descending the steep incline of the parking lot, guiding the babies in a double stroller, Candace ascending hand in hand with her fiancé, Daniel, who'd graduated from Darden last May. That day also, she and Daniel had stayed at the inn, a charming place not too historically oppressive, with comfortable furniture, good sunlight, and damp, warm cookies in the late afternoon.

But today she was on her own, Daniel now working for Sapient in Boston, though they hoped the job he really wanted would become available in D.C. after the first of the year. Her only reason to come back to town was a business meeting she'd volunteered to attend because she wanted to see Sterling. She might also visit a couple of places that could be nice venues for their wedding reception—they'd decided on a city hall wedding and a big party soon afterward—though more and more she was thinking of having the party at his parents' house in Sperryville. Everything could seem a bit too university-connected sometimes, even if the town was quite various, with its Street o' Liberals (as Sterling called Park Street), its horsey crowd, the arts community.

She walked to Mudhouse and ordered a café au lait. While others had gotten through school on caffeine, she'd existed primarily on milk (milk shakes: skim milk with Hershey's chocolate added, along with a packet of powdered vitamins, in the late afternoon), though a café au lait was the perfect combination of the two. The person behind the counter (her ears with many piercings) gave Candace a cup to put in the amount of coffee she wanted, then hand back for the hot, foamy milk to be poured in. "Do you like foam?" the barista asked. What a question. Who did not like foam except those people who did not like foam, though they might have thought it an important component of waves, or of laundering clothes, or of shampooing. It was one of those questions you couldn't trust to convey the right meaning if you put it in a time capsule.

Her new leather boots had cost five hundred and fifty dollars. She'd admitted to three, to Daniel. If Sterling commented at all, he wouldn't have any idea what they cost—he lived alone and cared nothing about fashion—so she wouldn't have to lie. She'd noticed that the woman checking her in earlier in the day had eyed the boots; since the woman had already commented on her ring, though, she wasn't about to keep complimenting her. Candace was wearing her favorite black skirt, with black tights and a cashmere sweater slightly silver-tinged, a gift from Daniel's mother. She didn't look like a college girl, and she didn't look like a faculty member, either. They wore sensible shoes and rectangular glasses and weighed too much or much too little. She was just right. At least that was what Daniel thought.

She checked her cell and saw that Sterling had called while she'd been in the coffee place. The message said he'd pick her up at six unless she told him otherwise. He'd be taking her to the restaurant in Belmont that she'd suggested for dinner—not too fussy or expensive, and Sterling was always interested in changing neighborhoods. He wasn't like her mother, who thought nothing ever changed for the better; he was appreciative of old buildings being saved, of new energy coming into the community.

*   *   *

On the porch of the inn, Sterling gave her a big hug—he felt thin—and commented on her boots first thing. "New shoes?" he said. There was no reason to wear them yet during this late, mild October, but they made her feel good. "You and your mother, always fashionable," he said.

He was driving his old Lexus with a crooked back bumper, an Obama/Biden decal, and a patch of paint gone from around the door handle on the passenger side. Ninety-three, he told her proudly as he opened the door from one of the few still-operating features, the button that unlocked all doors. The last time she'd been in his car, the window wouldn't go down on the passenger side. She settled back into the slightly cracked seat, pulled on her seat belt. No place to park in front of the restaurant; thirty-minute limit by the convenience store. Sterling made a right turn, then a left, then saw a place on the opposite side of the street. He made a U-turn and parallel-parked and turned off the engine. She opened the door, wondering whether it was okay that the bumper slightly overhung the white line by a driveway. He saw her looking. "Okay to park here?" he called to a man she hadn't seen, sitting on his front porch in the near dark.

"Yessir, that's fine," the man replied. From his voice, it was obvious he was old. There was another man sitting with him. Sterling gave a little salute and walked around to give Candace his arm. It felt bony. She wanted to talk about what he'd been through, but later, when they were in the restaurant and more comfortable, after they'd had a drink, not right off, which would seem aggressive. If her mother was forty-eight, Sterling was fifty-one, though he acted younger than his sister. Not immature younger, but tentative, without Claire's easy way of conversing, a little preoccupied and twitchy, like a young boy. He did hate to sit still.

The restaurant was crazy, and she hadn't thought to make a reservation: A young woman with a topknot was shrieking at the corner table; some blowhard was hectoring a table of fat, middle-aged people in suits and ugly dresses who looked at him puzzled, as if firecracker after firecracker was failing to ignite; waitresses made themselves mouse-thin to slide through the small holes in the crowd of people with their barstools pushed back into the aisles, or headed to the bathroom, or on their way to the second floor, or to the roof, from which they'd take flight and clutter the night sky, for all she knew. "Let's go somewhere quieter," she said. It was too chaotic in the restaurant. All wrong.

They walked back to the car, Sterling's hand guiding her elbow. Her mother had said, "Sterling got Papa's cancer, and I'm going to get Leigh's breast cancer, you watch." Her mother was in Florida tonight, visiting her best friend who'd moved there from Pennsylvania a year ago. They'd be drinking too much wine and doing other unhealthy things sure to lessen her mother's chances of escaping "the family curse," though as far as Candace knew, only one woman in the family had had breast cancer, and she'd survived it.

"Wait a minute, hold on, folks," came the old man's voice. They stopped outside the car, turning in his direction. "I've got something for you. It was polite of you to ask about parking near my driveway." He was tall, and his lanky arm was outstretched. Both reached out to shake his extended hand, but instead of shaking, he dropped something into each of their palms. There was enough lamplight that she could see hers was a dark origami bird. Two smaller birds sat in Sterling's hand: one white; one that seemed to have been made out of some lightweight cardboard.

"For us?" she said. "How did you do this?"

"I fold," the man said. "I hope you like 'em."

"This is very nice of you," Sterling said, staring at the little birds in his hand but not touching them. Actually, he seemed quite taken aback.

"Origami!" she said, realizing Sterling probably didn't know the word. "What a lovely present. Origami birds."

"That one's a swan," the man said, though the sentence was uninflected, not proud at all.

"Thank you very much," she said. "I can't believe you're giving these to us."

"More where they came from, sailing up and down Mother Nature's river," the man said. "You have a nice night."

"Really, thank you," Sterling said. "I've never seen anything like this."

"I'm a veteran," the old man said flatly. "You have a nice evening."

Sterling handed her his birds so he could insert the key into the lock on the passenger side. The three birds, with big beaks and lovely wings, really looked like treasures in her hand. She stepped into the car carefully off the steep curb, a little awkward about settling herself gracefully when one hand was useless.

She looked back at the porch in time to see the light extinguished, though it seemed the two men were still seated in the dark. She dumped the birds on her lap and reached across quickly to unlock her uncle's door, but he'd already inserted the key. The door swung open. "I don't know why he did that," Sterling said. "Do you think he took you for my girlfriend or something?"

"Of course not!" she said. "That's ridiculous, Uncle Sterling."

"Or he seemed to think I'd been in the military," Sterling said.

"Not with your asthma," she said.

"Honey, I never had asthma. I had pneumonia twice when I was a teenager, and your mother never got over it. I never tried to enlist. One idiot doing that in the family was enough. Cousin Coop going to fight in Desert Storm. Nobody in our family had anything to do with the military since the Second World War, when they had to. Coop—he'd do anything it took to push his old man's buttons. I guess he did, too, coming back with a blown-off pinkie and a lifetime of migraines."

"Mom said you tried to enlist, but they wouldn't take you because of asthma."

"Your mother lives in her head," he said.

"Really? She completely made that up? I've always thought it was strange that you felt so patriotic, but you never vote."

"Like I said: She lives in her head."

"But you did finish with chemo, right? And everything's looking good?" Why had she blurted that out now. *Why?*

"It's not a good kind of cancer to get. Without treatment, something like forty, fifty percent chance of recurrence, pretty quick. I think it halves it, something like that, if you do chemo."

"Oh. Well—I think Mom might have told me that, but I was just feeling very optimistic."

211

"She didn't tell you. I'll bet you anything."

"No, I don't think she did, actually. So now are you going to tell me my father's not such a bad guy, that with all her bitterness about money and broken promises, she was just living in her head?"

"Honey, I don't want to say anything about your parents' divorce. They're divorced. That's that."

"*Are* you going to vote?"

"America's run by a big machine, and we're not even a splinter of a cog in the wheel. They fixed the election the year Al Gore had it. I'm not gonna vote, I'm not gonna avoid having a beer tonight in spite of my medicine, and also, just to keep you fully informed, a few weeks ago I took on my girlfriend's car payments, which makes me a chump and a fool, because her husband's just waiting in the shadows, and when that car's paid for, you can bet he'll be back behind the wheel."

"You have a girlfriend?"

"Yeah, what? Your mom told you I was gay?"

"She never said that."

"Maybe she did and you were just optimistic."

"Stop it!" she said, shoving his shoulder. A bird fell from her lap to the floor. She picked it up, wiped it carefully, unnecessarily, on her jacket. Its finely pointed beak resembled the toes of her Italian boots. She dropped it on top of the others.

"So you e-mailed that you were going to check out some wedding places? What kind of places you thinking of?"

"You know, now I'm thinking about having the party at his parents' weekend place in Sperryville. It might be easier for our friends in D.C., and it's really pretty there."

"But your poor afflicted uncle would have to drive farther. Think about that. And now I've got a pet—now I've got a wild swan—so going north might mess up its migration."

"We could eat dinner at that place out 250," she said. "The one that's like a family restaurant."

"That's for old folks," he said.

"No, it isn't. I used to go there with my friends."

"Old-people vegetables. Brussels sprouts. Mashed potatoes."

"So where do you want to go?"

"I'll take you to my girlfriend's and we can order pizza," he said. "She lives in a cliff-hanger of a so-called townhouse on the way to the entrance onto 64, with crappy wall-to-wall carpeting and an addict daughter who comes and goes, who can't even make it through beauty school. I was reaching for a plate the other night, and the cabinet door came off in my hand. Particleboard."

"Why would I want to go there?"

"Because she cares about me," he said. "Because I shouldn't compartmentalize. It would be good for her to meet somebody from my family."

"This is someone you're serious about, Sterling?"

"The love of my life. At least up to this point."

"Well, sure. It would be nice to meet her, then. Sure."

"Her name's Lana. She's vegetarian, but she smokes. You okay with that?"

"With smoking? Will she absolutely have to smoke?"

"She lives there," he said.

He glanced in the rearview mirror and made a quick U-turn: They were suddenly headed away from town, past a

Food Lion and a dollar store. So her uncle wasn't asthmatic, he had a girlfriend, and he knew in detail his chances for survival. Since that was true, what else might he tell her? She'd probably hear more about her mother before the night was out, and it wouldn't just have to do with her cowardice about pneumonia thirty years ago. Claire had always been phobic about catching colds. She kept Ivory soap, which she maintained was much better than hand sanitizer, in not one but two soap holders on both sides of the sink in her bathroom and in the kitchen.

"You know what happened to Lana a week or so ago? She'd been working on the story of her life, a memoir thing about being kidnapped when she was a teenager and made to work on a ranch out west, and this one horse that she said saved her life. She had eighty pages, and it all just disappeared. We took her Mac to a place in town, but they couldn't get it back. She said it was like the horse dying all over again, working so hard on something and having it desert her, it just made her crazy. She'd been taking this course up at Piedmont at night, along with her nursing course: people's stories about how they got where they are in life. Not the kind of thing you probably studied over at the university, but—"

"Uncle Sterling, she didn't have it backed up in any way she could retrieve it? Do you mean the hard drive crashed or—"

"The one thing I know, I convinced her to keep the machine, to print the story every time she had a new part. She didn't have a printer before. Anyway, this guy who was teaching the course told us that for very little money, she could have everything backed up and it could go to heaven."

"What?"

"A service you pay for, where everything you write—"

"Automatic backup? It goes to the cloud?"

"That's it! I told you, up to the sky, like a moonbeam bouncing back! Goes to the clouds."

"Cloud," she corrected. "It's an abstraction, but—"

"'Buckets of moonbeams, buckets of tears!'"

She looked at him, confused. It was like having a conversation with a crazy person. " 'Buckets of moonbeams, buckets of tears . . . blah, blah, blah, honey, when you go,'" he sang in a good imitation of Bob Dylan. Aha!

She smiled with relief. "He was at John Paul Jones. I saw him with Elvis Costello when I was here. Did you see that concert, Sterling?"

"Don't go to concerts," Sterling said. "Those days are behind me."

Sterling was pulling into a new development—she'd imagined the girlfriend living in some old, outdated place, from the way he'd described the dreary interior—with bathmat-sized balconies off the front, bordered in metal railings. On one, someone stood in front of a glowing grill that puffed steam into the night's cooling air. Romney signs were draped over a few of the rails. In front of them, a boy pedaled slowly up the incline, the light underneath his seat weakly blinking as his bike moved up the steep hill.

"This feels good. This seems like just the right thing to do," Sterling said, and she realized by the way he spoke that he was perplexed by his actions, not certain. Had he been drinking before he picked her up? Or was the medicine having some bad effect on him? She could hardly ask. He'd

turned on the radio, and they were listening to Radiohead—
Radiohead!—as he pulled into an empty carport that looked
as flimsy as an opened tin of sardines, and turned off the
ignition. "You'll like her," he said. "Even if you don't, you can
tell your mother, and she'll be shocked. She won't believe I
introduced you to someone I've been dating, who lives in a
housing development with a bunch of Republicans."

Candace pulled her jacket more tightly around her as she
got out of the car. It was a part of town she hadn't known
existed; it had been a field the last time she'd driven past this
big outcropping of buildings on the hillside of bare earth, with
what looked like the devil tending his fire with a pitchfork
just above them as they ascended the stairs.

The door Sterling was heading toward was on the third
level, right in front of the stairs, a Coke machine making
noise beside it. It was the sort of room you'd ask not to have
in a motel. There was no light inside, but two doors down,
she could see a little boy in boxing gloves hammering his
father's leg as he tended the grill. Sterling knew someone
who'd been kidnapped? Like that girl the crazy couple took
in Utah? A large long-haired cat arched its back and darted
around the man and the boy, playing with something it batted
between its paws.

"It's me, Lana!" Sterling said, staring into the peephole
as if it would allow him to see inside. "I want you to meet
my niece, open up, darlin'!"

"Jee-*zus*," a young Hispanic woman said, peeking through
the door opened only a crack, its safety chain pulled on. "Did
you ever think of calling first?" She slid back the chain and
stepped aside. Sterling preceded Candace into the apartment

without an entranceway and gave the young woman a quick one-armed hug. "Where's your mother, darlin'?" he said.

"I thought you were sick," she said. "Who's this?"

She spoke as if Candace weren't present. The young woman seemed about her age, maybe younger. She was wearing three gigantic hair rollers and was dressed in black: black sweatpants; black turtleneck; black shoes with white laces. "Ooh la la," she said, whistling through the space between her front teeth. "Those are million-dollar boots. This is the way you dress your other girlfriends, Sterl?"

"She's my niece. The only family member who's willing to make a visit to her uncle. I'm feelin' fine now, darlin'. Where's your mother?"

"Community college," the girl said. "In case you forgot, she's working toward her nurse's-aide credentials."

"I didn't forget, but since when does she have classes on Wednesday night?"

"Since they canceled classes on Tuesday because there was a bomb scare," the girl said. "Pleased to meet you." She extended her hand. There was a tattoo of a spider's web on the back of her hand. "Somebody got a credit card? We can call Domino's," she said. Candace gripped the girl's hand, looking at Sterling for guidance. He gestured toward the single piece of furniture: a sofa in the living room. He took his credit card out of his wallet and handed it to the girl. "I like extra cheese," he said.

"You?" the girl asked Candace.

"Just . . . what he has will be fine," she said.

"What exactly is a niece?" the girl said to him. "It's the daughter of your brother or sister, right?"

"Sister," Sterling said, as if this were an often asked question.

"College girl?" she asked, still not looking at Candace.

"Used to be," Candace said. "Now I work in Washington."

"Ooh la la," the girl said. She texted the pizza place on the phone she'd been holding in one hand all the time, the motion of her thumb rippling the spider's web, then placed the phone on the table. "Pepperoni on half, extra cheese on the other," she said. "It comes with a free bottle of Dr Pepper tonight." She sat on the floor and stared at them. "That's not your niece, is it?" she said to Sterling.

"Candace, my niece," he said.

"Cool," the girl said, lightly fingering a hair roller. "It's between you and Lana." She picked up a magazine and twirled a bit of loose hair around a finger. "I been irradiated like you, I might do whatever I had a mind to do myself. You drink your protein shake today? I heard her call you this morning to remind you."

"I drank it," he said.

"Sounded like a little love buzz going on, maybe? She didn't tell you about the makeup class tonight?"

"No," he said.

"Well, maybe because you're not part of the family, proof being that you got a credit card that works," she said. "So I'm glad you've got your niece there, and your very own family."

"I am his niece," Candace said. "I love him very much."

"I've had some loving very much," the girl said, "so don't go claiming no superiority in that department."

Sterling sat on the sofa. He reached up and turned on the floor lamp, and his already pale face blanched white. He had hardly any eyebrows, Candace saw for the first time. Instead, there were a few scraggly hairs; above them, his skin was wrinkled like a Shar-Pei's. How could she not have noticed before? His hair was sparse, his thinness quite obvious with his long legs stretched in front of him. He'd looked healthier before he'd taken off his jacket. Candace's jacket was pulled tightly in front of her, and she had her arms folded over her chest. It seemed colder in the apartment than it did outside. She glanced to the side and into the small kitchen. There was a child's high chair. Every door to every cabinet seemed to be open. Piles of dishes sat on either side of the sink. She was thirsty, and wished for a drink of water, but not enough to get up and walk in there.

"I'm nobody," Sterling said to Candace, as if he were saying "Good morning" to a colleague who meant nothing to him.

"That's not true," she said. "You're my favorite relative. Somebody took a liking to you tonight and gave you a very nice present this evening, remember that? Things are going to be okay. I really feel like they are."

The girl was twirling her hair, listening to them talk and pretending not to.

"I'm a coward," he said, "but not in the way you think. They made me see a shrink in order to get my pain meds refilled. Every Friday I have to report in. He told me not to compartmentalize, to open myself up more. If that's what it takes, me making my report of success, I guess you came along at a good time for me, maybe not such a good time for you."

"It's fine," she said.

"Everybody understands everybody. I'll be back when the pizza shows up," the girl said, getting up and walking out of the room. They both stared after her; she went into another room and quietly closed the door.

"She's looking after her friend's kid," Sterling said. "She's got a good heart."

"There's a child in there?" Candace said.

Sterling nodded. "Asleep, I guess. Maybe it's better if I sit by the window and watch for the pizza guy. Maybe that way he won't wake up."

"Why would she walk out of the room like that?" Candace said.

"Not sure," Sterling said. "Not a hundred percent sure she's telling me the truth about her mother and where she is tonight, either."

Candace looked into the kitchen. "Maybe we should go," she said. "Let's go back to the inn and I'll order us a pizza. To be honest, I wouldn't mind having a beer from the honor bar. It's quiet there, maybe somebody in one of the rooms, but quiet. Warm."

"A perfect place, complete salvation," he said. "A cloud."

He took a twenty-dollar bill out of his wallet and put it on the table next to *Allure*. He picked the bill up, creased it, put it down again, folded so it looked like a little roof.

"Is it your child?" Candace said quietly.

"Mine? No. What would make you think that? Mine? It's her best friend's two-year-old, Jake. She took the train to Albany to visit the kid's father. He's in jail. She apparently always takes her time getting back to Virginia." Sterling looked at his watch. "Domino's usually gets here fast, because they're just down the street," he said. "Maybe it would be nicer to wait for the pizza guy. Have a slice with her, then leave."

"I think he's here," Candace said, looking past his shoulder to the stairs. She saw the top of someone's head, coming nearer. But it wasn't the delivery person, it was two EMTs. Below, in the parking lot, a white light blinked atop the ambulance. The pizza delivery person was, however, coming up the stairs as the two men returned, carrying an empty stretcher. She could hear them greet the Domino's guy as if it were all in a night's work, as Sterling stood with the door thrown open, his wallet removed from his pants pocket, another few bills pulled out to put in the delivery guy's hands. Some leaves blew into the room, and she thought: Autumn! Not the most colorful autumn, but autumn! Next, winter. Then her wedding in early spring, six months from now, May. She looked at her diamond ring. At her uncle. Who must have ordered from Domino's before, because he was on good terms with the delivery guy. They exchanged a quiet joke as the two men carrying the stretcher moved past them. Into the middle of it all streaked the big cat, but with fancy footwork, the man carrying the back of the stretcher avoided tripping on the animal. She looked at the twenty-dollar bill on the table. Had he forgotten it, or did he mean to leave it? He'd walked past Candace, box in hand, and when he returned from the room minus the box, he pulled on his coat and said, "You're right, Candy. Let's go."

She exited behind him, relieved that when the door was pulled closed, you could hear it lock. From the landing, the cat's eyes flashed as it stared down. She stopped briefly before following her uncle down the stairs. Somewhere, she'd scuffed the toe of one boot. There was a scratch, though there'd been nothing in the apartment but the ugly rug she'd heard about, so how had she done that? She followed Sterling down the stairs, into the driveway where the doors of the ambulance were open, and she saw, inside, an old woman being transferred onto a gurney. Candace instantly looked away, followed Sterling to his car, eyes averted, shivering a little as she waited for the click of the button that would allow her to open the door. She felt ashamed. Because she hadn't been nice to the girl, who, she'd decided, was much younger than she. Because she hadn't even had the courage to go get a drink of water. Why had she felt humiliated, why had the thought of eating the same pizza she'd eaten for years, all through college, washed down with milk, why had the thought of oily residue on her fingers depressed her so much? Sterling had left the apartment because of her, hadn't he? She didn't think she was better than other people. She really didn't. Even when she'd been in school, she'd realized there was animosity in the community because of the haves and the have-nots.

"I married her," Sterling said across the roof of the car, "but she kept thinking about her ex-husband, she was a lousy actress, so I said, 'Hey, I'll continue to make your car payments as a wedding present, and we can get this annulled.' Four days? What's four days? So I called a frat brother of mine, a big-shot lawyer in Ivy. But now Lana's daughter pretty much hates me. She thought I was a real improvement over him. She was a bitch tonight, but she's got her worries, taking care of that kid for however long she'll have to take care of him this time. She flunked out of the same program her mother's going to, and I guess she's flunking out of beauty school, too.

What the hell must that be like? She's twenty-two, and she hasn't pulled off one thing in her entire life."

"Sterling . . ."

"I *do* consider them family. Lana picked me up all but one time from the hospital, and she sent a guy who's a friend of hers the time she couldn't be there. Who knew all that cancer shit was going to broadside us? It's okay. It was a big mistake, a big mistake, but we've put it behind us, we're still friends. The ex-husband's got his nose out of joint, but maybe they'll work it out. I don't know."

"This is hard to believe," she said. "Did you know this is where we were going to end up, or was this just—"

"Impulsive?" he said. "Yeah, I'm a little impulsive sometimes."

She sat in the passenger seat mutely. Had they even been inside for half an hour? She thought back to the last time she'd seen her uncle. It had been at the zoo. They'd gone to the reptile house, which had been her favorite when she was a child. Her mother had been with them. What was it—three years ago, more? March or April? He'd bought her a balloon, saying that she could let it go any time she wanted, none of that little-girl fumbling, none of those clumsy attempts to tie it around her wrist, no little-girl tears if the balloon got away from her: It would be liberating to deliberately let it go high into the cloudy sky. And so she had; she'd released the string, her mother frowning, disapproving. Later, they'd had Chinese food on Connecticut Avenue, Claire sulking a bit as Sterling and Candace toasted liberation. Of course people became more mature with age, her mother had protested: Candace had grown up; of course a balloon didn't mean the world to her anymore. She just didn't get her brother, really she didn't. So her daughter being happily in collusion with Sterling—she didn't get that either. The day would have been better if Claire hadn't been along, though it was likely neither of them would have thought of a balloon if she hadn't been there as a witness. What was Candace going to say to her mother about this night?

Nothing. The next time she saw her uncle, he'd be dancing at her wedding. While all this had been going on, had Daniel tried to call? She wondered, but she didn't reach for her purse. Neither did she spit on her finger and hope against hope that the mark on her boot was dirt, not a scratch. Her throat was too dry to swallow, anyway. Dinner? Who wanted that? But a drink of water . . .

She opened the window—it rolled down—picked up the little cluster of birds, and extended her hand until the wind sucked them out the window. She thought of the eerie cat, of how it would find its perfect moment on Halloween. How it would have liked to pounce on the pretty birds. How much it would have liked to kill them.

Autumn leaves spun in the breeze under the streetlamps.

"I'm so sorry," he said, not speeding, but not braking for a yellow light, either. "Here, Sperryville, I'm not going to be able to come to your party." He reached down and gave her hand a squeeze, and again she realized that his hand was bony, much too light. Daniel, she thought. I'm engaged to a man named Daniel? The wind was whipping her hair across her face. It stuck to her lips, chapped from being bitten. Tears rolled down her cheeks. Her hands fluttered uselessly.

HOODIE IN XANADU

Most nights my neighbor, a middle-aged man in a red hoodie, would stand on his front porch, reaching up every now and then to knock the icicle Christmas lights dangling from the roof back and forth. He'd survey the street and usually smoke a cigarette. When he finished, he would fumble for his keys, then open his front door slightly, ducking his head to enter as if the doorframe were too low. If he saw me watching, he'd give a desultory wave, or I'd lift a hand in his direction. He didn't go out at night, and he seemed bored or not too bright or, like many Key Westers, pretty incomprehensible—at least he would have been in any other context. The icicle lights burned all night.

Sometimes I could hear Glenn Gould playing loudly, and then my neighbor—the drawstrings of his red hoodie tied under his chin—would emerge and stand with a blanket wrapped around him, shivering in his jeans and clogs, looking forlornly down the empty street. If Hoodie had anything resembling a life, you wouldn't know it by his chagrined expression and by the way he sagged in the chair on his

225

porch like a shot duck, too heavy-assed to rise, even when he needed to sign for a package: quite a heavy fellow, for someone who smoked dope—I've smelled it—and whom I've never seen carrying a bag from the grocery store. When, and how, had he put up the Christmas lights?

Hoodie—on the night in January we became better acquainted—silently greeted me as we stood across the street on our porches: "two citizens of Planet Earth," as my late husband used to say. What does Hoodie do all day? I'm in my sixties, so if anyone wonders about me—which I doubt—I'm sure they assume I creak and groan and sprout chin hairs. My own son, Roland, appears once or twice a year for a brief visit, then returns to Miami. He's never invited me to visit wherever he lives. He's never even given me an address. If Roland knows that Christmas has come and gone, he's given no indication. My best guess about Hoodie? He sleeps late (many in Key West do), then does errands (which occupy everyone, always, until the second you pitch over dead)—errands that, in his case, might include a certain number of doctor visits, given his weight. I assume he has a hobby as well, because of the number of boxes delivered to the house. I've been asked many times by the UPS or FedEx driver to sign in his absence. One recent rainy afternoon I'd taken in two boxes, then walked across the street with them later that day. The shippers had names like OxyLoxy, in Newtville, TN, and StarLady in Winches, NH. The boxes were heavy, they often smelled nice (though sometimes they smelled of smoke) and were more or less the same size. Once, when a box was shipped through the U.S. mail, I'd paid the postage due of thirty-four cents, for which Hoodie had thanked me profusely.

* * *

I arrived in Key West in 1986, leaving a cruise ship that could continue to transport its weary just fine without me: passengers tainted with flu; not-quite ex-wives, giving the marriage one more try; geezers under the delusion that the high seas were a watery limbo where they could revert to their youth and not take their medicine; shrilly entitled, run-amok grandchildren; the eccentric who came aboard with his parrot in its cage. My husband had died in 1985, Roland was in boarding school in Connecticut (courtesy of his grandmother), and I'd impulsively responded to an ad in *The Washington Post* for discounted cabins on a winter cruise whose first stop was Key West, Florida—which also became my last.

When I'd left, I'd gotten a job cleaning at Tra La La Tropics Guesthouse (I was also given a temporary room there and permission to swim in the pool). I had soon branched out—there's a pun!—creating displays for their entryway from flowers discarded after rich people's parties, or stuffed in florists' trash cans the night before garbage pickup. Fallen palm fronds have always been free, and a gold-and-silver glitter stick costs next to nothing and really adds panache. I would pinch-hit for the cook (Zachary "Zit Man" Chisholm) when his diabetes made him too weak to serve the last meal of the night. I've been retired for years, living on my—and my husband's—Social Security payments.

I still do the flowers for Tra La La, which morphed into Sea Breeze House when straight people bought it in the nineties—though I don't Dumpster-dive anymore. I supplement my income when I'm called upon to make bridal bouquets and—to my surprise—wrist corsages, which are especially popular in transsexual commitment ceremonies. Who knows what Hoodie made of me, with these people coming and going from my apartment.

Well, here's what he makes of me: He crossed the street, after all this time, wearing his customary red sweatshirt with the hood pulled up, which he untied and pushed off his head as if gallantly removing a fedora, and said, "I'm embarrassed to say we haven't really met," and I said, "Joe, I know your name because of the packages addressed to you," and he said, "Right, so let me ask: What's your name?"

Audrey Ann was the answer, but no one had ever called me either name, and Annie wasn't my favorite nickname—Flora was. It had been bestowed on me in 1986 by Zit Man, whose nickname had preceded our meeting. I told Hoodie I was Flora.

"Happy to know you," he said. "I'm taking a pill called Zoloft, and I find I'm able to extend myself to people now, so I think it's about time we made each other's acquaintance."

This, of course, made me feel bad. The poor man was depressed, and I'd never so much as introduced myself. After my husband died, I had retreated inward.

"I'd like to ask you in for tea," he said. "I'm feeling much better these days. We'll have a chat. Not about anything in particular, just a neighborly visit."

"Joe, that would be a pleasure. When would be a good time to come over?"

"In half an hour?" he said.

Half an hour! Well—why not? "Fine," I said. "Thanks so much."

I went inside and saw the answering-machine light

blinking. The red light upset me about as much as seeing a palmetto bug scurry under the sink. You can do it, I told myself silently. I hit play.

"Mom, hi, I'm calling because I've sort of got a situation here. Is there any way you could use your Triple A card to get us towed? I'm in Georgia. [!] Yeah, we're over here in Marietta, picking up Cindy's daughter, who's got an issue with school or something [?], and where I was parked in a parking space over here right on the street? Yeah, a tree fell on our car. I'm maxed out on my credit card, and I could use some help with towing. Cindy's cell is five-one-eight—" then silence. I stared at the answering machine; if I waited, the other digits of the telephone number might be magically filled in. Roland had a girlfriend named Cindy, who had a child, and they were in Georgia? Ohh-kay (as the exterminator always said when a bug started running). Surely he would call back.

But time passed, and there was no new message. I went into the bathroom and took a quick shower, toweled off, put the same clothes back on, looked again at the answering machine, then headed off across the street.

"Please come in, Flora," Joe said, stepping aside ungracefully in his doorway but not shaking my hand, though he made a move in that direction and then stifled the impulse. He was wearing enormous baggy jeans. He tried to stuff his unshaken hand into the pocket and failed. He had on what looked like a red cashmere sweater. He'd done something to slick back what was left of his hair.

"Oh! Isn't this something!" I said. I was in Xanadu. The front room was an enormous, vibrant, multicolored tent.

The materials were radiant; some sparkled with tiny mirrors that threw off light; others were woven with threads that seemed to lift off the surface like three-dimensional TV test patterns. I'd never been to Morocco, but maybe this was what things looked like there. Fabric was draped over the walls, and swags dipped from corner to corner. The walls were hung with quilts in various geometric patterns. Only the two front windows, with white shades lowered, were not somehow blanketed. Your eye was constantly drawn to where the material converged mid-ceiling, punctured by a dazzling pink spotlight that looked like it might have just vaporized a flamingo. This must have been what had come in the boxes: the quilts and fabric, the shimmering threads. People thought the back gardens were the hidden secrets of Key West? They should see this!

Joe reentered the room—I'd hardly noticed he was gone—wheeling a two-tier cart that carried a silver tea service. A lovely aroma mingled with the room's other smells: a bit musty, somewhat cinnamony, lemon-tinged. "White rooms drive me crazy," he said straight-faced, as if delivering the punch line of a joke. He poured tea into a china cup and handed it to me, the cup teetering on a mismatched saucer. "Cream and sugar," he gestured. He poured a cup for himself. His free hand swept in the direction of two black butterfly chairs, which of course hadn't been apparent amid the riot of color. We retreated to the chairs. "Lady Grey," Joe said, sighing the words, and at first I entertained the notion that it might be a new nickname for me—that he could be making a remark about the color of my hair. He held up the tea bag's paper tag, like a little magnifying lens, or a bit of unreflective mirror, or a tiny shape from one of the quilts: Lady Grey. "Thank you for coming," he said.

As you would imagine, we talked about how he created the room. It took a year, he told me. He had the AC revented at his own expense. He called the room "my personal vision." This was the guy who stood outside smoking, gazing at nothing? I felt like I was a shard inside a vast kaleidoscope. "It's for rent, now that it's exactly the way I want it," he said. "To be perfectly frank, it's something I hoped to interest you in."

"Me, rent your living room?"

"No, no. But I've seen your talent for flower arranging, and I thought that when very special people came, I might call on you to arrange some flowers."

"Special people? What do you mean?"

"Flora, if you promise to keep this in the strictest confidence, I can be specific about the first arrivals," he said.

In the second before he whispered their names, I wondered: Might they be the Queen of Hearts and the White Rabbit? The first name, the woman's, I recognized, but I wasn't sure I could pick her out of a lineup. The man's name meant nothing to me, but he was apparently the husband.

"You know, this is just incredible," I said. "Are they—I mean, they're checking in?"

"I'd say checking out," he said, pleased with his turn of phrase.

"You want me to do the flowers?" I said. "Where would you put them?"

"I have a table in the other room," he said, sounding a bit hurt. "I'll bring in the table."

We sipped our tea in silence.

"So these celebrities are on their way?" I asked. "When?"

"Saturday. They rented it from noon to midnight."

"I have to do the flowers for a wedding on a catamaran this Saturday, Joe."

"Won't they blow away?" he said.

"The vases have bricks in the bottom. I bundle the stems together and put sink weights on them."

"I'll give you five thousand dollars," he said.

"Well . . . do we know what kind of flowers they like?"

"I can ask."

I nodded. "I feel like that would be taking advantage, though," I said. "It's too much money."

"It isn't a lot of money to them, I guess."

I thought about it for a moment. Five thousand dollars was more than I'd make in many months of doing wedding arrangements.

"Well, I can't very well say no, can I?"

"Good. More tea?"

"No, thank you. But it's delicious."

"I'm glad you like it."

"No one could possibly suspect that walking through your front door, this is what she'd find."

"I never raise the shades," he said.

"How did you get the word out that—"

"Craigslist."

"They were reading Craigslist?"

"Their people were. It's an anniversary. Not a wedding anniversary. The day their child was conceived or something."

"Should I allude to that in the flower arrangement?"

"I wouldn't say so, no. I think that information was just

personal. For some reason, the secretary felt she had to explain herself."

"And you really do believe—"

"The deposit cleared."

"Wow. All right. Well, I'll have to give this some serious thought. I'm glad I've got time to get flowers flown in from Miami. This is really incredibly kind of you, Joe."

"I just look like a fat schmuck, don't I?"

The question startled me. If there'd been anywhere to put my teacup, I'd have set it down.

"No worries," he said, gesturing to the walls. "This is definitely the revenge of the nerd."

"It's truly amazing. To think this exists right across the street from me! So—can I come up with some sketches? How would that be?"

"You don't have to show me sketches. You're a genius."

"Oh, far from it," I said. "And you've barely seen my work."

"I didn't exactly level with you before: The UPS guy told me your name, because you're always so nice about signing for my packages, and I've got a book about designers who've done amazing Key West interiors, so I realized instantly who you were. I saw one arrangement where you wrapped lace around bamboo shoots and scattered snails on the table! It took a while to get up my courage to approach you."

"The UPS delivery person knows who I am?"

"He used to have a design store with his wife in Marathon. His wife used to be a guy. She was the roommate of a cook who used to be a friend of yours at Tra La La? I think he took photographs of your flower arrangements for their brochure, right? The cook?"

"Yes, he did do that. You know, I fell out of touch with him. I didn't know he had a roommate. I mean, except for work, I guess I didn't know him very well."

"I heard he's working at a restaurant in South Beach. His health is apparently much better. Has some pump in his chest."

"I see. So the UPS man married Zachary the cook's roommate, who had sex-change surgery?"

Joe nodded.

"That's a very Key West story."

"It's why we're all here, right?"

I momentarily considered the possibility that he'd been referring specifically to sex-change surgery. "What do you mean?" I said.

"So that everything can be a Key West story."

Relieved, I found myself on my feet, preparing to leave. "This has been quite the day!" I said. "To be continued."

He rose also, on the second attempt. He said, "I'll e-mail their secretary and get information about what flowers they like."

"Good. Let me know."

He reached out, but it was for my teacup, not to shake hands. Nevertheless, he did shake my hand because it was extended. Then he took the teacup and saucer and returned them, with his, to the cart. He said over his shoulder: "Isn't it really sad when you lose touch with people you once cared about? Technology has made everything worse, because you feel like you could potentially get in touch, so you assume you will, and then instead of writing a letter, you're looking for somebody on Facebook, and half the time they're not there."

He opened the door enough to let me out. A kid flew down the sidewalk on a skateboard, with all the dexterity of a fledgling. When the boy passed, Joe quickly stepped out behind me, unlit cigarette in hand, and pulled the door closed. "Now you know," he said.

The words echoed in my head as I reentered my apartment, which looked more than a little shabby, with an afghan thrown over an old chair and a picture hanging crooked. But who lived like Joe? There was something very odd about it—well: Of course there was.

The answering-machine light was blinking, and I knew who'd left the message: Roland, calling to get my help so his car could be towed. "Mom," he said the second I pushed play, as if his voice had been waiting to jump out of the machine. "Hey, Mom, we had that little trouble here, but some Good Samaritan gave us a ride to the school, so we met up with Frieda, no problem, but when we got back to the car, it'd been towed, so I was wondering if you could call the towing company and point out that a huge tree fell on our car and it wasn't just a matter of not respecting the rules by moving our car by five o'clock. We had no way to do that with some tree crashed down on it. I've got the name of the place here. The thing is, we're all going to have to get back to Miami, like get a bus or something, and the cash machine won't take Cindy's MasterCard. If you—" The line went dead.

I already felt like Alice expelled from Wonderland, but Roland's phone call was too much of this world. I would have loved to be able to tell my husband about my adventure, though if he'd lived, we'd still be in Washington, D.C. I had heard on the Weather Channel that Washington had gotten two feet of snow. Snow that deep would paralyze the place. I undressed and stepped out of my shoes to lie down and take a nap. I lay on my side, pulling the bedspread from the far side of the bed over me for warmth. What a sad little chenille cover it was, balding a bit here and there as if a caged animal had bitten its fur, a gloomy beige to begin with. Joe would disdain such a cover, though under its warmth I fell quickly asleep.

Her favorite flowers were anthuriums, birds-of-paradise, and proteas. Mixed in with these would be white irises, for which, when I ordered them, I requested the tightest buds possible, since once they open, they die in a day. It was risky, I knew, but it worked out. I found some white ribbon with red sparkles at Dollar Tree out on the highway and asked a friend if I could prune his bougainvillea—awful, thorny stuff, but it would just be at the base of the arrangement, and what was beauty without a little danger? I found some gallon milk containers in people's recycling and rinsed them out and cut off the tops with pruning shears. I would use bricks as platforms of various heights to support the gallon bottles, and disguise them under beards of Spanish moss. Under cover of darkness, I grabbed Spanish moss from a tree on White Street. I asked Joe if I could come in Saturday morning to assemble the flowers on-site. There were many flowers, brought at little expense, because Manolo's assistant (Manolo owned the florist shop in Miami) would be driving to Key West anyway, to deliver orchids to the Marquesa Hotel and to see his girlfriend. Manolo had a very entre nous way of talking. He thought two hundred dollars to deliver them was more than generous. If you're wondering whether the check to me cleared, there was no check. I had five thousand dollars cash, which Joe had handed me in a bank envelope the day after we spoke. It was a perplexingly large amount of cash to have, but I seemed unable to deposit it in my account. I just kept looking at the envelope, which I tucked in the Yellow Pages and put in a cabinet drawer in the kitchen. Joe told me I could come whenever I wanted that morning, and we agreed that I would begin around ten.

The night before, I had slept badly, and it took two espressos to get me going. I had hoped Joe would volunteer to help me carry the boxes—the birds-of-paradise had been too long-stemmed to keep in my emptied-out refrigerator, so they'd been in the sink overnight, soaking in the porous insert of the asparagus steamer—but he seemed so nervous, I didn't want to do any more than hint, making it a point to stagger during the three trips I made carrying the big boxes.

I arranged and arranged, repositioned, plucked, and tucked, and when I was finished, I used the tips of my hedge clippers to pick up the bougainvillea branches, feeling as powerful but as humble as a blacksmith dipping into the forge. It was a truly magnificent arrangement. Big-headed proteas dowsed above the bougainvillea. Birds-of-paradise shot upward like torches. The delicate, waxy anthuriums, in white and pink, added an odd texture and were perfectly interspersed with the white irises. I alternated the two, like the rails of a curving staircase Bette Davis would descend. Below the basket I scattered gold stars (appropriate!) that I'd gotten at CVS and musical notes that I'd cut from black construction paper, consulting one of my son's boyhood songbooks—its pages perforated by silverfish—to make sure I'd gotten them right. Move over, Martha Stewart. At exactly eleven A.M., Joe again pronounced me a genius. He had centered the table under the spotlight. It was really riveting. We hated to leave, but we did, Joe dropping his key in the mailbox, then withdrawing his hand and crossing his fingers. "This is sort of embarrassing," he said, "but I don't really have anywhere to go. Do you think I could spend a bit of time in your apartment?"

He could tell I was taken aback. My apartment? What would he think of such an uninspiring place? And how long might he be there?

"I'm agoraphobic," he said. "I can go a little way from home, but really not that far. This wouldn't be the day to pass out on the street."

"No, it certainly wouldn't. Well. Of course, come over."

"They had a lot of hope for the Zoloft. Although it's facilitated our friendship, it doesn't seem to have stopped me from feeling that if I go far, I might stop breathing."

"What a terrible affliction," I said. "I know something about what you're feeling, because my late husband had asthma."

"He didn't die from an asthma attack, did he?" Joe said, eyes wide.

"No, not from that. Joe, are you okay?"

He'd stopped in the middle of the street.

"I look up and down this street, practicing," he said. "It's easier at night. I made it to the library three days ago. Then today—wouldn't you know."

"Joe, let's just—" I took his hand, which was quite cold.

"Assholes, you think you're at a cocktail party?" sneered some skinhead who swerved around us on a bike. He puckered his lips as if spitting over his shoulder, but since the wind would have blown it back in his face, I doubted it was anything but pantomime.

"I don't think I can take another step."

"Joe," I said calmly, "there are chairs out in front of my place, and if you can make it there, you can look right over at your house. Let's try that."

"I'm dizzy."

"Well, Joe, it's not really safe to stand in the street."

He crumpled. He was almost bent over double, but he managed not to sink to his knees.

"Everything okay?" a young woman said, passing by, talking on her cell phone.

"Fine," I said, knowing I sounded doubtful.

"So sorry. I can't—" He was gasping. "Is there a siren behind us?"

There was nothing. Not even a car. Though as soon as the light changed on the next block, a line of cars would be arriving. The young woman stood on the curb, frowning as she turned off her cell phone.

"Joe," I said, "we don't want to call an ambulance or have the police drive up, you know? We don't want a scene outside when your company might be arriving. Joe?"

"It's good I haven't passed out. I'll be fine in a minute. If only that noise . . ."

The girl walked on. A man with his little boy on his shoulders held his son's ankles and pretended not to notice us. Slowly, inch by inch, Joe started to straighten up. He leaned on me heavily. His eyes were slits. "So sorry," he said.

"Much better! You see, you're coming out of it! You can do it, just over to my porch chair. You're standing up much better, Joe."

We lurched forward as the first car slowed to a halt. I met the driver's eyes, and he met mine. I understood from his eyes that he thought Joe was drunk. Just then Joe took off, a little lopsided, more or less dragging me with him. We made it to the other side. "All right," he panted, cupping his hands over his ears. "Okay, but I don't think I can make it to the chair."

"I'll bring it to you," I said.

"Yes, please, so sorry, thank you," he said.

I ran up onto the front porch, folded the wooden chair, and carried it to where he stood, sweat beading on his forehead. I'd found the chair curbside, then worried it might have termites, so I'd never taken it inside. Joe sat down and rubbed his hand over his face, then down the leg of his jeans. "So sorry," he said. His breathing was less frantic, but he stared straight ahead. If he'd been Superman, he would have been looking through the clapboards into the gorgeously swirling tent, where my flowers sat center stage. I stood at his side with my hand on the top of the chair. I felt a little rattled myself. I no longer seemed able to think beyond the next minute.

Time passed, and he got better. I went in to get him a glass of water. We chatted about his guests' arrival—how soon they'd be there, that sort of thing. "I was going to sit in the reading room of the library," he said, tilting his head to look at me.

"Well, when you feel ready, we'll have some tea, or whatever you'd like." I tried to sound encouraging, but I wasn't sure he'd ever make it into the apartment. I was worried that the famous people would show up and we'd be there, gawking.

We did make it inside, we had tea, and afterward Joe agreed to lie down for a minute to rest. He stretched out on the sofa and fell asleep. He snored a bit. The sun came out from behind the clouds, and I thought the light would awaken him, but he threw his hand over his eyes and continued to sleep. As the day went on and it got colder, I considered putting on the space heater, though the thing made an awful crackling noise, and I was afraid it might wake him. I lightly placed the afghan over Joe. I picked up the book I was reading, *In Transit* by Mavis Gallant. The stories were very involving, though every now and then I'd look up to see if anything was happening across the street. Gradually I let the worry I'd tried to suppress take over: What if they never came at all? Though he did—we did—have the money, at least. What would it matter if Xanadu sat there, unseen? I went on to the next story. I was so engrossed that I forgot about dinner, as I'd forgotten about lunch. To be honest, I might have been reading a bit desperately, as a way not to think about what was—or, more accurately, what was not—going on.

When Joe woke up, we had tomato soup, and we moved one of the chairs so we could sit side by side in the dark, watching a bit of late-night TV, trying to pretend to each other that we weren't watching his house. Not long before midnight, an enormous white shape appeared in front of the windows: a white stretch Humvee limo. We couldn't have

been more surprised if Moby Dick had beached himself. We
sucked in our breath. We raced to the window in unison and
closed the curtains, then peeked from either side, as if we'd
rehearsed this. "There they are!" he said. "My God! They're
here!" I whispered. It was like being a little child looking in
on Santa Claus. This was no Santa, though. As I'd read in the
tabloids at the checkout line, she was very curvaceous. She
had on a long white strapless gown, plunging in the back
and looking I don't know what way in front, because she got
out on the side near the curb and I never saw anything but
her coxcomb of fancifully upswept hair, her long neck and
back. A fur stole was handed out of the car, and then, on the
same side from which she'd disembarked, with the chauffeur
now holding open the door, the husband emerged, quite a
bit shorter than his wife, reaching up to place the fur around
her shoulders. She didn't stop walking, so instead he carried
the stole like a pet. I was trying to remember every detail as
if it had begun happening hours ago: for instance, that she'd
gotten out of the limo before the chauffeur had managed to
get to her door. "Look for the key, it's in there!" Joe whispered.
The chauffeur was reaching around in the mailbox for the
key. He pulled out the day's mail—hadn't thought about that
as an impediment to finding the key!—then he found it, we
could see that. He and the husband stepped in front of the
woman, who had on very high heels, probably as high as they
could be made. She took several perfect backward steps and
finally swept up her stole and tossed it over one shoulder.
Then they were inside and the door was closed. The chauffeur
was in there with them. Behind the limo, someone tried to
inch past, realized it was impossible, and began backing up.

The limo glowed brightly under the lamplights. We said nothing. Some people passed by, commenting on the limo. They stopped and stared, but since nothing was going on, their loud voices drifted away as they continued walking.

The chauffeur came out, closing the door behind him, putting on his cap. He went quickly to the trunk and took out an ice bucket and a stand. "They didn't say they wanted anything," Joe whispered, hurt. Our eyes met, but we didn't want to miss anything. With a bottle of something—champagne?—tucked under his arm, the chauffeur went back in, carrying the ice bucket in its stand. "There's no ice," Joe said. "I locked everything but the bathroom." I shrugged. "Well, you said they didn't tell you they wanted anything," I said uneasily. The chauffeur exited in about three minutes. He stood on the porch looking left and right, much the way Joe did at night, and then, removing his cap, he bounced down the stairs and got in the driver's seat and pulled away, some car honking behind him, a bicyclist, alone, sliding through the narrow space between the Humvee and the parked cars. Then there was darkness.

"Did you see the height of those heels? You don't see those down here, unless it's drag queens," I said.

He looked at his watch. "She has a phenomenal ass, if that isn't too crude to say," he said. "It's after midnight. How long do you think they're going to stay?"

"At least as long as it takes to drink a bottle of champagne."

"Let's open the curtains," Joe said. "They won't see us if we turn off the TV."

We did, then continued to sit in the dark. I wondered

whether the two of them might be in there all night, and what that would mean in terms of Joe.

Then the big white limo pulled up again, and the chauffeur, putting on his cap, got out and went around to . . . what? He lifted a big bag of ice from the floor. He carried it in the crook of one arm, and I saw how powerful that arm was. He went into the house and was out in another few minutes, in time to move before the car behind him with its pulsing, deafening sound system blared its horn again.

Joe yawned. I got up and turned on the space heater. I offered him the afghan, but he insisted I have it. I spread it over my legs. I had never known it to be this cold in Key West. She must be freezing in her low-cut dress. And doing what, inside? They didn't seem like the type who'd get down on the floor, but you never could tell. I wondered if Joe was thinking the same thing.

"Smelling the flowers, drinking champagne, dancing," Joe said, as if reading my mind. Then: "I hope neither one of them smokes. The ad very specifically said no smoking. I go outside, myself. They're probably not smokers, though," he said. "Although a lot of those people are."

"Did you make it clear that they had to leave at midnight?"

"It was very clear. Confirmed with the secretary."

"Why do you think they came so late?"

"Those people have no sense of time," he said.

Wait! The husband was standing on the street, talking on his cell phone. He was hunched over in the wind, hand to his ear, then he was reaching behind him for the hand of the woman descending the stairs, who threw the bottle into the bushes! Good God, it disappeared right into the hibiscus.

Joe and I looked at each other. The man and his wife clasped hands as she leaned her head, with its big tower of hair, on his shoulder—having to duck down a bit to do so. The stole was fastened around her collarbone. She bent a bit to kiss him. He slid his hand down her back as their lips locked. He clutched her but kept looking past her shoulder. Then she stepped out of her shoe and handed it to him. He dropped his cell phone in his jacket pocket and held her shoe. His other hand remained around her waist. She bumped down again and handed him the other shoe, and he tried to return it, but she put her hands behind her back. The dress had to be satin. Her husband stood there with his funny little pencil mustache, holding the shoes by their heels, searching the street. The limo pulled up, and the driver jumped out with another bottle of—I guess—champagne, but the husband put his hand up like a traffic cop and turned and pulled open the back door. His wife's shiny, amazing ass tipped into the air for a second, then she was in, headfirst. He tossed her shoes on the floor, rearranged something. He hopped in the back seat, and the limo idled for a minute, then the chauffeur got out, went up the stairs, put the key in the mailbox, returned, and drove away.

Joe and I were both so tired, we were rubbing our eyes. The question was: Could he make it back across the street? Or: Would I really prefer that he stay, just in a neighborly way, of course. Or did I simply dread taking the chance and being caught out in the cold again, with Joe unable to take another step? The same thoughts had to be going through his head.

"Your son that you were telling me about earlier," Joe said.

"You think he gets scared and can't continue speaking? Did you mean he suddenly seizes up, or—"

"I don't know. I guess I don't want to think he's drunk or stoned."

"He could be having panic attacks, you know. It sounds like he's finding himself in some strange situations—not that the most ordinary thing can't provoke an attack. I could talk to him. They have a lot of new drugs for that. Not that they've done me any good."

He's forthcoming, and he's willing to address my problems, and I like that. Maybe this is it, I thought. How much do I need to go out gallivanting, when I'm happy to take an afternoon nap and am yawning by midnight, even in the midst of a fairy tale? Also, he's proved he's no deadbeat. Between us, we've just made what used to be my entire year's salary. You miss out on life for years and years, and then you meet the guy across the street, who thinks you're a genius, and you've got money again, and love . . . well, it was hardly love with Joe, but it was clear that even though this was the last thing I expected, it was the way things did conclude for two citizens of Planet Earth, and in spite of all odds, I had a partner. I had a partner on a night when foxes sang and danced in the moonlight, and the old people sat and stared.

SAVE A HORSE
RIDE A COWGIRL

Heidi and Bree were rear-ended on Route 1 by Sterne Clough, driving his brother's Ford pickup. Neither girl seemed hurt. Sterne, though, felt the oddest sensation. It was as if someone had clamped an ice bag under his right armpit. It felt frozen and burned at the same time. Your body pulled all sorts of tricks on you when you turned sixty, and now he was seventy-four, so those tricks were less like pranks and more like extended jokes. He groped under his arm with his good hand but felt only sweat. Nothing accounted for the pain, which was worse in his knee. Damn! His bad knee had banged the dashboard when the little car in front had accelerated and then stopped with no warning just as the light turned green.

He got out of the truck, his knee none too helpful. It was distracting to have to stand there scowling at the damage while his armpit felt like a smoldering coal. Maybe later he could run a bamboo stick through a piece of steak and cook it in there. Meanwhile, he had some awareness that the car's driver was still sitting in her seat, not even looking over her shoulder. The other girl stood by the mashed-in bumper of the car—at least the thing had a bumper—her hands on her hips.

"Are you too senile to be driving?" Bree asked Sterne.

"Want to tell me why your friend started off and then stopped dead?" he asked.

"Because a squirrel ran across the road," Bree said. And because she's a total asshole, she thought, but she wasn't about to tell the guy that. They'd been headed to the outlets in Kittery to stock up on jeans, and maybe see if the Puma store had gotten in the shoes she'd seen in an ad earlier that summer. They both went to UNH, where the fall semester was about to start. Now this. Compounded by the fact that Heidi was currently outside the car, retching. Everything put Heidi in a tailspin, which was her way of ensuring that she wouldn't have to take the blame for whatever had gone wrong: another girl threatening to attack Heidi for having stolen her boyfriend; the produce manager at the market irately insisting that she help him pick up the bin of mushrooms she'd sideswiped with her elbow. Now here came the cops, sirens blaring. A total shit situation.

Sterne's younger brother, Bradley, was a lawyer. Within a few hours, he was able to find out that, at the moment the squirrel dashed in front of the car, the driver was texting. That, and the year before, she'd been on academic probation for physically fighting with another girl. Plus, she had an unpaid speeding ticket and had been cited in June for throwing a

Coke can out of a car window. It had been observed at the scene that she was driving barefoot. "Turn that off," the cop had said of the music on the car radio as Bree, not Heidi, complied with his request to see the car's registration, since Heidi kept gagging.

Bradley was upset that his brother had been involved in an accident, but a little damage to his old truck didn't bother him much. And a couple of phone calls had already guaranteed that Sterne was going to be fine. At worst, the insurance rates would go up. But it was six P.M. and Sterne was still fixated on the accident, cursing both girls as he helped carry the bookcase he'd been transporting into Bradley's new house.

Two years earlier, Bradley's wife, Donna, had been given the wrong medication at a hospital in Boston and died as a result. Bradley had wanted to stay in their house, but the cliché was true: There were too many memories. With the settlement check, he'd bought a smaller place, across the river from their old house, in a location that Donna would have loved. He'd gotten rid of a lot of their books—her cookbooks, along with her collection of poetry books, which he'd donated to Smith—but he still had a few left, and the new house had no built-in bookcases or built-in anything, so he'd kept an eye out for useful shelving at Leeward Landing Thrift Store, where lovely furniture appeared at the end of each summer.

Sterne had borrowed the truck because he needed to buy several large bags of mulch, and he had volunteered to pick up the shelf on the way. Almost every weekend, for one reason or another, Sterne borrowed the truck. He always brought it back with a full tank of gas, even if there'd been only a quarter tank to begin with.

In the house, the bookcase looked smaller than Bradley had expected. They'd positioned it between the living room windows that looked out toward the river, but now he thought that it might be better in the dining room, which had a lower ceiling and not much furniture. Decorating was not his strong suit. What he wanted, basically, was to get the remaining books shelved. Sterne had finally quieted down about the day's events and was assessing the bookcase with his hands clamped under his armpits.

"It doesn't look right there," he said.

"Maybe when it has books in it," Bradley replied vaguely. "Where are they?"

"Upstairs. The movers carried all the boxes up to the second floor by mistake."

"Why didn't you make them carry them down?"

"I wasn't here. I had a trial. Margie Randolph's niece came over to supervise. She needed the money because her babysitting job disappeared."

The Randolphs, Bill and Margie, had been Bradley and Donna's neighbors on Seagull Way. Bradley and Donna had had the corner lot, which gave them the advantage of great air circulation as well as a peek at the harbor. Their next-door neighbor, Miller Ryall, had spoken to no one, and no one had spoken to him, though his house sat between the Cloughs' and the Randolphs'. It was said that after losing his job on Wall Street, Ryall had sold his New York condo and moved his family into their summer house, though the wife, Constance, had quickly decamped with their two-year-old son and the Haitian nanny, and Miller had lived in the house alone for years. He kept the blinds closed, though sometimes in the evening he walked barefoot onto the front porch and sat in the porch swing, bare-chested and wearing his bathing trunks (although the pool no longer contained water), revealing the same perfectly sculpted body that the wives had all noted when the Ryalls first moved in.

Through Donna's binoculars, which she had used to watch birds, Bradley could clearly see their old house. Maybe it was a little maudlin, but he liked watching his old home disappear into the darkness every night, and he liked equally well the interior lights on either side of the second story that came on at dusk and remained lit until ten P.M. He was asking a lot for the house and was not inclined to come down on the price.

"What say we check out that new oyster place in Portsmouth?" Sterne said. "I hear they've got twenty local brews on tap, and I owe you, after crashing your truck into those bimbos. It's on me, bro."

Odd that Sterne had become obsessed with beer in his old age. The same substance he'd disdained in college—all three colleges he'd attended, starting with Michigan and ending with Bates, and not even a degree to show for any of it after seven chaotic years. Neither alcohol nor food held much attraction for Bradley after Donna's death. He ate just to keep going. But it was a nice offer—an apology and an attempt to cheer him up, no doubt—so he said jokingly that if Sterne would drive, he'd enjoy such an outing very much.

"You don't enjoy anything very much, but a few oysters and a brewski might help you get back on your feet," Sterne said.

"Back on my feet? Do you remember that I won a trial

last week that was a grand slam? I can pick and choose any case that interests me."

"You want to avoid the subject. That's fine. Not my place to nose in. I'm only thinking of you. Nobody knows what to do for you, me included."

"Nobody has to do anything. Life goes on."

"I don't think you think it does," Sterne said, "but I'll keep my big yap shut."

Portsmouth was sort of a nightmare, though they found a parking place in a bank lot where somebody had taken down the chain. Bradley felt sure they wouldn't be towed. They started off toward the center of town, a boy on a skateboard clattering the wrong way down a one-way street as a couple of girls watched. What tattoos they had. What crazy earrings, feathery hippie things that hung to their jawbones. One had on a necklace of black skulls. The other wore flip-flops on her enormous hennaed feet. "Make way for two old men," Bradley said, using his arm, Darth Vader–style, to cut through a cluster of boys who were smoking and holding their iPhones to the sky, jostling one another, checking out the girls. Sterne remarked on how much Portsmouth had changed. Bradley had to agree with him. In Prescott Park, a wedding was concluding, two little girls in lavender skirts so long the material almost tripped them as they threw flower petals everywhere they shouldn't.

At the restaurant, the brothers were told that there was only a half-hour wait if they were willing to sit at the bar. Sure. What was half an hour? They sat on a stone wall with the buzzer the hostess had given Sterne. Bill Randolph and his daughter from his first marriage wandered over to greet them. A nice girl. Peggy? Patty. She lived somewhere far away, like Newfoundland. Somewhere Bill had to take a ferry to get to. Margie was attending a therapy session. She'd insisted that they go out and enjoy the lovely summer evening; she'd even thought to make a reservation for them at Mombo.

When Bill and his daughter first approached, Sterne had hopped down off the wall to greet them as if *he* were the former neighbor. Bradley had gotten down, too—rude to sit there like Humpty Dumpty—but although he was glad to see Bill, he didn't really know what to say. Bradley didn't think this daughter had ever married, and he wondered if she might be gay. Her hair was cut like a man's, though many women her age wore their hair that way. He'd need another clue. Which would be what? A T-shirt emblazoned with the rainbow flag? Yes, he did think she was gay, standing there smiling a big unlipsticked smile, her feet, in Tevas, planted far apart. Donna would have figured it out in a flash, but there was no Donna, no flash.

Bill said that he missed having Bradley close by. Not that he'd moved far, but still, with him gone, there was only crazy Miller Ryall and all the noise he was causing.

"Noise from what?" Bradley asked. It was some sort of adult jungle gym that he was constructing, Bill said. The swimming pool was intact, but it had a different lining. Bill could see only a sliver of it from his attic window, peering through Tarzan's jungle. (Ryall had wisteria growing on arbors all over the property, plus trumpet vines and roses that made his front door all but invisible.)

Eventually they took their leave, Patty clomping, Bill quite demure beside his big-boned fortyish daughter. Sterne picked up the suddenly madly flashing, vibrating black box and held it as if it might explode. Bradley found himself hoping that there wouldn't be loud music they'd have to try to talk over, though sitting at the bar was good in that situation. They'd be close together. Donna . . . she could hear a whisper across a room. No, of course she couldn't if someone was blaring music, but in the silence of the house she could hear—really—she did once hear the sound he made while using a toothpick on his back teeth behind the closed bathroom door.

Oysters, yes. Fried calamari. An order of steamers. They ate so much they decided to share a main course. Sterne ordered a hard cider. Bradley agreed to another T and T, even though the tonic had been borderline flat. It was a fine idea, coming to the new restaurant. The noise level was atrocious, but after a while you got used to it. He felt proud of himself for knowing that it was Macy Gray on the sound system. Interesting to observe this summer's fashions: clothes splashed with orange; cashmere scarves carried so that you could bundle up in the AC. Bradley knew the difference between cashmere and other wools. On their long-ago trip to India, Donna had bought the loveliest cashmere shawl. His secretary had taken Donna's clothes away, promising she'd donate them. Somewhere tonight, someone else could be wearing one of Donna's dresses. How bizarre would that be, to see another woman in Donna's clothes.

They decided on grilled swordfish with a mango compote ("compote" basically meant a little cup containing not enough of a substance), french fries, and lemon-peel arugula "slaw." Why the menu put the last word in quotation marks was open to interpretation. When they finished eating, Sterne grabbed for the bill. Bradley wondered if his brother really would pay for dinner, or if he'd expected Bradley to insist on picking up half the check.

Bradley dropped Sterne off at home and took his leave. At his own front door, he turned on the hall light, then turned it off again and stared into the house, wishing that he could feel the new configuration of hallways and stairs and rooms. In the old house, he could have maneuvered well even if he'd lost his sight—it was all so familiar. He turned the light back on and went into the living room and sat facing the windows, though he could see nothing through them. Well, now he could have things his way: no blinds, no curtains. He sat there trying to make up a little jingle, but nothing seemed to rhyme with "curtains." Exertions, maybe? Lately everything seemed to require twice the energy it had when Donna was alive. He closed his eyes but didn't sleep. That would have been depressing: falling asleep after a big dinner, sitting alone in his living room. He sprang up, switching on the table lamp, but didn't know what to do next.

He decided to get the iPad and look up the pictures he'd taken the week before, when, with almost no warning, the temperature had dropped and hail had begun to come down—hail the size of mothballs—a totally bizarre August hailstorm in southern Maine. When it finally stopped, he'd taken pictures of hailstones filling the birdbath and the recycling bin like Styrofoam peanuts. It had done in his new hostas. According to a phone call from Margie, Miller Ryall had come out on his front lawn during the storm, wearing Jockey shorts, not even bathing trunks, raised his hands to heaven, and laughed and danced like some deranged freak on *Twin Peaks*, whooping and pirouetting. She'd taken a picture of that through her front window. Bill was already joking about using it for their annual Christmas card. Now Miller Ryall was building . . . what was it? Something with high crossbars and netting slung beneath, a weird exercise system where the pool used to be. It sounded like a contraption Bradley might have seen in Vietnam, either for the troops to exercise with or, more likely, to torture prisoners.

He placed the iPad on top of the bookcase and popped open a can of seltzer. He should review the long message a client had sent him earlier in the day—he knew he should—but the weekend was coming, and that would be soon enough. He sorted through some mail, threw out half of it unopened, took another sip of seltzer.

I am dull, he thought. He knew he was. But there was something to be said for not feeling conflicted or tortured, just empty. Done in. He picked up the binoculars and looked at his old house. It must now be past ten P.M.—yes, it was— because across the river, his upstairs lights had gone dark. Aiming the binoculars downward, he saw two figures swaying. At first he thought he was seeing low-hanging tree branches. But no, out in front of his old house, two people were dancing down the middle of the street. This was impossible. The entire block was asleep. So what was he looking at? It was Ryall. The stars cast enough light that he now saw Ryall's long, thin nose highlighted—but who was the woman? On the same day he'd found out about the adult jungle gym, he was now seeing the reclusive Miller Ryall dancing outdoors with some woman? He thought about calling Bill and Margie but didn't want to wake them. Also, he didn't want to seem to be fixated on his former neighbor because . . . well, because he disdained Ryall.

He finished his seltzer, peed, and undressed, draping his clothes on the bedpost. The next day was Saturday, so he'd wear them a second day. He'd go to the market and buy a few locally grown healthy things. Take care of himself. You had to at least contribute to a depression lifting. You couldn't just stare into the darkness with binoculars, looking at your old life, or at foolish people outside your old house, which you once occupied with your wife, your wife who was killed by an inept twenty-five-year-old nurse. What the hell was Ryall doing, though? The guy usually stayed hidden like a rabbit in its warren. And all that construction noise certainly wasn't going to help sell his house. Not that Ryall ever thought of others.

Bradley turned back the covers and slid into bed. He'd be up in two or three hours to pee. That happened when you drank: You thought your bladder was empty, but it filled up as soon as you lay down. And he'd had seltzer on top of the drinks. And ice water at the bar. He was never going to sleep, he thought. It was his last formed thought of the night.

"In a million years, you are never going to believe what I have to tell you," Margie said to him at the market the next day.

He was standing there with kale sprouting upward from his bag like green fireworks. The tomatoes weren't well enough cushioned at the bottom. They'd bruise. Perhaps the skin would break. He'd also bought a bunch of flowers, because some kid was trying to raise money to go on a trip with the high school orchestra. They were things you'd find alongside any road: Japanese knotweed, Queen Anne's lace, and some limp-stemmed vine with a few dark-purple flowers that would probably drop off immediately. He looked at Margie neutrally, though he was eager to hear what she had to say. He'd cultivated this blank expression for the courtroom, and over the years it had become incorporated into his response to almost everything.

"Ryall's got a live-in girlfriend," she said. "He met her through Match.com. She waved to me and walked right over and introduced herself. I was seeing my niece off, and suddenly she held up a hand and ran over, so I had to shake it. Her name is Bree. Daniel is her middle name. You'll never believe this: She was named for some woman in an old movie starring Donald Sutherland."

"*Klute*," he said.

"Cute? Well, I wouldn't say so—but with him, the presence of any woman is cause for wonder."

"No, no. The movie *Klute*. Jane Fonda played the woman. She was a prostitute, I think. Go on, Margie."

"She told me she was working at a store in Portsmouth, so she got a discount on the clothes. She was wearing a very swirly skirt that looked expensive. She'd dropped out of school and was going to be living next door. She brought up Match.com. I almost asked her if she knew that he didn't speak to any of us. But then I thought, No, she'll find out soon enough. That is, unless he's decided to be a human being. Isn't that amazing?"

"I suppose it is. Do you think there's any connection between the contraption he's having built and his new girl-friend?"

"You were born to be in your chosen profession, Bradley. That's an interesting question. You're thinking she might be an acrobat or something? One of those high-wire per-formers?"

He splayed his hands to pantomime not knowing. ("Stop pretending I'm a jury. I'm your wife," Donna would have said if he'd gestured that way in her presence.) He was tempted to tell Margie about what he'd seen the night before, but he couldn't imagine what she'd think of him, just happening to have binoculars, just happening to see the first real sign of life at Miller Ryall's in whatever it was, ten years. Also—and this was the real reason he decided not to say anything; he was quite aware that Margie wasn't likely to judge him—he'd awakened that morning with a very disconcerting thought. A really troubling thought that, for a few seconds, he'd felt en-tirely convinced of. Shaving, he'd continued to think, Maybe it was Donna. Maybe she came back, and I wasn't there—there was only Ryall—so she had her elegant, life-affirming dance with him. Such a thought was odd, he knew, even as he thought it. Yet it lingered, and he'd already decided that he'd jump in the car if he saw dancing again.

Now, after time had elapsed and he'd had two mugs of coffee, it occurred to him that the idea had popped into his mind because of some of the stories he'd heard in Vietnam—

bizarre things that the Vietnamese believed about ghosts who could be seen only as long as you looked at them, who vanished if you so much as blinked. By implication, the Americans were not only killing but blinking people away. Blinking them back into invisibility. He'd heard this from a nine-year-old boy who'd befriended him. He wondered what had happened to that boy, with his bloody knee and broken thumb, splinted with a tree branch, while at the same time he knew. That whole village had disappeared, though not while he was there; its end was not something he'd had any part in.

He and Margie said goodbye after a peck on the cheek, and he started down the well-trampled hill with his bag of vegetables he didn't really know how to cook. He should have kept at least one of Donna's cookbooks. He'd boil water and drop the stuff in. The corn would cook just fine, and if the kale wasn't edible, he'd know better next time. The Queen Anne's lace was dropping tiny flecks of white, like dandruff, on his car seat.

He drove out of the lot, a stream of tourists' cars facing him at the intersection by Stonewall Kitchen, where they came off the highway. Maybe he should invite a tourist over for dinner. He could be like the squeegee men in New York City, setting upon drivers stopped at lights, rubbing filthy water over their windshields and demanding tips. But he would ask them to dinner instead. After all, in a world where people met their life partners on something called Match .com, what would be the harm in accepting a mere dinner invitation? Free food! Kale boiled with corn. Sliced tomato sprinkled with garden basil. He also had a package of chicken sausages. Sure, come on, happy summer people, enter into life as it's really lived in Maine! The idea was starting to amuse him even as it made him feel horrible, like a condescending, ill-tempered human being.

To his surprise, he found that he had driven not to his new house but to the old one. When he saw where he was, he couldn't remember how he'd gotten there. On autopilot, that was how. Abashed, he pulled into his driveway, only to find himself fenced in: Emil Andressen, his real estate agent, had pulled in behind him in a silver Infiniti, transporting a couple of potential buyers. Bradley got out with a faint, false smile. Emil was not happy to see him. This was bad timing. He'd been warned: Buyers wanted to see nothing personal inside a house, no framed pictures, no scraggly plants, no memorabilia—and certainly not the owner. They needed, according to Emil, to have no obstacles to imagining themselves there. Anything could throw them off and ruin their imaginative projection—even the wrong fabric on furniture.

So then why had Emil blocked him in? Why hadn't the man at least parked at the curb, or where a curb would have been, had one existed? The second he realized he was angry, another thought occurred to him: Bree? The Match.com girlfriend was named Bree? How many Brees could there be? What would it mean if it were the same young woman whose car his brother had hit in the fender-bender? Could it be that small a world?

"Awfully sorry," he managed to say to Emil. "I was just going to take a look around, make sure everything was okay."

"Are you the owner?" the woman said, throwing open the car's back door. "If you are, will you give us a special tour of your lovely home? It's number one on our list of places to see. We're hoping it'll be our forever dream house in vacationland."

This squealing woman seemed disastrously stupid. The sort of woman he couldn't abide. Donna had been able to talk to anyone, but he had no facility for casual chatter. A forever dream house in vacationland?

Emil's body jerked as if he'd been hit by a big wave he'd turned his back on. His scrawny arms were actually flailing.

"I'm sorry," Bradley said, addressing Emil rather than the woman. "Why don't you back up and I'll go on my way, Emil?"

"Oh, no," the woman insisted. "Don't y'all think that is too silly, having everybody disappear as if nobody owned the house, as if we couldn't possibly learn anything from y'all?"

Her husband, texting, got out of the car. He looked at Emil. "This is the house's owner, who lives across the river now," Emil said. "As he says, he was stopping by to check on things, but we should probably—"

"You should, but you've got me blocked in, Emil," Bradley said, more testily than he'd intended.

Emil was a former tae kwon do instructor turned nurse's aide, as well as a part-time real estate agent, supporting his girlfriend and her ten-year-old son. He was also a four-years-and-counting member of Alcoholics Anonymous. A friend of Bradley's—a twenty-year A.A. member—had recommended Emil when Bradley decided to sell the house. Why he hadn't listed it with Sotheby's, he couldn't imagine, but he had only himself to blame.

"And what all is that?" the woman said, twirling to look at the couple dancing in formal attire up the road. It was not yet ten A.M. God, they'd danced out from under the massive bowers of wisteria without a sideways glance and were doing a salsa, or something hippy and swiveling, up the middle of the road.

"Fred Astaire and Ginger Rogers," the woman said, grabbing her husband's arm. "We are gonna have to refresh our ballroom-dancing skills to live in y'all's neighborhood!"

"What's that about, do you know?" Emil said to Bradley rather urgently. "A prank? They're playing a joke?"

The young woman dancing with Ryall had long bleached-blond hair and bony knees and wore black high heels with straps—official dancing shoes—and if everyone standing in the driveway was lucky, she and Ryall would do their pas de deux around the block, and the couple would indeed assume that they'd been the victims of a practical joke. The dancing woman was so obviously not Donna—just some foolish girl, probably either drunk or stoned, enjoying her sudden romance with a guy who, out of a job or not, had big bucks and was putting her on big-time by pretending to be up for anything, full of exuberance.

"Oh, I like this place already!" the woman buyer said, bouncing on her toes.

Emil was backing up his car. For a quick second, Bradley caught his eye, and that glance said it all. It said, I am my family's only source of income. It said, Get out of here now. It said, I will lose this sale. It said, Jack Daniel's with two cubes and a cherry. Then it said, No, no, no.

"I have just got the best feelin'!" the woman said as Emil steered her toward the house. "Can't we even ask him if he was really happy here?" Bradley heard her say as the front door closed.

Had he been really happy there? His wife had allowed him not to think about such a question at all. They'd carved out days and never realized that they were limited in number. "Carved" days. Why had he used that word? He didn't know. He could "get in touch with his feelings," an expression he detested, if he had to. But to whom would he reveal them? Not Sterne, who was afraid of his own shadow. Had Donna not died, he wasn't sure they'd be close at all. There had been years in which they'd seen little of each other. His brother had also been in Vietnam, though his collapsed lung had gotten him sent home early. Sterne had been present for their mother's death, just as Bradley had been there for their father's.

As he pulled out of the driveway, he reversed so abruptly that the bag of vegetables toppled off the passenger seat and spilled onto the floor. He'd automatically reached out, as he had so many times to brace Donna when she'd sat there, but it wasn't her; it was only a bag of kale, tomatoes, and corn, all of it bought for under ten dollars. At the stop sign around the corner, he leaned over and picked up most of the things, which seemed more ordinary and less fascinating now than they had at the market. The truck in front of him inched and braked, inched and braked, waiting for an opening in the traffic. A sticker on its back window said, in big red letters, SAVE A HORSE RIDE A COWGIRL. What was it with America and saving things? Yes, he got the slightly dirty joke. But really, Americans felt they had to save everything from tadpoles to foreign countries. The argument was always that it was in their interest to do so; no one was naive, no one a romantic. He supposed he should be thinking in terms of "we" rather than "they." He was, after all, an American, too.

A little girl peeked out the back window of the truck and waved just as the truck lurched forward, taking off with squealing tires and a backward spray of gravel. No crash followed. Now Bradley watched for an opportunity to accelerate, but no one was giving an inch. A steady string of cars stretched in both directions, drivers feigning obliviousness of anyone trying to enter the stream. He wondered if he would ever be able to make the turn, if any car would flash its headlights or simply stop. Was there even one civilized person left on the planet? He felt he might sit there until he turned to stone or drew his last breath. Until he died of old age—which was, of course, better than dying of someone's ineptitude. These were the things that went through his mind as he sensed something bearing down on him from behind. His eyes flicked up to the rearview mirror. With that slight motion, he became conscious of a headache forming. It was the idiots, continuing their dance, emerging from some clever shortcut, since he hadn't seen them turn onto the road leading to the stop sign.

Time passed. A convertible hesitated but sped up when he removed his foot from the brake. Stone, he thought. Death. He and his car would be covered by the dust of time, just as his new hostas had been buried under the avalanche of hail. Eyes up! The couple was gaining on him, though he couldn't imagine—and hoped he wouldn't have to find out—whether they'd acknowledge his presence or merely dance around him. Were they completely in their own world? How much of it was a taunt? That had always been one of the crucial questions you needed to consider before you made a move in-country: Was something really happening, or was it a mirage, a hallucination?

The dancers came close, her smile lipsticked red. His crazy neighbor's eyes blazed. They'd dance around him. He was invisible, the car a mere shell. His sense that he was idling at a stop sign in his old neighborhood in Maine, where some middle-aged Southern belle was inspecting his house and oohing over Donna's Persian carpets, was just an illusion. He would exist only as long as the dancers didn't blink, and so far, wild-eyed and disheveled, they seemed not to.

They were almost upon him when he finally had a chance to shoot into traffic. Eventually the road would take him to his new house, just as, years before, a plane had lifted him out of Saigon: *plunk.* There you go. Sweet dreams. Or better yet, none at all.

How long could people dance that way? How far could you get, pushing yourself beyond exhaustion? He knew the answer. He'd learned it. He'd learned also that whenever you thought you were having your moment, life tapped you on the shoulder and cut in. That was the cruel blink of fate's eye. You were all wrapped up in each other, dancing? Oh, no, you don't get to do that.

SAVE A HORSE RIDE A COWGIRL had pulled in to the local ice-cream stand. He gave a two-fingered salute as he passed, in case the little girl was watching. It would have been nice to see her fine blond hair again. Her little fingers. But things didn't work like that. He was inside an anonymous car. He'd been only a moment's diversion for her. Still, he wiggled his fingers in imitation of the way she'd moved hers, remembering as he did the horrible Chinese bird spiders, bigger than her palm, the poisonous spiders for whose bite there was no antivenom—one of which had once so startled Callahan by springing out of his empty boot that he'd screamed and raced into Bradley's arms.

Another time. Another country. The stakes were so different now, though the old life-or-death thing still took its toll.

What would he dream, if he could determine his dreams? Years ago, he'd seen a man named Dr. McCall who had asked him just that. The man had written with a pencil with a sharp point. He wrote only when something impressed him. It didn't seem very professional, in retrospect, that he had let his patient see how infrequently his pencil moved. "Oh, a nice trout stream with burbling water and leaping fish, and wading boots in the right size for once, and clouds to block the sun but not the light," Bradley had said. No movement of the pencil. "Or the opposite: working in a skyscraper in New York City, beautiful women throwing themselves at me, the whole male-fantasy thing." Nothing. McCall had said, "You're just going with the usual all-American fantasy? You don't wish to banish any memory of the dead?" McCall sat behind his desk in a wheelchair. He was said to be the best shrink at Walter Reed. He'd once been a patient there himself, and he had a low tolerance for fairy tales. "Any answer?" the doctor had persisted.

McCall must not have been married. In those days, shrinks were cagey: If it worked to wear a wedding ring, they wore it; if it didn't help, they left it on the dresser. Still, there was often the telltale white circle. What he wouldn't give for one more chance to look at the doctor's hand. But McCall had disappeared from the VA. Maybe the guy had found his own trout stream. Maybe he was happily married to some woman who sewed his buttons back on and gave him a push uphill when he needed it. Back then Bradley had been just one of thousands of Humpty Dumptys who needed to be put back together.

Now he wore Donna's gold wedding band on the chain from which he'd removed his dog tags. It dangled so low that no one could mistake it for a necklace. Not that he ever showed it to anyone. No one could have known that the way the ring warmed up or cooled reminded him constantly of her. She'd been killed, as so many had, by friendly fire. That girl—the so-called nurse—was on Facebook. She was married, with a son and a daughter. He wished her nothing good: no dream answered, no summer vacation. A terrible illness, of the kind that so often ironically befell those in her profession, could not make her sick enough to satisfy him. His thoughts were nothing but uncharitable. And if her children grew up to fight in their own war? Well, it would certainly be sad if they never came home.

In his living room, he raised the binoculars and looked across the river. No sign of the dancers. Maybe—because his own life seemed to move so excruciatingly slowly—Miller Ryall and the girl were living in sped-up time. They had already married, had children, sent them off to college, attended their weddings, and were waiting excitedly for grandchildren, who'd come to play on the wooden contraption that could dangle them upside down for hours, or break their ribs if they sprang free.

* * *

The house sold for almost eighty thousand dollars more than the asking price. Bradley and Emil drank a Newman's Own lemonade at the ice-cream place to celebrate, sitting under a big umbrella. Emil was riding high, astonished at his good luck. "I don't know, man," he said, shaking his head. "I mean, it's funny now, but the four of us standing there, watching that weird mating ritual going on down the middle of the street? It's something I'll tell the grandkids, and we haven't even gotten around to having our own kids yet."

"Don't do it. Enjoy your lives with each other," Bradley said.

"Beg pardon?" Emil said.

He didn't repeat himself. Anyone who didn't want to hear didn't have to. His own brother never asked him any personal questions. Not about what had happened in the war, not about why he and Donna had never had kids (how would he dare ask that, since he'd never married?), not about his sessions with Dr. McCall. It was really cowardice that Sterne asked nothing. It almost made Bradley want to call his brother and force him to talk about those things, but his hostility was misplaced. His brother was a fuckup and had been all his life. It had protected him from many things, so who was Bradley to say that it wasn't an effective defense strategy? Sterne couldn't speak Donna's name, but Bradley forgave him for that.

Donna had never taken pleasure in anyone else's pain, but she might have been intrigued by the mental breakdown that resulted in their old neighbor being carted off to the hospital. Emil had been there, working the night shift as a nurse's aide when Miller Ryall was admitted, and he gave

Bradley the details the next day. Bree had disappeared as quickly as she'd come.

"Why would we live on a street called Seagull Way?" Donna had asked him when they were young and they'd first made an offer on the house. She would have been surprised by the last-minute bidding war that drove up the price, and surprised as well that when Ryall's house was listed, Bill and Margie moved instantly to buy it, later constructing an enclosed passageway that led from one house to the other. Bill's sister lived there for a while, following her stroke. But Donna would have thought Bradley silly for giving Sterne her expensive binoculars. He'd decided that he wanted to know less, not more, about his former life. He gave his brother the truck, too; he really didn't need it anymore. When he stopped returning Margie's calls, she stopped calling and only nodded if they crossed paths. What had he said to Donna when she'd asked that question about living on Seagull Way? He forgot so much. Not his feelings toward her, just what, exactly, they'd said. Maybe he'd answered, "Because that's what this pretty street happens to be called." Once it had seemed an unusually pretty street, safe, predictably quiet, a street where—even if some pride was involved in assuming such a thing—everyone else seemed worse off than they were. She had no doubt nodded in agreement.

ABOUT THE AUTHOR

Ann Beattie has been included in four O. Henry Award Collections, in John Updike's *The Best American Short Stories of the Century*, and in Jennifer Egan's *The Best American Short Stories 2014*. In 2000, she received the PEN/Malamud Award for achievement in the short story. In 2005, she received the Rea Award for the Short Story. She was the Edgar Allan Poe Professor of English and Creative Writing at the University of Virginia. She is a member of the American Academy of Arts and Letters and of the American Academy of Arts and Sciences. She and her husband, Lincoln Perry, live in Maine and Key West, Florida.